In the sunroom of an assisted living facility, four wrinkled old women confess the details of their involvement in a forty-year-old crime. Newspaper editor, Gloria Larson, plans to write a book about their story, and to make them confess to something more—
Which one of them is her birth mother

THORNS OF ROSEWOOD

ROSEWOOD SERIES— BOOK 1

Gina M. Barlean

Less Traveled Roads Publishing
http://lesstraveledroads.wordpress.com

"Each time I had to shut down my kindle between chapters of *Thorns of Rosewood*, I couldn't wait to get back to the cast of characters and twists that G.M. Barlean created.

That is what I'd call a successful cozy mystery."

—Kay Bratt, best-selling author of *The Tales of the Scavenger's Daughters*

"This is one mystery that caught me completely by surprise, in more than one way! The characters made me laugh, and made me cry. I loved the story, and the ending couldn't have been more perfect, or more satisfying."

—Victorine Lieske, NYT best-selling author of *Not What She Seems*

Acknowledgments and Dedication

I dedicate this book to my friends. So many of you have inspired and guided me. I appreciate every person who has shown me support or kindness during this journey.

Thank you to the Thorns. You know who you are. Thanks to my writing group, the Local Muse for cheering and correcting along the way. Thank you to my team of beta readers who brought so much expertise to my work. Dr. Joyce Sasse, for your insight into the field of psychology. Scott Gray, for your legal knowledge. Laura Cooper, for your police experience. Thank you to my hometown's local newspaper editor, Larry Pierce, for your beta read. To Donna and Wayne and anyone else who read and offered suggestions. To Lisa Kovanda, the President of the Nebraska Writers Guild, who gave me great insight from an adopted child's perspective. It takes a village to write a book and I have a pretty great village.

1

Hard, cold eyes whitewashed from a camera's flash stared up at Gloria Larson from the yellowed newspaper. The 1974 headline read *Thorns of Rosewood Go Free*. The four women in the black-and-white photograph had been informally accused of foul play in the missing-person case of a judge's wife.

One set of eyes in particular held Gloria in an inky gaze. She traced her finger around the woman's face, wondering what thoughts were behind her glare. The other women's faces had also become familiar over the past couple of years. She'd read this paper many times.

Below, another article showed a picture of a striking woman with flowing red hair and high cheekbones. The title read *Naomi Waterman Talbot Still at Large*. According to the item, Naomi Talbot had been a prominent woman in the community. Came from money. The judge's wife.

Gloria's eyes trailed back up to the first article. Not enough proof, apparently. The women either weren't guilty or had gotten away with... murder?

Too many questions were unanswered. Her reporter's instinct wanted facts the newspaper of the time hadn't given. She had some of her own questions, too.

Gloria had lived in Rosewood for six years and had told herself this job as editor of a small-town weekly paper was a stepping-stone to something bigger and better. But somewhere along the line, she'd forgotten to step.

This story about these four women—the Thorns of Rosewood—is what was holding her here.

Her parents were none too happy about her moving to Rosewood, Nebraska, a small town nestled in a valley along the Platte River. The peaceful Midwestern community boasted brick-paved streets and sleepy storefronts in hundred-year-old buildings. Very Mayberry.

And Gloria Larson loved small-town life. The fresh air and green lawns, the fences trimmed in roses, and those big blue skies. It was idyllic. A comfort—like a warm blanket in a soft bed.

Boring? No. Gloria had always been able to turn wherever she was into someplace interesting. It was the reporter in her—full of questions and a desire to learn every last detail.

Moreover, this little town had a long-kept secret she was determined to get to the bottom of, which was why her parents had balked in the first place. When she found out why her parents didn't want her to move to Rosewood, Gloria became even more determined to take the position.

From as early as she could remember, Gloria had sensed she was adopted. Her auburn hair, green eyes, and athletic nature were different from everyone else in her family. They didn't act or look the way she did. They were short, blond, and brown eyed for the most part. She'd asked the big question when she was five and they'd answered her. "Yes, Gloria. We adopted you. You are so special to us. We chose you and will love you forever. This will always be your home, and we will always be your family."

She'd grown up believing she'd been selected like the freshest, most perfect fruit picked from the vine. But when Gloria was around twelve, she could no longer fight the festering question of why the woman who'd given birth to her had chosen to walk away.

Gloria had questioned her parents. They'd kept their answers short and factual, said her birth mother had been a woman in her forties who was incapable of raising a child at that age.

At twelve, forty had sounded ancient to Gloria. And once again, her parents smothered her with love and it helped her put the issue aside.

But when Gloria was in high school, the subject once again demanded attention. It gnawed at her as she lay in bed at night. Who was this woman? Why didn't *she* think Gloria was special? Why hadn't *she* loved her enough to keep her?

"Did you ever meet her?" Gloria asked her mother.

"No." Karen Larson wiped the already-clean counter with a dishcloth.

"I wonder what she was like." She pushed.

Mrs. Larson shrugged and kept wiping.

"Do I look like her?"

"We were told she was very beautiful." Karen rinsed out the cloth and began to wipe some more.

It was like pulling teeth. Her parents obviously didn't want her to know any more than she had to, but why not?

"And you said she was in her forties? I have a friend in my class at school whose mom had her when she was in her forties."

Her mom only shrugged again, still wiping that counter.

"She must have had a good reason, dear. Maybe it was her health." Her mother wrung out the dishcloth, draped it over the edge of the sink, and left the kitchen slowly, like she was secretly creeping away.

By college, Gloria had stopped asking questions altogether. She got busy with getting her own life started.

After college, she worked at a few different journalism jobs around the state. Magazines, reporter gigs at papers—and when the job opening came up for editor of the *Rosewood Press*, she was ecstatic. She'd thought her parents would be thrilled, too.

But instead, they'd balked.

"Why? Because I'm moving out of Omaha? You think I'll get bored in a small town? But I'd be the editor. It's what I've always wanted to do."

Yet they continued to act far more concerned than she would have expected. Pacing, hand-wringing, the exchange of furtive glances. There had to be something more to their behavior.

After numerous conversations over several days, Gloria finally badgered them until they coughed up the information.

It blindsided her.

"My birth mother was from Rosewood?" Gloria's mouth hung open in shock. "Is she still there?" Gloria couldn't believe the woman had been so close... *so findable.* "Why didn't you tell me this before?" The air in the room seemed to have disappeared.

Gloria became more confused when her mother began to weep. Then her father, stoic Roger Larson, left his easy chair—a rare event—and returned with a glass of scotch in his hand.

"Scotch? Dad! It's ten thirty in the morning. What the hell?"

It turned out her birth mother hadn't been just any forty-year-old woman from Rosewood.

"She was suspected of murder?" The blood drained from Gloria's face.

Dropping into the chair beside her father, she grabbed his glass of scotch and drank every last drop in one gulp. It burned like hell all the way down, kind of like the new information about her birth mother.

She not only took the job, she practically put an exclamation point after her name on the application. And the first free moment she had, Gloria began searching the old newspapers in the archives for stories. How many significant crimes could there have been in the small town of Rosewood, Nebraska?

Turned out pretty much just that one.

Her birth mother had to be one of the Thorns of Rosewood. Which one, Gloria was determined to find out.

2

Gloria had heard about the almost forty-year-old story when she first moved to Rosewood. It remained a legend in these parts—the sleepy town's claim to infamy. Old folks in the community still spoke of it in hushed tones. Some believed Mrs. Talbot had met her demise at the hands of the Thorns of Rosewood. But the accusation had never been proven.

And to this day, a body had never been found.

The newspaper had done a thorough job of sensationalizing the story. The editor's opinion pieces all but prosecuted and sentenced the four women. The articles must have worked the sleepy town into a lather.

Other headlines in previous week's papers were equally slanted. *Guilty or Innocent?* and *Women Refuse to Confess.*

So much for journalistic integrity.

But I bet they sold papers.

She felt guilty about even thinking such a thing, but she was, after all, the editor of a newspaper and selling subscriptions was a hurdle she had to jump each week.

After investigations found no proof, all news articles about the incident became small stories buried in the sports section. But the people in town hadn't buried the speculation. They spoke of it to this day.

Of the four women, the only one who had ever given a statement to the press had been Debbie Coleman—the face with those hard, cold eyes. And all Debbie had ever said was "No comment."

Smart women. Whether they did or didn't have anything to do with Naomi Talbot's disappearance, keeping their mouths shut seemed to be the key that unlocked their cell doors, so to speak.

So, for the years she'd been editor of the *Rosewood Press*, Gloria had allowed herself a certain amount of time each week, reading all the articles from 1974 about the Thorns of Rosewood. At first she'd been gung ho to start the search for her birth mother. But something held her back. A strange panic rose in her chest at the idea of crossing the line and looking for the truth. With all the love and support her parents had given her over the years, she knew searching for her birth mother would cause them pain. They didn't deserve that. She loved them and would always consider them her real parents. They'd earned the title. Yet, the woman who gave her life sat like a shadow at the back of her mind.

Gloria stared at the old newspaper once again. Then she closed it and hung the dowel back in its rungs on the wall of the archive room. She tucked it in like a faithful bedtime story. The account of these women from 1974 gripped her imagination. The faces frozen in time… in print. At first glance, their eyes seemed so angry—but fear and anger often spooned in the bed of emotional turmoil.

She clicked off the light and shut the door behind her. The basement stank like the old room it was. The newspaper office had been built in 1889, back when the town was birthed, back when newspapers were important. It reeked of antiquity. Like dust. Like mold. Like the aroma of old people—just that much closer to death.

As she trudged up the stairs, her cell phone vibrated.

It was her mother. She hesitated for a few rings, then answered.

"Hi, Mom."

Gloria listened to Karen Larson's voice as she went into her office, closed the door behind her, and stared out the tiny window at the sleepy Nebraska town. Population 2,500 if you included the traffic driving through to Lincoln on a Husker game day. Her office was no more than a closet, and her old desk sat shoved against the wall like she'd been put in the corner, punished for bad behavior.

"Yes, Mom. I'm getting enough sleep." Did moms ever stop worrying?

"Well, I hope so. Eight hours are essential. And are you eating right? Leafy greens are important," Karen Larson said.

Gloria shifted the phone to her other ear and watched a dusty red pickup sputter down Main Street. The old man behind the steering wheel leaned forward like those extra five inches were going to help him see what was coming.

"Yup. Eating healthy, too. Lots of greens. Healthy colon and all that."

The pickup continued to creep down the brick-paved street. Gloria knew where he was headed—to the NAPA store to meet his brother. They'd go over to the diner for lunch like they did every day of the week. The small rural town ticked along like a clock.

Her mother still asked questions which didn't need asking. They did this dance every Wednesday.

"Nope. No boyfriend. Guess I'm destined to be single."

Karen heaved a sigh on the other end of the line. The kind of sigh that always vacuumed up a little piece of Gloria's soul, then spit it back out like a bad penny. Her mother reassured her she was only concerned, but somehow Gloria managed to hear disappointment in the question.

Pulling her attention away from the small office window, Gloria leaned back in her chair as far as it would allow—just short of falling over backward. Her mother was going on about the joys of a loving relationship. Gloria stretched and yawned but gave no answer. She wondered if Debbie Coleman's line would work. *No Comment.*

"Well, you'll find someone. You're too pretty to be single," her mother said.

"So you keep telling me."

"You'd have better luck if you lived in the city."

She sighed. Not this again. You'd think her mother would be happy she lived in a safe little town, but no, she wanted her in Omaha.

"There just aren't jobs available right now, Mom. The economy sucks, remember."

Since Gloria had moved to Rosewood, she'd fallen deep into the small-town rut. Slowed way the hell down. Even developed her own predictable routines. Oatmeal for breakfast. Two-mile jog every day after work. Exactly forty-five minutes of reading before she turned out the light to go to sleep at night. And truth be told, she really wasn't even looking for a job anymore. She liked it here. Rosewood wasn't her problem.

"But are you happy, sweetheart?" Karen asked.

Happy? What kind of question was that? "Sure, Mom. I'm happy." Lying to her mother. Going to hell for sure. Happy wasn't a word she would associate with her life, or her personality for that matter. She just wasn't the cheerful type. Her life was acceptable. Uncomplicated. Pragmatic. Safe.

But if she was being honest, she'd admit she felt stagnant and a bit empty. Something *was* missing. And she knew what it was.

Heat climbed up her neck. Time to breach the topic her mother didn't like to talk about.

"Mom. I've decided to find her."

Karen Larson fell silent.

Gloria could hear the TV in the background. Her dad had on the *Andy Griffith Show*. Old Roger never tired of it.

"Mom?"

"Are you sure you want to do that? Won't it take time away from looking for a job? From dating? From the job you have?" Mrs. Larson was grasping at straws.

"You mean the important things?"

More silence.

"You know I'm just worried you won't like what you discover." Karen's voice wavered.

"Well, stop worrying, Mom. This is my decision."

More silence.

"Sorry." Gloria cleared her throat.

"If there's one thing I've always known about you, Gloria Marie Larson. You will do exactly what you want to do, regardless of what I think." Gloria's mother didn't sound angry as much as resigned.

The corner of Gloria's mouth pulled into a half grin. "It's your fault. You raised me to be independent."

"Yes. I did raise you."

She knew what her statement really meant. "I love you, Mom. I will always love you."

Uncomfortable silence took over like it always did when Gloria talked about finding her birth mother.

"I'll always be here for you. No matter what."

"I know, Mom. But I need to know why she wasn't."

3

Gloria said good-bye to her mother, then dropped her head on the desk with a thump. It was as though she watched the world from the bottom of a lake. Glimmers of life were happening up there, but she lolled underwater, holding her breath. And it had begun to feel like her air was running out.

Was she really ready to find out who her birth mother was?

Her thoughts trailed back to the story of the Thorns of Rosewood. Even if this search for her biological mother proved fruitless, she still wanted—no, needed—to put fingers to the keyboard and get some kind of start on writing, and not any story, it had to be *this* story. This was the one exciting thing to ever occur in this small town. And Debbie Coleman and her friends were, in so many ways, exactly the characters she was looking for. Betty Striker, Tanya Gunderson, Josie Townsend. *Their* story was the book Gloria wanted to write. *This* was the direction she needed to go. She knew it. She could feel it pulsing like a rhythm in her brain.

"You okay, Gloria?"

She jolted and sat up straight. The ad manager of the paper paused at her door.

"Great." Gloria offered a false smile with wide eyes.

They had a conversation she barely heard or participated in—something about the weekend. Nothing important.

Ideas for the book consumed her thoughts, and she'd already made a mental list of questions she wanted to ask these women once she found them.

It was time.

She was going to investigate the story about the Thorns of Rosewood. She was going to write a book. Be an author. Make a name for herself. And if she could, she would learn some truths about her own life. Maybe even find her birth mother and ask the most important question: "Why?" But she was adamant for the story to come first—and on that count she was kidding herself.

Internet research helped Gloria find that the women were still alive and all resided at the same assisted-living facility. In Lincoln, Nebraska, no less. One hour away. Seemed like it was meant to be. Some kind of weird twist of fate.

Phone in hand, she dialed the number to Meadowbrook Assisted Living and asked to speak with Debbie Coleman.

She held her shaking breath and tapped her fingers on her desk as she stared at the wall's old brown paneling. She glanced back at her door and hoped no one would barge in.

"This is Debbie." A voice scratchy from years of smoking rasped on the other end of the line.

Giddy excitement fluttered in Gloria's stomach. "Debbie, my name is Gloria Larson and I'm the editor of the *Rosewood Press*."

Silence.

"I wondered if I could come talk with you about the incident in '74?"

The pause seemed endless.

"Uh... who?" the old voice asked.

"Gloria Larson. *Rosewood Press*," she repeated.

"Oh dear. No comment."

Click... dial tone. Conversation over. Same thing Debbie had said again and again back in '74.

So much for life falling into place.

But Gloria really never had been one to take no for an answer. She'd call the next woman on the list.

When her call was answered, she asked for Josie Townsend. Another old voice picked up moments later, but this one had a bit of a chirp to it.

"Yes?" The shaky voice quaked.

"Josie Townsend?" Gloria asked.

"Yes. This is Josie." The old woman sounded excited. "Who is this?"

A reasonable question. "Ma'am, this is Gloria Larson. I'm from Rosewood. Actually, I'm the editor of the *Rosewood Press*. I was wondering if I could visit with you about the incident in '74." *Come on, old woman. Give me a chance.* Gloria held her breath.

"Oh. Gloria? Well. I don't think I should talk about that. I'm sorry."

Gloria couldn't let her slip through her fingers. "Ms. Townsend, please. I really just want to learn your side of things."

"My side? Oh dear. Well. No. I couldn't. Now, I can't talk to you anymore. I'm sorry."

"Wait..." Gloria didn't get a chance to go on. The click of the phone sounded apologetic, or frightened, somehow.

This was strange. And even more intriguing. Gloria sat and thought about the two voices she'd heard. Josie's and Debbie's. Did either of their voices sound familiar to her? Maybe like her own? Would she even be able to tell? Probably not.

Gloria did know one thing. She wasn't about to give up. She had two more women to talk to. She probably needed to see them in person. Being hung up on twice was enough to prove the point.

The next day Gloria drove down to Meadowbrook. It was a pretty drive, and she tried to keep her nerves at bay. She wanted this story but was also anxious to meet these women. She would be looking for resemblances but couldn't be too obvious about it. One of these women had to be her birth mother, and she was determined to find out which one. Oh, and to get the story, too, of course.

She barely noticed her surroundings when she walked in. Her nerves were on fire, and she blazed up to the nurse's station to ask where to find Tanya Gunderson. The nurse raised an eyebrow and waited. She apparently needed more. Gloria pulled out her card. "I'm with the *Rosewood Press*. I need to visit with her about a story the *Press* did several years ago."

"Does she know you're coming?" the nurse asked with a side-eyed stare.

"I called." Not a lie. She had called here. She wasn't going to get the story by being a pansy. Hard-nosed newswoman. This would be her role today.

After a moment, the nurse said, "I think Tanya is in the solarium." She pointed down the hallway, but her gaze remained suspicious.

Gloria nodded and headed in the direction the nurse had pointed. Sunlight at the end of the hall came through panes of glass. Green plants. Tile floor. Looked like a solarium to her.

She turned the corner and found two women sitting in the sunshine, one drinking a glass of iced tea and the other a cup of coffee. They looked up from their newspapers and over their reading glasses. Gloria stared at them. Gray hair. So many wrinkles. How could she possibly see herself in these aged faces?

"Can we help you?" the woman with the coffee asked.

"I'm looking for Tanya Gunderson." Gloria smiled, but her heart was pounding in her ears so hard she suspected it showed—a rhythmic pulse on the side of her head.

"I'm Tanya," the old woman who'd been drinking coffee responded as she put down her cup.

No time to pause. "I'm Gloria Larson, editor of the *Rosewood Press*. I wanted to talk to you about the story from '74—the Thorns of Rosewood." Gloria strode forward, her hand out to greet Tanya.

Tanya's mouth dropped open and she crunched the newspaper in her gnarled fingers.

The other woman stood up, rising to her full height, which for an elderly woman was still very straight and tall. "She will not visit with you about any such thing," she said. "How did you find us?"

"And who are you?" Gloria asked the tall woman.

"Betty Striker, not that it's any of your…"

"Oh good. You were next on my list!" Gloria exclaimed.

"I don't appreciate being on anyone's *list*," Betty said, making air quotes.

"Well, you were, along with Mrs. Gunderson, Mrs. Coleman, and Ms. Townsend. You were all the Thorns of Rosewood, were you not?" Gloria launched into her questions and pulled a notebook out of her pocket, pen already in hand.

"Young woman. I'll have you know, we do not appreciate you coming in here like gangbusters, as if we owe you any kind of information. We are law-abiding citizens and minding our own business. For crying out loud. We're just a couple of little old ladies in an assisted-living facility. How dare you charge in and assault us like this!"

Gloria stepped back. Did she sound that aggressive? She hadn't meant to. But in the midst of Betty's tirade, Gloria noticed how the eyebrow above the woman's left eye rose higher than the one above her right. Gloria's eyebrow did that, too. Then she glanced at Tanya. There was something about her ears. Unattached lobes. Gloria reached up and touched her own.

"Did you hear us?" Tanya was standing now, leaning on her walker. "We are going to get someone to help us if you don't leave right away." Tanya shooed Gloria, her old hands moving like she was fanning away a bad smell.

Gloria backed up. "I... I..."

"And I'll tell you another thing, missy. You'll catch a lot more flies with honey instead of vinegar!" Tanya was rolling her walker toward her now, one-handed, shaking her finger and with a look of determination on her face.

Gloria backed up. This had been a bad idea. She hadn't been ready to do this, after all. She turned to leave and almost mowed over two more old women. Stepping back, she stared at them.

Betty hollered out to them, "Josie, Debbie. Don't you two say a word to that woman. She's nosing around for a story about '74. She's a reporter!"

Tanya and Betty were now storming—well, inching—in Gloria's direction.

Gloria quickly scanned the faces of the new women she now stared at. Round cheeks and a small mouth on Josie. Sharp, hard features on Debbie. Her mind spun. Which one had given birth to her? She wanted to turn and scream the question at them all. Instead, she scooted sideways around them with ease and fled, not that she needed to run, down the long hallway.

She definitely hadn't been ready to do this. She didn't have her motives in the right place at all. This had been a terrible idea.

After Gloria returned to the paper, she decided to ruminate on things for a couple of weeks. She must have been delusional. Writing a book hadn't been her main objective at all. She was just trying to hunt down her birth mother, and in a very unprofessional way, too. It wasn't even fair to them, pouncing on them in crazed-reporter style, especially under the lie of wanting a story.

And they were awfully aggressive.

Or had *she* been the aggressive one?

Yes. It *had been* her.

Shame on her. Gloria owed every one of them an apology. She had a lot of thinking to do. Did, or did she not, want to write a book? If she did, then she needed to put the notion of finding her birth mother away. The story had to be the main focus or she wouldn't do the women, or herself, any justice. No wonder they were leery of her. She had shown them nothing but greed and self-serving intentions. She had to approach things with some kind of tact. Professionalism. Detachment.

The audacity of just calling Debbie and Josie and asking them to talk. Going down and confronting Betty and Tanya. Then running out like a scared rabbit.

They must think her a fool.

But a few weeks later, Gloria had her head on straight. She *did* want the story. Finding her birth mother was important, too, but the story had invaded her brain. It kept her up at night and it's where her mind wanted to wander. She decided to try again. This time, she knew she had to not only be more grown-up about the whole thing, but that she would also have to find some way to make up for her previous behavior. She wanted this story. And she wanted to know which woman was her birth mother. And she could have both of those things if she used her brain. Poured some honey on it, like Tanya suggested.

This time she phoned Linda Weldon, the administrator of Meadowbrook.

Gloria explained who she was and what she wanted to do. The administrator listened in silence. The dead air on the phone proved painful. At the end of the call, though, Ms. Weldon agreed to visit with the women on Gloria's behalf.

A week later, Ms. Weldon phoned to invite Gloria to come for a visit.

Gloria almost choked on her tuna-salad sandwich.

4

Gloria drove down the narrow stretch of highway on her way to meet the Thorns of Rosewood again. To say she was nervous would have been like saying water is sort of wet. She had a lot of face-saving to do—groveling. Her stomach gurgled at the thought. What had motivated these women to grant her an audience after the stunt she had pulled the last time they met?

As blue-green soybean fields and tasseled cornrows flew past her car window, Gloria thought about Debbie Coleman in particular.

Looking at the pictures of Debbie in the old newspapers had been like staring into the eyes of unbridled rage. Bone thin, a hard line to her face, and threatening eyes. Her dark hair framed a face with a darker attitude. She was a peculiar combination of frightening and absolutely intriguing.

The other women in the newspaper had appeared less intimidating. Sure, they scared her enough to make her run away when she'd gone to see them, but they'd only been defending themselves. She couldn't really blame them.

In the '74 newspaper, Tanya Gunderson's visage held a look of worry. She seemed like an average small-town wife and mother. Josie Townsend, from what Gloria read, had been single, a teacher. Not at all the type one would have thought capable of hurting someone. And Betty Striker—tall and aloof with intelligent eyes—seemed far too poised and in control for what she had been accused of. Except for Debbie, Gloria couldn't imagine the women doing anything more nefarious than cheating at bingo.

But could she see herself in any of their faces? Similarity in one particular set of eyes? She would find out.

The facility came into view. Tall oak trees and manicured green grass surrounded the building. Red brick and ivy, white-trimmed windows and black shutters—Gloria half expected people to be playing croquet on the front lawn.

She parked her car in a visitor spot, popped a breath mint into her mouth, and finger-combed her hair. Time to meet some shady ladies involved in a crime, or victims of a setup, whichever the case might be. One way or the other, in the back of her mind the main theme remained—it was time to meet her birth mother.

She gathered up the folder of information, a tape recorder, and her laptop from her back seat. Arms full, she shut the car door with her foot, then began to trudge up the long sidewalk to the front door of Meadowbrook Assisted Living.

Gloria hoped the women would be more talkative than they were in '74. Certainly more receptive than when she'd visited before. They had to be. They had invited her to come.

The more Gloria thought about it, the more energized she became. She was finally going to write a book. All her life she'd scribbled stories in notebooks, hoping someday to develop one into a full story. It was oddly frightening, to stretch your wings and see if you can do such a thing... whatever that thing may be—to try and possibly fail, or possibly succeed. She'd worked hard, paid the bills, and now it was time to allow herself to realize her potential, follow her dream, and find out if she had what it takes to be an author.

The smell of ammonia and musty old people was what Gloria expected when she opened the door to the assisted-living facility. Honestly, she hadn't paid any attention to the surroundings when she'd been here last. She had been busy bulldozing her way into the lives of the four women.

A big yellow lab with a happy tail approached. Had this animal even been in the front room the previous time she visited? Then a fluffy orange cat began to saunter in Gloria's direction. This unlikely couple seemed to be the greeting committee, and they had their ritual down pat. The dog sat down at her feet, looking up, waiting for her to acknowledge him. The cat brushed against her leg. How did she miss all this before?

The smell of warm cookies met Gloria's nose. A short woman with a big smile and happy crinkles at the corners of her eyes rolled up with a serving cart holding a big plate piled high with the delicious cookies filled with chocolate chips.

"Hello," the small woman chirped. "Can I help you find someone?" Chubby little thing. Coiffed hair. One of those women who had a standing appointment at the beauty parlor, Gloria suspected.

Reaching down to pet the dog, then scratching the cat's ear, Gloria pulled her business card out of her pocket.

"I'm Gloria Larson. I have an appointment with Linda Weldon, the administrator." Her eyes wandered to the cookies. *Offer me a cookie, woman.*

"I can take you to Linda's office. Follow me." She turned and headed around a corner, the wheels of her cart squeaking as she went.

Gloria followed. Her eyes darted around as she looked for the women. It was like she expected them to jump out from behind every corner.

Blue parakeets chirped in a birdcage by a tall ficus tree. Several women in a room off the entry played cards and laughed. In another room, an elderly woman was having her nails done. This was nothing like the care facility she remembered visiting her grandmother in so many years ago.

Busy gawking at the accommodations, Gloria almost ran into cookie-cart-woman when she stopped beside an office door.

"Here we are. Now, how 'bout a cookie?"

"I thought you'd never ask. They smell wonderful." Gloria almost sighed in relief. She accepted the warm treat on a little pink napkin.

A voice came from within the office. "Come on in, and have a seat." The administrator of Meadowbrook sat behind an unassuming desk stacked high with piles of documents and files. She had a kind smile but controlled eyes. Linda Weldon stood and held out her hand. A firm handshake, as one would expect.

"So you're Gloria Larson?" Linda asked. "Editor of the *Rosewood Press.*"

"Guilty." She nodded, then took a bite of her cookie.

"Have a seat and let's talk about the story you want to write." Linda pointed to a chair, then sat back down at her desk. She cleared away enough papers to see through the piles, then leaned forward attentively. "And about your previous visit."

Gloria swallowed hard. "I was out of line," she began.

"Yes, you were. Honestly, I can't believe they're willing to talk to you. They were absolutely livid after you left last time."

"I'm sure they were." Gloria expected this admonishment and was ready. "Ms. Weldon, I'm incredibly sorry for my behavior. I came on way too strong. I approached them like a rabid reporter, as if it were still 1974. I feel terrible about it. I'm glad for the opportunity to apologize to them. My enthusiasm got the better of me."

Ms. Weldon nodded, but her eyes didn't show empathy. "These are some of the nicest women I've ever met. You must treat them with respect or I won't be able to allow you to go any further with this project."

Gloria felt like a naughty child in a third grade class. She nodded and heat crawled up to her cheeks.

Linda continued. "From what the women have told me, they visited at length about you. And they actually want to talk to you. I don't understand it, but it's their choice. They're all of sound mind, and as long as you visit with them here, in a safe environment, we all feel good about it. But please, don't upset them. This is their retirement. They aren't on trial."

"I understand. I promise to be respectful." Gloria hung her head in shame.

"Okay, so on to the positives. What are your plans?" Linda steered them back to the business at hand.

Gloria had taken a bite of the cookie. She chewed quickly, then swallowed. "I've read all the articles in the archives. Plenty to choose from when it comes to the missing person and accusations of foul play. But, there aren't any personal interviews with the women. I want to know what *they* have to say… their side of the story. A body was never found. Then the paper dropped the story. The rumors remain about the Thorns of Rosewood getting away with murder. I guess I'd like to write about the facts. Maybe put an end to the rumors and hear their side of things."

Linda nodded her head as she listened. "I see you've put a lot of thought into this." She smiled, her hands resting lightly upon each other. It seemed the storm of threats had passed. Kindness washed over her face.

"Yes, I have," Gloria answered with a smile. "I want to focus on facts—do a fair and unbiased story. That's my goal. Tell the truth from their perspective."

And she also wanted to know a lot more about the woman who went missing, Naomi Talbot. An idea she'd keep to herself for now.

"Sounds like this could be a good book if written well."

"I think it will be. And it will be well-written." Gloria wasn't sure if she was offended by the comment or not.

Linda's words were encouraging, but the look on her face was serious. Gloria felt a little sweat at her temples.

The administrator stood and came around the desk to sit beside her. "I've thought a lot about this, too. The first thing you need to know is we here at Meadowbrook take the safety and peace of our residents very seriously. It's our job—my job—to protect our clients."

Gloria held her breath. The winds of cooperation seemed about to change. She'd thought this whole thing had been too good to be true.

"But I've visited with the four women and they've told me they *do* have something to say, after all."

Gloria perked up.

"The women have contacted a lawyer. With her help, they came up with a contract we all feel will be suitable."

Contract?

"Provided you honor the contract, they are amiable to being interviewed."

Linda picked up a blue folder lying on top of one of the many the piles on her desk. She handed the legal document to Gloria.

Gloria scanned the papers. Although her excitement blurred the words together, she could see it was the real deal. She hadn't expected anything so formal. No fly-by-night writing would be acceptable here, not that she intended to do anything less than her best work.

"Don't be intimidated." Linda's voice remained friendly. "They have to protect themselves. I'm sure you understand."

Gloria understood. Legal issues came with the territory of running a newspaper. But she hadn't been prepared to be handed pages and pages of legalese.

Leaning back in her chair, she nibbled on the cookie as she read. The contract had all the expected bells and whistles. Plenty of legal jargon laced throughout. She flipped to the page with the terms. Her eyes grew wide and she swallowed hard. Then she looked up at Linda with questions ready to spill.

Linda's face showed she'd been waiting for Gloria to read those words on the last page.

Before she could ask any questions, Linda began to explain. "Basically the bottom line is if you publish without the women and their lawyer's approval, there will be legal consequences. They will not approve the contract if your work is anything less than honest and fair. If you publish without them signing off on the product, they will prosecute to the fullest extent of the law." She smiled stiffly.

Then came the one-two punch. "And you can't publish this book until the women have passed away."

Bomb dropped. Big explosion. Her brain blanked. It was all Gloria could do to not let her jaw drop.

"Until they've passed. You mean died? They have to die?"

That could be years and years from now. These women could outlive her, for all she knew.

Linda leaned back in her chair and folded her arms across her chest. "It's the only way they'll work with you on this. I'm sorry, but these are the women's stipulations, and I agree with them. So does their lawyer. This information will bring attention they don't want—never wanted. They'll only meet with you if you agree to these terms."

Gloria tapped her fingers on the papers in her lap. She gripped the contract tight in her hand. Her face sagged in disappointment. She wanted to write this story, but waiting for people to die? So morbid. Like an ambulance chaser. A ghoul.

She began to mull it over. It *would* take time to write the story. Time to find an agent. Time to lock in a publishing contract. It *could* realistically take years for the project to reach completion. Of course, she would do this all while she continued to work at her full-time job. And, although she was a small town newspaper editor, she was nobody's fool. She'd done her due diligence. Being published was no walk in the park.

Then something occurred to her. "How is their health?"

Even as the words left Gloria's mouth, she couldn't believe she'd asked such a revolting question. "I'm sorry." She looked down in embarrassment, releasing her grip on the contract and letting it fall into her lap. "Forget I asked that."

Linda smiled and answered. "It was a logical question. They're all in pretty good shape actually. This is assisted living, not a nursing home. The only reason they're even here is because they were all alone and missed each other. The women simply wanted to spend their final years together. All of them may well be here for many years to come… although one never knows."

Gloria could feel her forehead wrinkling. She took a deep breath and tried to weigh the pros and cons. The main thing she kept thinking was how much she wanted to learn the truth—even if only for herself. It was as though she had to know. Damn inquisitive-reporter personality of hers.

"Did I mention"—Linda's eyes locked with Gloria's—"the women want to give you a full confession?"

Gloria put her hand over her mouth to cover a gasp. *Confession? That could only mean…* Her mind began to race and she felt her heart accelerate.

Linda's voice pulled her back to the moment. "So, you see, it's going to be a big story. It *will* sell books. And it's going to rock the town of Rosewood. It should be worth your wait."

That settled it. Gloria needed to write this story. Two years, five years, ten years. It didn't matter.

"I'm in," Gloria said with a quick nod. She had to meet these women. Birth mother or not, these four women held the secrets to a story she had to write.

Gloria started to dig through her purse. "Let me find a pen?"

Linda handed one across the desk and Gloria's hand twitched in excitement as she accepted it with a broad smile.

5

Linda Weldon and Gloria shook hands. The deal was done. "Send someone to show Ms. Larson to the sunroom," Linda said over the intercom. "I'd take you down, but I have another appointment." She was already shuffling papers around on her desk.

"No problem." Gloria only had to wait a moment before an aide arrived.

Walking down the hallway of the facility, they met old people in tracksuits and tennis shoes with little weights in their hands and looks of purpose on their faces. Not one room held any evidence of people withering away, ignored and forgotten.

Her escort opened a set of French doors into a large sunroom. Trees and gardens filled with flowers beckoned from the wall of windows facing south. The aide directed Gloria to a glass patio table with padded wicker chairs. Air filtered into the room through two windows cranked open near the table.

Sun beat in and she could feel sweat forming on her brow. She fished a tissue from her pocket. "It's pretty hot in here." Fanning herself, she hoped the aide would take pity and put them in an air-conditioned room.

"Debbie likes the sun room so she can smoke." She made a face and shook her head. "Terrible habit, but she's been doing it since she was thirteen, so there's not much hope of her quitting now." She shrugged. "Amazing she's made it to eighty." The aide shook her head, then shielded her mouth as she leaned over to Gloria. "I'm pretty sure Josie sneaks a smoke when she can." She pursed her lips and rolled her eyes. "I'll turn on a fan for you and bring you a pitcher of ice water, how's that?" She bustled over to a tall oscillating fan and directed it at Gloria.

The breeze fluttered the curtains and chilled the beads of sweat now formed on her neck. "Thank you."

Once alone, Gloria set out her laptop, tape recorder, and a folder filled with information. Then she heard the sound of elderly women in the hallway.

They were coming.

She stood and faced the doorway—more than a little nervous. Blouse adjusted. Hair pushed behind her ear. She dabbed at the sweat on her face and neck. She was going to show them she wasn't mean and pushy. The shuffle of walkers and thumps of canes neared the doorway. It was time to face the women rumored to be killers, and the first thing she had to do was apologize.

Yellow tennis balls on the ends of a walker, then the toe of a thick-soled white sneaker hinted at the approach of one of the ladies. A bent-shouldered, white-haired woman came into view. The walker's yellow balls squeaked on the sunroom's tiled floor. She entered the room, then stopped to adjust her pants. She looked up at Gloria through thick glasses and scrunched up her nose.

"Damn pants fit too soon," Tanya said with a Midwestern drawl.

Gloria nodded, but had no clue what "too soon," meant.

"They fit too tight, Tanya. Not, too soon. Too tight." A scratchy voice came from the second woman now entering the room. Gloria recognized the voice and the face. This one had told her "No comment." Debbie.

Carrying her own ashtray and a colorful cigarette case, Debbie held a long white cigarette in her knobby fingers, waiting and ready to light up. She used no walker or cane, stood straight, and walked with a slow, lanky gait. She was thin and stringy-looking, like tough meat. Elbow and shoulder bones poked out of her tan sweater, which was buttoned at the neck. Gloria recognized the hard edge to her eyes from the black-and-white photo she'd studied so many times.

"Tanya always gets that wrong." Debbie shook her head as she spoke to Gloria.

Tanya swatted her hand at Debbie as she passed her. "It's not wrong, it's just how I say it. I'm colorful, dang it!"

Debbie landed by the window and lit up her smoke, inhaled deeply, and blew it out the screen. "Ahhhh." She leaned her head back and closed her eyes. Smoke curled in the air above her.

Gloria turned to a new voice coming from the doorway. "Tanya, I love it when you say too soon. Don't let Debbie pick on you."

A roundish woman with a cane, stylish glasses, and a pleasant smile entered the room. Her hair still held a hint of auburn. She laid her hand on Tanya's shoulder and smiled at Gloria. This was Josie. She, too, passed Tanya, who had only made it midway across the room, and it really wasn't so big of a room.

Josie sat down by Debbie and held out two shaking fingers in a peace sign. "May I have a puff?"

Debbie opened one eye and handed over the cigarette. Josie took a drag. It looked like an age-old habit these two women shared.

"You ought to quit smoking, Debbie. It's going to kill you," Josie said with a wry grin as she blew a thin stream of smoke out the window.

Debbie laughed until she coughed. "I've lived long enough. At this point, I'm just a pain in the ass."

Josie smiled. "Oh, you've always been a pain in the ass, dear."

Debbie took another pull of nicotine, closed her eyes again, and ignored the comment.

Tanya and her yellow-balled walker finally reached the table. She eased into a chair across from Debbie.

Gloria gazed at the door, waiting for Betty, the tall, striking woman with a confident face and posture. She entered, wearing a powder-blue tracksuit and white tennis shoes—and not the thick-soled kind like the others wore. Her shoulder-length white hair was pulled back in a ponytail, and she stood straight with a certain air of dignity. She made eye contact with Gloria and extended her hand.

"I take it you're prepared to grovel?" Betty raised her eyebrow in question.

Gloria took Betty's hand and shook it as she attempted to look as humble as possible. "I am so incredibly sorry for my bad behavior when we first met."

Betty stared a hole right through her, then gave a curt nod and took her seat.

Turning to the table, Gloria looked from face to face, examined wrinkles and laugh lines, gray hairs and hunched shoulders. She realized the women were not threatening or mean like she'd expected them to be. They looked... forgiving.

The flutter in Gloria's stomach settled.

Josie cut through the air with terse words. "No need for niceties. We know why you're here, and you know who we are. Let's get down to business." She put her thick-soled shoe up on the last chair at the table and pushed it out. It screeched on the tiles and sat empty—an invitation Gloria had best not refuse. They stared at her in silence until she took the chair.

"Yeah. Let's get to it." Debbie squinted her eyes as smoke curled up past her face. "And you'd better behave today. You may not know this about me yet, but I'm kind of cranky sometimes." Debbie met Gloria's eyes with a knowing glance, held her in the gaze, and nodded slowly.

Gloria swallowed down a lump in her throat as she met the hard eyes staring at her. And to think, one of the four women in the room had most likely given birth to her. The thought was daunting.

"Good Lord, no need to be pushy. We're scaring her." Tanya scolded her friends, then turned to Gloria. "Dear, relax. We won't bite. And if anyone understands the need to be forgiven, it would be us."

Gloria cleared her throat. "Well, as you know, I'm Gloria Larson. I'm the editor of the *Rosewood Press*." She saw Tanya wince. "I don't want to do a news piece on you. I want to write your story in a book." She paused and searched their eyes.

They waited.

"I came across articles about you when I was going through archives at the paper."

Gloria opened up the file and passed around copies of the articles from the papers.

The women's eyes followed her hands and darted over the bold headlines and harshly lit photographs of them when they were forty years younger. Gloria watched them, looking for resemblances, gestures, and expressions—any kind of connection she might have with any of them.

But as the room fell silent, the remaining sound only Debbie's rattling breaths, Gloria knew their story was going to be what she had to focus on. Would want to focus on. She was going to have to put her genetic origins second, and it wasn't going to be as difficult as she'd expected.

Tanya's shaking hands with papery skin reached out, then drew back away from the articles to touch her mouth. She looked away.

Josie murmured under her breath.

Debbie scowled.

The Thorns of Rosewood continued to stare down at their past, pared down to so much black ink on copy paper.

"Here's the water and some coffee for Tanya." An aide's voice pierced the silence. Only Gloria started. The women remained transfixed.

"Set it down over there." Gloria stood and pointed at a small table at the back of the room, then walked to it.

The aide began to arrange things.

"I'll take care of it." Gloria reached to take the pitcher.

"Oh, hon, I can pour for you. No problem."

She put her hand on the aide's shoulder. "Can we have some privacy?" Her voice was firm.

The aide looked up and her eyes flicked from Gloria to the table of elderly women.

"Oh, I understand," she whispered and nodded. "I'll shut the door behind me so you're not bothered anymore."

Gloria smiled and mouthed, "Thank you."

Once the aide left, Gloria finished pouring five glasses of water and a cup of coffee since it sounded as though Tanya preferred it. She walked back to the table and set them down. Josie picked up her glass with a trembling hand and gulped down half the water. The room was too quiet. Too tense.

Gloria cleared her throat. "I want to write your story. The town of Rosewood only remembers the one-sided articles they read in the newspaper. You were all silent to reporters. It left everyone with

43

more questions than answers—and questions breed gossip." She paused and waited.

No response.

"And of course, the biggest question is, what happened to Naomi Talbot?"

Tanya's hand rose to her mouth.

Josie began to rub her arthritic hands.

Betty kept her fingers laced together on top of the table as she stared out the window with worry in her eyes, as though the answer was somewhere out in the trees.

Gloria realized her own fingers were laced together in much the same way.

Then Debbie leaned forward and stubbed out her cigarette with sharp, angry motions. She locked eyes with Gloria. Dark memories shrouded the old woman's glare as she blew the remnants of smoke out of the side of her wrinkled mouth.

Gloria held her breath, then Debbie's raspy voice escaped like a threat. "You sure you don't have any other agenda?"

Gloria swallowed hard. Was now the time? No. Not yet. "I'd like to know why you decided to see me after the way I acted when we first met."

"I guess there's just something about you." Debbie's eyes sparked. "We visited and decided to give you one more chance."

The others nodded in agreement and watched Gloria closely.

"And you know what, sweetheart? We do have a helluva story. So buckle up. This story may get a little bit weird. But it's a good one. I promise you that. And when it's all said and done, you may learn a little something more than you even realized you came for."

Goose bumps crawled up Gloria's arms, but she kept her mouth shut. Not only was now not the time—she was beginning to wonder if there would ever be a good time to ask any of these women if they had once given a child up for adoption. Maybe she'd just as soon not know. Maybe her mom was right after all. She might not like what she found out.

6

Gloria readied her pen. She could sense by the women's furtive glances at each other that they were about to start telling their story.

"Where do we start?" Betty asked the other women.

Debbie banged her fist on the table, shaking the ashtray and the stubs within. "At the funeral!" she yelled.

Everyone jolted in their chairs, and Gloria began to wonder about the stability of Debbie's mind.

Tanya set her mouth in a hard line and tears formed in her eyes. "I think we should start on the night Mari died." She pushed her finger under her thick glasses and rubbed a tear away.

Gloria's eyebrow rose. Mari? Who was that? But she didn't have time to ask. More ideas flowed from the four women.

"Or the night we…" Josie left the remainder of the sentence hanging in the air like the smoke from Debbie's cigarette.

Gloria held her breath. *Yes.* It was right where she wanted them to start.

Betty shook her head. "No. We need to start in the beginning. This all began back in high school, senior year… We were seventeen."

The group of women nodded in agreement and murmured to each other.

When you were seventeen? Dear Lord. This is going to take forever. Gloria imagined sitting in this room, listening to these women chatter on about their youth for months on end. Patience was not one of her virtues. She groaned, but not out loud. But the more they talked, the more story she would get. And if they wanted to start back in the stone age instead of where Gloria would have liked them to begin, so be it.

Betty stood up and began to pace back and forth. It looked like she was putting her thoughts together. After a few minutes, Betty took her seat and faced Gloria. She took a deep breath. "It was a long time ago—1950. We were all in the same graduating class with Mari." She glanced around at the other women as if asking permission to begin the story.

They nodded in approval. Even Debbie.

"Who is Mari? Gloria asked.

"Mari Brent was our friend. We were all like sisters." Betty reached out and grabbed the wrinkled hands of the two women on either side of her. The others did the same, forming a circle that excluded Gloria. It looked to be a bond stronger than anything the world could throw at them.

"We were always together. We went to grade school and high school together, raised our kids together, went to the same church. Our kids even ended up going to the same high school we attended."

"And then that bitch, Naomi, killed Mari." Debbie banged her fist on the table again, almost sending the ashtray flying.

What the hell?

Gloria scooted her chair back and stared at Debbie, then looked around at the other women. This was new information. Naomi had killed someone? This was something that hadn't been in the papers.

Josie put her hand on Debbie's arm. "Calm down. Naomi is long gone. She can't hurt us anymore."

"I know, but she didn't suffer enough. *We* ended up suffering more than she did, and it wasn't right." Hatred shadowed Debbie's eyes. Her words hissed out between gritted teeth.

"Calm down, Debbie. Anyway," Betty continued, "it was 1950, and we were all seniors in high school. It was a wonderful time in our lives, and we were all having a grand year."

For a moment, Gloria hesitated. Maybe she *should* tell Betty she had to start the story in '74 when Naomi went missing. But the women were all smiling. A flash of youth filled their faces with joy. Memories of poodle skirts and saddle shoes, ponytails and sock hops, danced across their faces. Betty had such peace in her eyes. If the old woman wanted to start the story with their glory days, there had to be a reason.

Betty's face darkened. "Then Naomi Waterman moved to town."

The mood in the room went sour in a split second.

"She waltzed into that school and ruined our senior year." The wrinkles in Betty's brow deepened.

"And she tried to ruin the rest of our lives." Tanya's tears began to flow.

"We let her ruin our lives," Josie mumbled as she pulled her handkerchief out from the end of her sleeve and dabbed at her moist eyes.

Betty waved her hand to shush them. "Anyway, it was homecoming. Mari had always been the nicest girl in the class. Everyone loved her."

The other women nodded.

"She was never mean to a soul, was she?" she asked the others.

They shook their heads.

"And Mari and Doug Talbot were going steady—going to get married after he graduated from law school."

Gloria perked up. Talbot. Naomi's last name.

"Mari and Doug started dating sophomore year. No one thought of only Mari or only Doug. It was always Mari and Doug. They were the perfect couple."

Tanya sniffled.

Josie sighed.

Betty continued, "I was out on the dance floor, a few steps away from Mari and Doug when Naomi Waterman walked through the doors of the school gym."

Betty's voice was mesmerizing, taking Gloria back—way back—to a time filled with school dances, pretty dresses, and nostalgic music. As

Betty spoke, the words came alive, painting scenes into Gloria's mind as she settled back and listened, nearly forgetting her role as a reporter while she fell comfortably into the tale.

Betty Starts the Story—1950

Jack Anderson gazed into my eyes. He spun me out and my dress twirled, brushing against my legs. I loved that dress. Made me feel like a princess when I danced.

He was trying hard to hold me close, but I wasn't much interested in him. I kept exchanging glances with Mari… rolling my eyes about Jack's advances.

Mari and Doug were homecoming king and queen, and Jack and I their runners-up, sharing the spotlight dance.

Mari's head leaned against Doug's shoulder and his chin rested on her head. Their arms hung down by their sides and their fingers were clasped together as they swayed in the center of the dance floor. I remember watching them and wondering what it would be like to be so in love.

Nat King Cole was singing "Mona Lisa." Mari wore a light pink skirt dress with little burgundy dots and a white lace collar. She was the Olivia de Havilland of the school and Doug the Jimmy Stewart. Doug's dark blond hair and strong jaw, Mari's soft eyes and graceful smile… the dim lights, the soft music… everything was perfect.

Then the gym doors opened and closed with a heavy clang. Heads turned and the new girl, Naomi Waterman, came strutting in like she owned the place. She wore a silky red dress and her full bosom almost burst from the bodice. Her pointy-toed, black spiked heels clicked on the floor, and her long red hair flowed over her shoulders like Bette Davis in *All About Eve*. She'd moved here from California and held her nose high, looking down on us small-town girls.

The eyes of every boy—and most girls—in the gym were drawn to her like magnets. She'd come to the dance alone, something not many of the girls had the courage to do. Her dress was sleek and expensive—most likely something she'd bought in California. The rumor was her parents had money.

Most of us wore crisp cotton with rounded collars and soft hairstyles, pink lipstick, and a little light blush on our cheeks. But Naomi slinked around like something from the pictures in *Vogue*, painted up and full of curves, like nothing any of us had ever seen in person. Those emerald eyes with long false lashes, the clear and obvious outline of her hips, those shapely calves, the bright red lips and heaving cleavage… how could we not all stare?

But not Mari. Her eyes were closed as she smiled and snuggled into Doug's shoulder while they swayed to the music. She was completely oblivious to Naomi's grand entrance.

Doug, on the other hand, couldn't take his eyes off the vixen.

It soured my stomach. But what worried me more was the glance of acknowledgement Doug and Naomi exchanged—like they already knew each other.

I told Jack thanks and left his grasp. He wasn't really my date, just the guy I shared a title with for the night. His face drooped—but those big ears and freckles—he wasn't my type.

As I walked up to Mari and Doug, the spotlight dance ended. Doug caught his knuckle under Mari's chin and lifted her face to his.

He nodded toward Naomi. "Naomi is here and she came alone. I feel bad for her being the new girl and all. Do you think I should ask her to dance... to make her feel welcome?"

I put my hand over my mouth. What a farce. Did he think Mari was going to buy such a phony line?

But sweet-natured Mari only beamed at her guy. "That is so nice of you, Doug. You absolutely should. Betty and I will go visit with the girls while you dance with her." Mari gave me a nod.

I stared, openmouthed. Doug kissed Mari's nose and headed toward Naomi. Mari watched him for a moment, gave me a smile, and turned to go meet up with the girls by the punch table.

I followed her off the dance floor. How could I explain she had made a big mistake? Before I could put in my two cents, the other girls jumped in with their opinions.

"What are you doing?" Tanya stared past Mari at Doug, who was leading Naomi out onto the dance floor with his hand resting on the small of her back.

"What do you mean?" Mari asked.

"You can't let Doug dance with the new girl. He belongs to you." Tanya held up her hands in alarm.

Josie added, "It's a slow dance, Mari. A slow dance! Look." Josie pointed toward the couple.

Doug held Naomi close and she had her arms draped over his shoulders, her head cocked the way girls do when they're flirting. She stared up into Doug's eyes, wearing a sly grin.

"That girl is a man-eater," Josie added as she crossed her arms over her chest.

Mari shook her head and smiled, but it was a tight smile. There was a hint of doubt behind her bravado. "Not my Doug," she said. "He's not like that. He's just being polite. Besides, her father is Mr. Talbot's new law partner. Naomi and Doug have been friends all summer. He says she misses her home. It's hard to move to a new school in your senior year. I think we should all be nice to her." Mari picked up a glass of bright red punch and tried to change the subject. "So, where is Debbie?"

"Where do you *think* Debbie is?" Tanya giggled. "Same place she always is at school dances."

We all looked toward the bleachers right as Debbie and Bud Coleman came stumbling out from the dark, straightening their clothes and hair. They couldn't hide their mischievous grins. Bud strutted, his ducktail a mess, gelled locks hanging down on his forehead. They parted ways, Bud off to brag to his friends and Debbie sauntering toward the punch table with long, lanky steps.

"Debbie, if Mr. Franks catches you and Bud behind those bleachers, he's going to kick you out of the dance. You're asking for trouble." Josie wagged her finger, one hand on her hip.

"Yeah. It's a disgrace," Tanya added, then leaned in and whispered, "So, what all did you do?"

"Tanya! It's none of your business." Debbie unwrapped a stick of gum and popped it in her mouth. "Besides, we weren't doing anything unnatural." She winked at me.

"Your shirt's on inside out." I stared at her seams and winked back.

Debbie glanced down. "Oh crud." She ran off to the girl's restroom.

I shook my head, then looked back to Mari. "And if you aren't careful, that siren you let Doug dance with is going to lure him off behind the bleachers, too."

Mari held her head high. "Nope, Betty. I trust my fella." She sipped the red punch.

"Are you sure?" Tanya pointed out to the dance floor, her eyes wide.

We watched Naomi twirling a lock of Doug's hair in her fingers as she whispered with those red lips right by his ear.

Mari straightened up and her eyebrows peaked.

I began a slow boil. Mari and I had been friends since we were little girls. I wasn't about to let some new girl waltz into the school and steal her guy. "That's it. I'm going to put a stop to this," I said, then took a step toward the dance floor.

Mari pulled me back. "No, Betty. You'll embarrass me." Her voice was firm.

"Being embarrassed? That's what you're worried about? Mari. Doug is only human. He needs help." I pulled my arm away from her grasp and started again.

"Betty, I will be furious if you do this. I do not want to be one of those jealous girls who sends friends to do her dirty work. I'll talk to Doug later."

I stopped. "Do you promise you'll talk to Doug?"

"Yes, I promise." Mari's eyes pleaded. "Besides, I still trust him. He wouldn't do anything like that."

Tanya interrupted our conversation. "Well, I hope you're right because they're leaving the gym together."

Dumbfounded, I watched as Naomi led Doug through the gym doors and out into the dark night. I could see a tear form in the corner of Mari's eye, but she pushed it away with a quick hand.

Tanya and Josie both shook their heads and started whispering to each other. I didn't know what to do other than offer encouragement.

"There has to be an explanation." I patted Mari's shoulder, but I could see her faith in Doug shattering.

The minutes ticked by and I was praying Mari would come to her senses and storm out of the gym to find Doug and Naomi.

Then we saw Debbie and Bud leave the gym.

"Where are they going?" Mari asked.

"They can't get enough of each other. They're probably going to his car to tongue wrestle some more," Tanya said.

"Doug's car is out front, too," Mari whispered. It was clear she realized what Doug and Naomi were doing outside.

Debbie burst back into the gym. "Mari, come quick!" she yelled from across the gym.

Mari's face turned every shade of red imaginable and she froze.

"Now!" Debbie ordered.

The command pushed Mari into action and we all hurried with her. When we reached Debbie, she grabbed Mari by the hand and dragged her out onto the steps in front of the gym. She pointed her finger toward Doug's car. We stopped and stared in shock. Every window of the big Ford was steamed and the car rocked ever so slightly. Then a black stiletto rose above the back seat and was planted on the rear window.

Debbie turned to Mari. "Well? Aren't you going to go kill him?"

Tanya and Josie covered their mouths with their hands.

I expected Mari to break down and run to the restroom to cry her eyes out, but she surprised me. She clenched her fists, marched down the steps and over to Doug's car, then swung open the back door. We stayed back, still on the steps but close enough to hear and see the whole sordid episode. Most of the kids in the gym had poured out from the big double doors to see what the fuss was about. They were about to get a good show.

Doug scrambled off Naomi, his suit coat wrinkled, his tie loose, and his face covered in Naomi's bright red lipstick. He had a dumb grin on his face like he couldn't leave the last moment he'd experienced to face this new one.

Mari reared back and slapped him so hard she let out a scream. Doug stumbled and fell back into the car, right on top of Naomi.

Apparently amused, Naomi laughed as she pushed him off.

Doug stood back up. "Mari. I don't know how this happened... I... It's not what you think."

Doug reached out to grab Mari by the shoulders. She pushed his hands away, then slapped him again and shoved him back down into the mess he'd made. Mari straightened up, proud and tall, and glared at him. He continued to blather on, trying to find the words to make her understand, but she turned and stormed away, leaving him red-faced and pleading.

Mari stomped past all of us—the whole school it seemed. She marched up the steps and went back into the gym, the doors now clanging shut behind her.

Josie, Tanya, and Debbie ran down the steps to take their turn at Doug and Naomi. They screamed at Doug and yelled insults at Naomi while the school of onlookers watched and shouted encouragement as they giggled and squealed.

Naomi exited the car and adjusted her dress like nothing had happened. She even put on fresh lipstick while the girls yelled at her.

I stayed back, trying to decide what to do next. My best friend had been crushed and Naomi Waterman thought the whole thing was a joke. "Girls!" I yelled out to Josie, Tanya, and Debbie.

They turned, left Doug, and ran up to me on the steps of the school.

"Don't waste your time. Doug's a bastard and Naomi's a slut. Everyone knows it now. You're wasting your breath on them. Let's go help Mari."

That was only the beginning of our problems with Naomi.

7

Gloria clicked her pen in and out—a nervous habit. Then she noticed Debbie glaring at her hand. Gloria put the ballpoint down and began to think about the story Betty had told. Naomi was clearly a piece of work, but high school drama wasn't enough reason to kill someone. "Sounds like the catfight began right there and then." Gloria started to yawn but tried to keep her mouth closed to hide it. A sleepless night was coming back to haunt her.

Anger flared in Debbie's eyes and Gloria realized she hadn't hid her yawn.

"Oh, bored are you?" Debbie cocked her head to the side and pursed her wrinkled lips.

"No, no. I'm just tired. But, I *am* most interested in the story about Naomi going missing in '74."

Gloria didn't want to upset them, but her mother's words about taking time away from her job lurked at the back of her mind.

"Well, don't you worry, precious. We're starting at the beginning for a reason. You'll understand soon enough." Debbie crossed her spindly legs and drummed her fingernails on the table.

Gloria hadn't meant to upset anyone. "I'm sorry. I shouldn't have interrupted. Really. I'm sure it will all make sense in the end."

"You're darn right it's gonna make sense in the end." Debbie mumbled curses under her breath. "*I'm* gonna tell the next part of the story if it's all the same to you, Betty." Debbie scooted up to the table and shot a defiant stare in Gloria's general direction.

"Absolutely. Go right ahead," Betty said, then relaxed in the chair and sipped her water.

Then Debbie took everyone back in time.

Debbie Takes Over—Summer 1951

Charlie O'Dell ran the soda fountain at the back of Mickey's Dime and Drug on Tenth Street. Whenever it was my turn to pick where we went, I picked Mickey's. I loved the white paper hat and fresh, clean apron Charlie wore every day. He served malteds and sodas with nice long red-striped straws. To me, there was something about the long shiny counter and the bright red stools. Everything at Charlie's counter was spic and span, and I needed to be in a clean place once in a while.

I always got a Black Cow and Tanya a strawberry soda unless it was winter, then she drank coffee. Then we'd argue about why our drink was better than the others. I love a good argument, especially with Tanya.

"The thing is, Debbie, with the strawberry soda, you get whipped cream and a strawberry. Everyone knows more is better." Tanya popped the fresh fruit into her mouth.

I took my gum out and stuck it behind my ear to save for later. "No contest, Tanya. A Black Cow is pure—just root beer, soda, and ice cream. Whipped cream and strawberries are for amateurs. Less is more." I was used to having less.

Josie rolled her eyes and sipped on her cherry Coke. "Seriously, who cares?"

Mari and Betty glanced back toward the pharmacy counter. Something had gotten their attention. I followed their gaze and saw Naomi and her mother, Mrs. Waterman, talking to the pharmacist.

Mari shifted her attention back to her chocolate malt, but I fumed at the mere sight of Naomi and continued to stare. I hated Naomi so much. The way she flaunted Doug on her arm our entire senior year. The embarrassed look on Mari's face every time she saw them together. The joy on Naomi's face every time she saw Mari look away from them. The way Doug had fallen head over heels for Naomi had been pitiful.

"I'm going to get closer so I can hear what's going on." I stood and crept over behind the rotating display of postcards. I could see Naomi and her mother between the wire and paper, and I could hear them, too.

"It's just that she's so sick to her stomach in the mornings," Mrs. Waterman told the pharmacist. "I was hoping there was something you could suggest." The blue hat Mrs. Waterman wore sat low on her forehead and a dark black pin curl blessed her cheek.

"Mother, keep your voice down," Naomi said through gritted teeth.

"There'll be no denying it soon enough. You'll be showing within a month." Naomi's mother snapped at her sullen daughter, then returned her attention to the pharmacist behind the counter.

I hurried back to the girls. "You're not going to believe this," I whispered in Tanya's ear.

"What?" Tanya asked too loud.

"Yeah, what, Debbie?" Josie repeated, and they all leaned forward, a row of inquiring eyes looking at me.

"Naomi is in the family way," I told them, my face dead serious.

"You're kidding!" Tanya declared, loud enough to stop Charlie in the middle of making a malted. The pharmacist, Naomi, and her mother also turned their heads our way to see who had yelled out.

Josie elbowed Tanya. "Hush up."

Tanya slapped her hand over her mouth and turned to see if Naomi was looking at her.

She was.

Tanya turned quick and whispered out of the side of her mouth. "Oh no. Here comes the wrath of Naomi."

Naomi stormed toward us with her head held high, her shoulders back, all arrogant and pissy. She made a beeline toward Mari.

"Mari, dear, have you heard the news?" Naomi's voice high and fake.

Mari looked up into the long mirror behind the soda fountain. She met Naomi's eyes in the glass but didn't answer her.

"No?" Naomi asked. "Well, let me be the first to tell you. Doug and I are to be married in September. Isn't that wonderful?" Naomi clapped her hands together, then laid her hand on Mari's shoulder and squeezed.

Mari cringed.

"He proposed last week. Very romantic. He's the best. Of course, you know that already."

It was time for me to put an end to this show. I stood up and went to face off with Naomi. "Why do you think Mari would care about any of this?"

"Well, Debbie, I saw you all over here whispering like silly girls. I assumed you were talking about me. I thought Mari would be the most interested as she and Doug used to be friends." Naomi smiled.

I crossed my arms over my chest and stuck out my chin. "So, is it true you're knocked up?"

Naomi stiffened and her face flushed red.

"Because if you are, you won't be able to wear white for your wedding. Won't that be a shame?" I cocked my head and raised my eyebrows, waiting for her reaction.

Tanya snickered under her breath and even Mari couldn't stifle a smile.

Naomi turned red in anger and reached up to slap my face, but I was quicker and I grabbed her by the wrist and shook my head. "Oh no you don't."

Naomi jerked her hand away. The staring match continued.

I stood up as straight and tall as I could, pulled the gum out from behind my ear, and popped it in my mouth and began to chew with a fury. Squinting my eyes, I stared into hers. My glare never wavered as I stood there with my shoulders back and my chin out. "You ever try to hit me again, Naomi Waterman, I promise you'll regret it."

"Oh yeah? What would you do, you little white-trash rat?" Naomi hovered over me.

I searched my mind for what I might do to Naomi, and came up with no end of ideas. I thought back to times men beat up my mom. Things I wished I hadn't seen. The bar fights I'd witnessed while being dragged from one sleazy dive to another when I was a kid. Yeah, I'd seen plenty of the underbelly of Rosewood in my short life, and Naomi was one more human disappointment. The kind of disappointment that had made me tough and prepared.

I reached into the pocket of my dress and pulled out the jackknife I kept there. I showed her just enough for her to see the glint of steel.

Naomi backed away a step. Her hand rose to her mouth. All of the girls fell silent.

From the corner of my eye, I saw Naomi's mother storming over. I shoved the knife back deep into my pocket.

Mrs. Waterman reached out and grabbed her daughter by the elbow. "Come along. We have errands." Mrs. Waterman pulled Naomi behind her, and by Naomi's pale face, it appeared she was more than happy to be taken away from the situation.

I sat back down, took my gum out and stuck it back behind my ear, then slurped my melting Black

Cow through the red-striped straw. No one said a word for a while.

"Are you okay, Debbie?" Josie asked in a hesitant voice.

"Yeah, I'm fine." I shrugged.

"Would you actually use that knife?" Tanya's words quivered.

I thought about it for a minute. "I would if I had to."

And I was pretty sure I meant it.

8

Debbie scared the hell out of Gloria. A teenager carrying a jackknife? She tried to imagine the old woman in front of her ready to rumble. Oddly enough, the image came easily. And if this was the woman who gave her up for adoption, Gloria could consider herself fortunate to have been raised by someone else. Karen Larson would never be so bold or easily angered. Yet it couldn't be denied that Gloria always did have a problem with patience and a bit of temper. She shuddered at the thought, but now wasn't the time to think about such things.

"Sounds like you and Naomi were archenemies." The term sounded like something from a cartoon, yet it was apt.

"You could say that." Debbie eyed Gloria, suspicion hanging heavy on her face. "But the next part of the story seals the deal."

Debbie took a sip of water, cleared her throat, and continued.

Debbie Remembers the Reception—Fall 1951

The large green lawn, perfectly manicured shrubbery, and whitewashed brick of the sprawling home screamed "We have money! Lots and lots of money!"

A life I couldn't even imagine living. Although I'd tell anyone who asked I wouldn't want it, deep inside I guess I wouldn't have minded trying it on for size.

As I stood at the end of the sidewalk, I tried to figure out how I might be able to get out of going to this wedding reception. There really wasn't any good reason in the world for Naomi to have invited me or the others except to rub our noses in her money. And to remind Mari she had stolen her guy. It was like crawling into a spider's web, knowing we would all be wrapped up in silken strands and eaten alive.

Slipping my hand in my dress pocket, I fingered the cold jackknife. It gave me confidence.

Music and voices from the reception lilted over the high white fence of the backyard. Tall wicker vases filled with ferns flanked the garden gate. They were tied with balloons, which bobbled in the breeze. A sign on the gate read Waterman/Talbot Reception.

Unfortunately, I was in the right place.

I trudged up the sidewalk, then paused. Just beyond the closed door, I overheard Naomi.

"We'll be living in the Grafton house on Sunderland Lane. But only until something more acceptable becomes available to buy."

I pushed the gate open a crack and saw her visiting with a blue-haired elderly woman who was wearing pearls and a lace-trimmed hat. The putrid scent of the lavender perfume the old woman had obviously bathed in latched on to the breeze and slapped me in the face.

"I see," the blue-hair said with a raised eyebrow and a look on her face as though she'd caught whiff of a sewage lagoon. "The Grafton house. Hmmm."

Apparently, the Grafton house was subpar, I thought.

The gate tugged at my hand as a man pulled it open, exposing me to the crowd. Ice and alcohol clinked in his glass. Gin. I could smell it. My mom's drink. His eyes had a glassy, bloodshot vagueness I recognized too well. He glanced past me. I guess I wasn't important enough to acknowledge. He staggered by.

Money did not mean good manners. Nothing I didn't already know.

Naomi turned to me and we locked eyes. Searching past her glare, I sought out my friends. If I'd have gotten off work earlier, we could've come together. Showing up alone to a snake pit like this took all the guts I could muster.

A hand grabbed me from behind and pulled me back away from the gate—away from Naomi's piercing glare.

"Wish I could come in with you, sugar baby."

I grinned at the sound of Buddy's comforting voice. I spun around and threw my arms around his neck.

"This is going to stink. I don't wanna go. Let's get on your motorcycle and drive away," I pleaded, enjoying a glimmer of hope that I might not have to endure the stuffy party.

"Debbie! Over here!" Tanya's voice squealed over the music of the small band as they played, dressed in white sport coats.

I glanced back through the gate and into the crowd, past Naomi's judgmental stare, the blue-hair's downturned mouth, and the turquoise waters of a swimming pool. There was the gang, all waving frantically, glad for one more body to fortify their numbers.

Damn. For a moment, I thought I'd be able to blow that pop stand and have a fun afternoon with Buddy.

"Looks like you're not going to get out of this one so easily." Buddy's bottom lip pouted.

I reconnected with Naomi's glare. Between hugging Buddy and Tanya hollering across the pool, I had created a scene unpleasing to Her High Haughtiness.

Good.

I gave her a grin, leaped into Buddy's arms, and Frenched him like a woman sending her sailor off to sea. Buddy didn't shirk his end of the deal. I heard the blue-hair gasp. A round of applause rang out from my friends across the pool.

Breathless, I pulled away, turned back to Naomi, and winked. She glared at me, a sneer on her lips.

"Thanks, Bud. I needed that." I ran my thumb along the edge of my bottom lip and cleaned up my lipstick.

"Always happy to oblige." Buddy bowed. "See ya later, sugar baby." He wore a smudge of my lipstick on his mouth.

I turned to make my entrance into the back yard and sauntered up to Naomi. "I guess I'm supposed to congratulate you or something." I snatched the gum from behind my ear and popped it in my mouth, put my hand in my pocket, and jiggled the knife. I was feeling full of myself, satisfied everyone there knew I was every bit as wild as the townsfolk rumored me to be.

"I see the old saying is true." Naomi glared. "You can't make a silk purse from a sow's ear." She looked down her nose at me, smiled, and raised her eyebrows..

"Don't be so hard on yourself, Naomi. I think you cleaned up okay," I said, then pointed at her protruding stomach. "Seven... eight months pregnant, and you still wore white." I shook my head. "Your mother must be so proud."

Naomi's face froze, but I didn't wait long enough for her retort. Doug stood a few steps away. He gave me a smile and a nod as though commending me for a job well done. Maybe he wasn't as happy about this marriage as Naomi would have liked us to believe.

I would have chatted with him like old times when it was Mari and Doug, but he'd stabbed Mari in the back. No self-respecting friend would do anything but hate him for it. I turned up my nose and held my head high as I passed him by. He knew what he'd done. He'd fallen from our grace. From the looks of the snooty crowd and his bulging bride, he was paying for it, too.

"Debbie, I can't believe you were making out with Buddy right there at the front gate." Tanya giggled as I sauntered up.

"That was nuthin'. You shoulda heard what I said to Naomi." The girls gathered around as I relayed the details.

"Here's what I want to know," Josie said, putting her hands on her hips. "Why are we even here?"

"Because we were invited," Mari answered.

"I know, but *why* were we invited?" she pushed.

"To rub our noses in... this." Betty swept her hand out, indicating the garish display of wealth.

Young girls in black dresses and white aprons served hors d'oeuvres. Flowers in hanging baskets decorated the patio around the pool. Tall vases filled with white roses adorned tables covered in white tablecloths, loaded with champagne glasses waiting to be filled.

Every guest—the hangers-on, the wannabes, the social climbers, as well as the big shots and la-de-das of the community—stood around, mumbling quietly about golf scores, theatre, and politics. They all behaved with stiff superiority. Each of them acted as though they were better than everyone else while at the same time, they were wary of making a mistake and being exiled from the clique.

A strange game, this being important and wealthy, I thought. I'd take my Buddy and a motorcycle any day of the week.

"What's going on over there?" Josie pointed at Naomi, who was whispering in a man's ear.

"Who is she talking to and why are they staring at us?" Tanya asked, her voice shaking.

"They're not staring at us. They're staring at me," I answered. "And that's the chief of police."

He'd been to my mom's house a few times, breaking up disputes between her and whatever man she'd dragged home.

Naomi and the chief began to walk my way. I swallowed hard and clenched my jaw.

"What's going on?" Tanya whispered.

Josie put her arm around Tanya. Betty began to step forward, but Mari glided past us all and approached Naomi and the chief.

She extended her hand to take Naomi's. "Naomi, you look so beautiful today. And this reception is wonderful. Thank you so much for inviting us."

I watched as Mari tried to run interference, but it took more than a pleasant smile and kind words to stop Naomi's freight train once it hit the tracks.

The bride hesitated, gave Mari a sickly smile, then stepped around her, her eyes still trained on me.

"Chief Danby, this is the girl I was telling you about." Naomi pointed at me. "She's crashed this reception. She was not invited."

"You liar. I sure as hell wouldn't come here unless I was invited." This I hadn't expected. The hairs on the back of my neck prickled and I knew things were about to get even worse.

Naomi laughed. "You're delusional. We would never, ever, associate with someone like you." Naomi made a face as though she smelled some of the sewer lagoon the blue-hair had caught whiff of earlier. "Chief Danby, I want you to search her. I've been told she carries a weapon. I don't know why she would break into my reception unless her plan was to cause trouble."

Naomi's words were loud—loud enough for every guest in proximity to hear. Gasps escaped the crowd like balloons hissing air.

"Young lady, are you carrying a weapon?" Chief Danby took a formidable stance and glanced at the pocket of my dress. "Perhaps a jackknife?" He reached toward my pocket.

I exploded. Naomi's scrawny neck needed my fingers around it. I lunged, wanting nothing more than to choke the lies out of the conniving backstabber.

Chief grabbed me by my shoulders and put me in a hold I couldn't wiggle free of.

I screamed, "You bitch. You filthy bitch!" The chief held me up off the ground, my feet kicking in the air. Then he put me down and twisted my hands behind my back. I cried out in pain.

"Oh, no. Stop," Mari begged. "None of this is necessary."

Too late. The chief had already begun to push me toward the gate. "Time for you to cool off in a jail cell," he bellowed.

More gasps escaped the crowd.

Accusing eyes glared at me. Hands covered appalled mouths, and judging stares bore into me. People backed away in disgust, as though I were rabid and foaming at the mouth.

Maybe I was.

It's the way I felt.

I'd come into this party knowing in my gut I was walking into a place I had no business being. But I left knowing one thing very clear. Someday I would make Naomi Waterman Talbot pay for what she'd done.

9

The stuffy room couldn't overcome the chill of the threatening tone of Debbie's story. Gloria shivered. "I can't deny it. At this point, I don't like Naomi, either."

"I know, right?" Betty put up her palms and nodded. The other women all bobbed their heads in agreement.

Gloria understood why someone would want to teach the shallow, self-absorbed witch a lesson. But murder her?

None of this information had ever come to light before. These were great insights into the emotions that led to whatever had happened between these women and Naomi. And as far as writing a book went, these *were* the colorful characters Gloria had been looking for. She would listen as long as it took. But for today, she had to go.

"Gals, I've been here a few hours and it's time for me to go, but it's been enlightening." Gloria stood and began to gather up her things.

Tanya's eyebrows peaked with concern and she cradled the cup of coffee in her hands. "When are you coming back?" She seemed a little needy, but also motherly.

Gloria's heart warmed to her and she searched the old woman's face for anything similar to her own. "How about I come every Tuesday and Thursday at two o'clock? I'll try to stay until four thirty or so. That sound okay?"

The women looked around at each other and nodded happily.

"Don't forget," Tanya said with a grin. "Maybe I should text you a reminder on Tuesday and Thursday mornings." She dipped her hand into the pocket of her ivory sweater and produced a smart phone. Gloria didn't even try to hide her surprise.

"Didn't think I had one of these, did ya?" She winked.

Josie laid a hand on Tanya's arm. "Oh, Tanya, Gloria won't forget. She wants this story. It's gonna make her famous." The old gal gave Gloria a heart-squeezing smile.

Josie was right about her not forgetting, at least.

On her drive back to Rosewood, Gloria remembered her own mother complaining about a woman in their neighborhood. "Gold digger" and "snob," were words she had used in connection with the particular name. Maybe every neighborhood had one or two women abusing positions of power. Lording their money over others and bossing the world around. Funny thing was, her mother really hadn't ever been the type to gossip or speak ill of anyone. It's why she remembered her saying it. People like Naomi had a way of getting under one's skin.

Gloria chuckled as she thought about how angry the old women's faces had been. All scrunched up, twisted old mouths, and furrowed brows. This Naomi had to be more than a socialite power monger to make these women so mad they still carried anger to this day.

From what Gloria could tell, the women all seemed like normal, intelligent people. Even Debbie. Maybe *especially* Debbie. Her outbursts and rough exterior were like a little drama inside the bigger show. Gloria was going to enjoy getting to know her.

She pulled up to the driveway of her little house. Twelve hundred square feet of low-maintenance living. One potted plant on the front porch, barely alive. Gotta water that, she thought, but knew she'd forget.

She showered, put on some yoga pants, went to the kitchen, and started digging through her cupboards. Brown rice, a can of black beans, and some diced tomatoes would do the trick, but meat would be nice. Not even as much as one can of tuna.

The fridge didn't hold any more promise. A head of lettuce and a bottle of mustard—not even a piece of bologna haunting the meat drawer.

Time to get some groceries. She grabbed her house keys, locked the door behind her, and took off at a jog down the few blocks to Hinkle's Food Haven.

As she ran along the street, she gave little waves to folks already sitting out on their front porches for the evening. She flipped open her cell phone. Five thirty—after supper for most of the senior set. She lived in a neighborhood chock-full of elderly folks. It was like having a dozen grandmas at your disposal. She was the only one in the neighborhood who moved above the speed of cold syrup. And these old folks thought she was plain crazy for jogging.

Gloria saw Mabel Piper sitting at the end of the block. The old woman had bad vision and couldn't see folks from her front porch, so she dragged her aluminum lawn chair right up to the sidewalk by the street and plopped herself there. Didn't miss a thing that way. Mabel made it her personal business to know everything about everyone, especially Gloria, it seemed. And right now, Mabel was waving like someone bringing in a plane for landing.

"Gloria, what are you doing? Running away from someone?" Mabel's chins shook as she laughed at her own joke. Three odd curlers clung randomly in her hair and she fussed at them with plump fingers.

Mabel always had an extra lawn chair for the potential guest. "Sit down." The loose weight under Mabel's arm wiggled as she shook the armrest of the extra aluminum chair.

"Can't tonight, Mabel." Gloria panted a little as she jogged in place. "Gotta get to the store. Out of groceries. Haven't had supper yet." Mabel put a lot of stock in taking meals on time. The old woman had once scolded Gloria about making sure she ate nutritiously. Like her own mother didn't remind her enough. Gloria hoped her empty stomach would appease the old gal.

"Out of everything? Did you forget to do your marketing this week?" Mabel's expression showed an absolute lack of understanding.

"I guess I did. Just got busy." Gloria still jogged in place, waiting to be dismissed. It wasn't that she didn't like Mabel. She just wasn't in the mood for an inquisition today. Especially on an empty stomach.

"Too busy to think of eating? Well, land sakes. Never heard of such a thing. Get on out of here you skinny thing. You need to eat more. And stop all this crazy running. It's not healthy. Jumbles up your reproductive organs is all that does."

As Gloria jogged away, Mabel hollered out, "Buy meat. You need protein. And vegetables. Don't forget vegetables!"

Later, Gloria cut up a hot dog into her rice, beans, and tomatoes. She suspected this wasn't what Mabel had in mind when she suggested she eat more meat.

She washed up her few dishes, then began to review the tapes from the afternoon. She paused to think about all the old people staring out at the world from their front porches in her neighborhood. Gloria realized these people might have light to shed on this whole Thorns of Rosewood issue. Maybe she'd have to sit down and chat with Mabel to see what she remembered.

Then it occurred to Gloria—tomorrow she could visit the old-man table.

Seemed every town had an old-man table at some eatery or coffee shop. This one happened to be at the truck stop on the east edge of town. Plenty of gossip was passed around at those tables. And endless cups of coffee. How old people could drink so much coffee, she'd never understand. They drank it like their lives depended on it. And hot— they demanded it be hot. Like they'd lived too damn long to tolerate lukewarm liquid.

Gloria had inserted herself into the old-man table conversation her first week in Rosewood and made it a priority ever since. It's where she found leads for some of the paper's best stories. The old men had welcomed her and done what they could to rattle her at first. Told some tall tales. Still did. But she could tell by their winks and exaggerated expressions which stories had merit and which ones were meant to send her off chasing her tail. She'd come to love those old guys.

Tomorrow she'd ask them about the Thorns of Rosewood and see what they had to say. They'd talked about them before, but this time she would pay closer attention. She had a feeling it would be worth the price of coffee.

It was called *The Last Stop* if you were heading out of town going east. Coming in to town going west—The First Stop. The timeworn diner sat on the east side of town right on the highway, directly across from the hospital. Everyone joked that it was a good thing since the food was a heart attack waiting to happen.

Most of the waitstaff at the Last/First Stop were older women who had been working there since the place opened back in the late sixties.

Except for Tildy Hoffman—Tildy ranked as the youngest waitress of the group at only fifty-eight. But she moved as quick as a forty-year-old and had an attitude capable of handling not only truckers but also the smart alecks at the old-man table. The old men often proved the more difficult of the two.

Tildy dropped a tray down onto the table Gloria and the old men occupied. Cinnamon rolls jumped on the plates as they rattled against each other. "I can't believe you boys haven't ordered a cinnamon roll yet this morning. These are the last four." She left the tray on the table, hustled over to the coffee station to grab a carafe, and came back to pour them another round. She filled all the cups full to the point of running over—one of Tildy's trademarks. Customers came as much for Tildy's show as for the chicken-fried steak the joint was known for.

"But, Tildy, I probably shouldn't have a roll. I'm watching my figure, you know," said Chevy. His eyebrows danced and he reached out to poke Tildy in the ribs.

Chevy was the tallest of the bunch. The ladies' man in his younger years, Gloria suspected. Old smooth talker had sold cars back when he was still a workingman.

Tildy pushed his hand away and pointed a threatening finger at him. "You're buying rolls. No arguments, and I mean it. And you all better leave me a decent tip today. This fifty-cent crap ain't gonna pay for my retirement."

Tildy unloaded a plate with a cinnamon roll in front of each of the old men, and they all looked as though they knew better than to argue.

After Tildy stormed away, Gloria ventured her question. "So, what do you fellas remember about Naomi Talbot?"

Delbert whistled.

"What is that supposed to mean?" she asked the retired dentist with bushy eyebrows and slouching shoulders but darn straight teeth.

"She was a hot one," Bart answered for Delbert. Cinnamon-roll frosting clung to his mustache. Bart loved sweets, as his round belly attested.

"Oh yeah, smokin' hot," Wayne added. Wayne was sometimes quiet, other times a comedian. He had the deepest pockets of the bunch and owned a few apartment buildings in town. He was well respected, which only made his statement about Naomi being smokin' hot funnier.

Gloria shook her head. *Old perverts.*

"I remember Naomi's husband, the judge, didn't seem nearly as upset as he should have been. Wasn't even him who questioned his wife going missing. He seemed satisfied to assume she left him." Wayne popped the last bite of roll in his mouth and licked his fingers.

"Could hardly blame him what with how she'd cat around on him," Delbert added.

"You know, I had a shot at her once." Chevy leaned back and crossed his arms over his chest.

"In your dreams." Delbert poked Chevy in the shoulder.

"Not a chance." Wayne shook his head.

"You finally went senile," Bart added.

Gloria waited for them to finish their chorus of insults. "So what did you guys think of the Thorns of Rosewood?"

The old men quieted down and the conversation from there became more hushed... reverent.

Bart twisted his coffee cup in its saucer. "Josie Townsend was a real good teacher. She actually helped my boy understand math. Never thought I'd see that happen. I got nuthin' bad to say about her."

Wayne nodded. "I always liked dealing with Betty Striker at the law office. She knew her stuff. Good gal. Always a lady." He slurped his steaming coffee.

"Debbie Coleman had a tough row to hoe. She grew up rough. Her, I wouldn't have put it past." Delbert played with a packet of sugar but avoided eye contact.

"Well. I can't even imagine Tanya Gunderson killing a fly, let alone a human. Even if it was that mean woman," Chevy added. "And don't forget their friend, Mari Gestling. The girls claimed Naomi murdered her. That's why folks figured they went after Naomi to begin with." He downed the last of his coffee and motioned to Tildy to bring him a refill.

"So, do you think they killed her or not?" Gloria asked outright.

Wayne shook his head. "Nah. They couldn't have. They wouldn't have known how to even go about something like that."

"I don't know. How hard is it to kill someone?" Delbert shrugged.

"Harder than you think." Bart stared solemnly into his cup.

The table fell silent for a moment. Bart was a veteran. "There wasn't any proof. That's why they were let go, wasn't it?" he asked.

"Yes, yes. That was why. I remember that." Delbert agreed and nodded.

"I think for the most part, we all would say those gals were innocent." Wayne smiled at Gloria and stirred sugar into his hot coffee.

But Gloria noticed Delbert's almost imperceptible shrug. Opinions were still split, like she suspected it had been back in the day. It only reinforced her desire to learn the rest of the story.

10

Thursday, around twelve thirty, Gloria started to watch the clock. Tanya had sent her a reminder text, but she hadn't forgotten. There'd be no denying Gloria was eager to hear more of the story and to spend more time with the four women.

When she arrived, they were all waiting for her in the sunroom. The yellow walls beckoned, as did the old women's smiles.

"Hello, ladies." Gloria greeted them.

"We have cookies!" Josie pointed at the plate on the table and clapped her hands together. "Oatmeal raisin."

Gloria would have to mention peanut butter was her favorite and see if wishes really could come true.

After settling in, eating a cookie or two, and making some small talk, Gloria brought out her notepad and pen. "Are you ready to tell me more of the story? I believe Debbie was being hauled off to jail, last we talked."

Debbie nodded, but Betty looked to be preparing to do the talking.

"Yes she was, and it was our job to spring her," Betty said and cleared her throat.

"That's right. We had to save our Debbie." A cookie crumb fell onto Tanya's sweater. She searched for it to no avail. Josie picked it off for her.

Gloria's heart warmed.

She sat back and grabbed another cookie as Betty reached back in time.

Back at the Reception with Betty—1950

We were still at the reception, and I wanted to get the heck out of there so we could go help Debbie. I hurried everyone along. "Go, go... before Naomi turns on us." But it was too late.

Naomi reached out and grabbed Mari's arm.

"Wait, Betty," Mari said to me as she slowed, then stopped.

"Ignore her," I begged as I clutched Mari's hand to tug her along.

"Just wait," Mari insisted. She turned to face Naomi. For a smart girl, she was certainly a glutton for punishment.

We paused by the gate. I knew talking to Naomi was going to make more problems. I knew Naomi had nothing but more ill will to spread. Damn Mari's good manners.

"What is it?" Mari asked, stiff but gracious. Always gracious.

Naomi placed her hands on her stomach and stared into Mari's eyes. Her attempt at a Madonna-like expression didn't fool me. I could hardly stand the sight of her act. What kind of show was this going to be?

"I'm so glad you're being such a good sport about everything, Mari." Naomi waved back toward Doug. He stood several feet away, talking to other guests. "I mean, you had some kind of little crush on him, didn't you?" She offered sarcastic sympathy with a slight pout of her bottom lip.

I crossed my arms. "Mari, you don't need to listen to this."

She ignored me. Her face turned crimson, but she squared her shoulders and raised an eyebrow. "It was a bit more than a crush, Naomi. Doug and I dated for several years."

"Really?" Naomi threw her head back and laughed at Mari. "Well, Doug hardly mentioned you. It must have been far more serious for you than for him."

"Yes. Apparently it was more important to me," Mari said, then began to turn. "Come on, Betty, we should be going."

But Naomi caught Mari's arm again and pulled her back. Nothing was ever enough for her. She wasn't happy until she drove her knife in deep.

"You do realize a man with Doug's future requires a certain kind of wife?" She twirled the new diamond on her ring finger and it glittered in the sunlight. "I mean, his father is an attorney. Doug will be an attorney. As his wife, I'll be part of high society." Her stiff smile hid her teeth but not her intentions. "It's the kind of thing people with money understand. You really wouldn't have been able to handle it."

A tear glistened at the corner of Mari's eye.

I'd heard as much as I could take. If Mari wasn't going to stand up for herself, I'd do it for her. "Naomi, the truth is you're nothing but a shallow snob. All the money in the world couldn't buy you the manners Mari comes by naturally."

"Well, excuse me, Betty, if I'm not offended by comments from your kind." Naomi laughed, then looked down her nose at us.

Then Tanya's temper kicked in. "Our kind? What the heck is that supposed to mean?" She stepped forward. "You mean the nice kind? The normal kind? The not-having-to-get-pregnant-to-catch-a-man kind?"

Doug walked up right at the end of Tanya's small tirade. We all stiffened and fell quiet. "What's going on here?" He searched our faces.

"Doug, these friends of yours... they're upset about their criminal friend being hauled away. Now they're taking out their petty anger on me." Naomi pouted, her bottom lip jutting out, and clung to his arm.

"You started it," Tanya blurted out and moved toward Naomi with her eyes practically shooting fire. "You came and stopped *us*. We'd have been long gone by now, but you had to get your licks in." Tanya's fingers curled into fists.

Naomi pointed at Tanya's hands. "See, Doug. They're ready to fight. What am I to think? Debbie keeps a jackknife in her pocket and this one looks like she wants to hit me. What kind of mob are you girls, anyway? Really, Doug, you're lucky I came along and saved you from this unsavory crowd."

Naomi looked back toward her father, who kept protective eyes on his daughter. He began to move toward her as though she drew him on a leash.

I held my breath. Now what lies would she spin?

"Naomi, I don't think you need to insult our guests. I've known these girls for a long time. They're all good eggs." Doug smiled at Josie, Tanya, and me, then let his eyes drift down to Mari. He smiled at her, too.

Naomi's face paled, then she flared. "Are you taking their word over mine, Doug? On *my* wedding day, no less?" She looked as though she might sprout fangs and rip his head off.

Doug reddened and turned away from her, then looked back with a glare that said he wasn't about to be embarrassed by his wife... on *his* wedding day. "Yes, I guess I am. I saw what happened. They didn't pick the fight. You did. Why don't you let them be?"

Naomi's eyes squinted with hate. She reached up and slapped Doug's face, her nail dragging across his cheek. A long red cut sprouted red.

Mari covered her mouth and gasped.

Class act, Naomi. Things were getting interesting.

Naomi's father rushed to his daughter's side, her mother coming up right behind. "What's going on here?" he bellowed.

"Daddy, I'm not feeling well." Naomi grabbed at her stomach and swooned.

Her father put his arms around her and glared at Doug. Naomi's mother fanned her daughter with a cocktail napkin, but I caught something in her eyes other than worry. Disappointment?

"Oh, for heaven's sake. Get her in the house. Put a cold cloth on her head." She shooed her husband and Naomi away.

The bride clung to her father and he hugged her tight, cooing as they went. "My poor baby."

Mother Waterman glared at Doug. He mopped at the blood on his cheek with the white handkerchief from his coat pocket. Her stare finally caught his attention and he looked into her formidable expression.

"Well, go on. Help your wife," she snapped.

Doug hesitated, looking from the red-stained handkerchief to the girls, then back to his mother-in-law.

"Now," she hissed in the loudest whisper she could manage.

Don't want the guests to know your dirty laundry?

Not only was Naomi pregnant out of wedlock, but she'd made two ugly scenes at the fancy wedding reception, which must have cost her parents a small fortune. I could tell Mother Waterman was less than pleased.

Doug hurried off, escaping her wrath.

Then Mrs. Edith Kern Waterman of the Boston Kerns and the fourth generation of Watermans in Hayes County turned to us. I braced myself but stepped forward to face her.

For a moment, it looked as though she would slice us with her tongue, but instead, she let out a deep sigh. Her face altered and she closed her eyes. When she opened them, they had filled with exhaustion.

Mrs. Waterman swallowed hard, then said with as much poise as she could muster, "Thank you all for coming. Please see yourselves out."

As I watched her turn and hurry away to the house, I wondered how many other things Naomi's mother had put up with from her daughter over the years.

Disapproving stares from guests around the patio shot our way. I hurried the girls out the gate and beyond the fence, then looked back and realized what a false front we'd passed through. It felt good to be back in the real world.

"Betty, wait up," Tanya panted.

I was running up the sidewalk to the door of the police station and the girls scurried behind me, their shoes scraping the concrete, their conversation rushed and worried.

I'd known Debbie forever it seemed. I understood everything about her—the need to protect herself, the rebel living inside the skinny girl, the brave face hiding a frightened young woman. And, Debbie, the girl who would act like being put in jail was a badge to wear, not a shame to hide.

There wasn't much she *could* hide. The whole town knew her mom was a drunk, and no one, including her mom, had any idea who Debbie's father was. She owned the right to be brash and loud. She'd earned the ability to wear her troubles behind a mask of toughness.

And it was easy for me to feel guilty. My dad was an upstanding citizen of Rosewood. A banker.

A councilman. So although I couldn't relate to Debbie's troubles, there was one thing I could do: take care of things. I knew how to be responsible, and that's what I would do right now.

Pushing the door open wide, I led the others into the front room of the police station.

"I've never been here." Mari's eyes darted from wanted posters to sale bills and finally landed on the woman standing at the counter. Debbie's mom. The woman who had turned Debbie into the tough cookie she pretended to be.

I cringed. Mona Jenks was drunk as usual, which translated into angry. Essentially, she was always yelling at someone.

Mona pointed at us, then swayed as though she might topple over. "Those girls. Put them in jail, too!"

The policeman behind the counter reached out, grabbed her arm, and pulled her back upright. "Mrs. Jenks, settle down. You've had too much to drink again."

"Me? I ain't been drinkin'. You shut your lyin' mouth." She shoved his hand away.

Mona turned to glare at me. "Betty, you gonna bail my Debbie out or stand there starin' at me?" She took a step forward. I took a step forward, too, and held my ground.

Mrs. Jenks stepped back. "Well, are ya?" She turned to the officer. "'Cause I ain't got enough money."

I turned back to the girls. They looked collectively horrified.

Josie lived with her grandmother. She spent more time in church than the rest of us. She'd most likely never been near a bar, let alone seen the likes of a drunk like Mona Jenks.

Mari was as pure as the driven snow and looked as though she'd melt at any moment.

Tanya's face was white as a clean piece of paper. Her eyes bugged out of her head as she pushed up her blue horn-rimmed glasses with the little rhinestones at the corner. She would be talking about this for weeks.

"Girls?" I asked. "Do we have money?"

"How much, Betty?" Mari stood tall.

"Officer, how much to bail out our friend, Debbie Jenks?" I asked.

Mrs. Jenks had laid her head down on the counter and looked to be in a drunken stupor.

"Twenty bucks." The officer walked away from the gin-soaked aroma of Mrs. Jenks and came to stand at the counter near us.

"I have two dollars," Mari offered.

We all dug in our handbags and came up with $10.42 between the four of us. I walked over to Mrs. Jenks and cleared my throat.

She didn't respond. The sight of her sickened me.

"Mrs. Jenks!" I shouted.

Mona jerked her head up, a long stream of drool dripping from her mouth to the countertop. Her red eyes stared at me but didn't seem to really see me. She was probably trying to remember where she was.

"What?" Mrs. Jenks shouted and almost fell over.

"We need money to get Debbie out of jail. We don't have enough. Do you have any?" I shouted back.

Mona appeared stumped by the question at first, but began to paw into her purse with clumsy hands. She pulled out a fistful of money and slammed it down on the counter. Pennies rolled to the ground, and nickels spun on the counter top in little tornadoes. "That's it. It's all I got." Then came an outburst of tears—a drunken sob about everything and nothing at the same time.

I reached around her to count out the money she'd slammed down. "Now we have a total of $14.32." I looked at the officer. "I guess we'll have to go find more money."

I turned to leave and nearly ran into Doug Talbot, who was standing in the doorway of the station. He looked more than out of place with his tuxedo and white carnation still pinned to his lapel.

"How long have you been there?" I asked.

"Long enough," he answered. "I'll cover the bail, Betty." Doug reached into his pocket and pulled out his wallet. He went up to the counter and put a twenty down. The policeman raised his eyebrows but brought out a clipboard with papers to be signed. We stood back and watched.

When Doug finished, he turned to us. "I'm sorry. None of this should have happened." His eyes fell to Mari. "None of it at all," he whispered, shaking his head.

Mari's eyes filled with tears. She turned her back to him. Even I could see Doug was talking about more than what happened at the wedding.

I stood there with the fourteen dollars and change clenched in my fist. Mona Jenks stormed over to Doug. He turned in time for her hand to come down hard across his cheek.

Mari gasped and stepped forward... then dropped her head and retreated.

"Mrs. Jenks!" I shouted.

"You rich bastard. Who do you think you are? You come in here like you own us. Throwin' your money around. You think you're so perfect, don't you?" Her eyes cleared for a moment. "Well, don't forget—you knocked up the little bitch you married. You ain't any better than the rest of us." She put her hand on Doug's chest and pushed him like she was picking a fight in a bar.

Doug said nothing but met her stare.

"Well, let me tell you this, you snotty little prick. Your slut wife will get what's coming to her for putting my little girl in jail. I promise you that." Mona's words growled through her yellowed teeth.

She turned to face us. "You all get Debbie home. I got stuff to do." She turned and staggered out of the jail.

We watched her stumble across the street to the Shady Bend Tavern. Stuff to do. Lives to ruin, money to waste, I thought.

"Good old Mom. Sets quite an example, doesn't she?" Debbie stood in the hallway behind us, escorted from her cell by the police officer.

We all turned. I stayed back, but Tanya, Mari, and Josie ran over to hug her.

Doug hung his head and turned to leave. I touched his arm as he passed. "Thank you, Doug. I'm sorry, too."

He looked at me with confusion. "What are *you* sorry for, Betty?"

"I'm sorry for you, Doug. I'm just sorry for you."

We left the police station arm in arm.

"Sorry about my mom," Debbie offered, her hands shoved down into the pockets of her dress. I knew she was playing with the jackknife the officer had returned to her.

"Hush. Don't even talk about it." Mari wrapped her arm around Debbie's shoulders.

"I can't believe Doug left his own wedding to bail Debbie out." Tanya pushed her glasses up her nose.

"I know. Naomi's gonna kill him if she finds out," Josie added.

"But it was the right thing for him to do," Mari said, and it seemed obvious to me she was still proud of Doug.

"Well, if I were Naomi, I'd be worried about my safety. Your mom isn't someone I'd want to mess with." Tanya's voice wavered.

Debbie fell silent—her brows furrowed and the corners of her mouth turned down. "Someday Naomi will get what's coming to her. Of that I'm sure."

11

No wonder Debbie viewed life like a person looking in from the outside.

"Sorry." It was all Gloria could think of to say. Her own childhood had been lovely, and it was hard to imagine anything different.

"Save your pity. I turned out great, if I do say so myself." Debbie lit a cigarette and blew the smoke out the window.

Even though the old bird was rude and mouthy, Gloria couldn't help but respect the strength it took to be who she was.

"Nineteen fifty-one was a tough year for you ladies. I assume, though, more trouble followed." She searched their creased faces.

"Oh, it never seemed to end." Tanya threw her hands up in the air.

Gloria hadn't heard much from Tanya yet, but she had a feeling she was about to.

"Naomi was like a bad cold. You'd think you had it cured, but damned if it didn't come back."

Gloria grinned. Tanya was so colorful. Her white hair, those big eyes behind glasses, a hot cup of coffee always at her lips. It was fun to watch her fidget and some of the things that came out of her mouth were golden.

"Sounds like you had your own problems with Naomi, Tanya."

"Kid, you have no idea."

Tanya's Boss—1960

I remember staring at the door with the gold lettering. It read Naomi Waterman Talbot, Chief Lending Officer.

I never thought that someday Naomi would be my boss. The idea turned my stomach.

Every morning, I would change the calendar on the wall of Naomi's office. I ripped off yesterday's page, and a large red number seven stood out below the word March. Rosewood National Bank headed the cardboard holding the date. It was 1960.

I turned on the radio to the local news station. The announcer repeated a story from the day before. President Eisenhower had sent 3,500 American troops to South Vietnam. At least Elvis Presley had been honorably discharged on Saturday—one less thing for me to worry about. I was his biggest fan.

I put a note on Naomi's desk to remind her about her one p.m. appointment. Glancing around her desk, I noticed the picture of her son, Douglas Junior. I picked up the photograph and shook my head. Poor kid. I wondered if Naomi ever gave him any attention. He was almost ten at the time. The kid had been handed off between Doug and Naomi's parents while both of them went to college. Doug took over his father's law firm, and of course Naomi began running the town's social calendar. It wasn't long before she landed a snug loan officer's job at Rosewood National, thanks to her father-in-law's position on the bank board. She was a pro at looking as though she was working hard while making everyone else do her work.

I left, went to my desk outside Naomi's office, and began to go through the mail. It was eight o'clock and the bank was about to open. It would be at least an hour before the great and powerful Naomi swished into the building like she owned it.

Ten after nine, the sunlight glinted off the chrome of Naomi's Corvette as she pulled up to the front of the bank. Everyone else parked in the rear of the building, but Naomi always had to be front and center. I watched her long legs stretch out of the car. She stood and adjusted her silk scarf and sunglasses, then pulled down her tight skirt.

When Naomi pushed the door to the bank open, the president jumped up and scurried out of his office. "Good morning, Naomi," he called out as he gave a wave. The fool looked like a puppy wagging his tail. Two other men on staff snapped to attention and echoed his greeting.

"Good morning, everyone." Naomi had her wiggle on and her tight skirt didn't go unnoticed by any of the men at the bank. A contented smile showed she had made the entrance she'd intended.

Naomi approached my desk, her smile replaced by a look of disdain. Taking off her sunglasses, she sniffed at the air. "Tanya, what is that smell?" She crinkled her nose and sniffed around my desk.

I sat up straight. *What game was she playing?* "I don't smell anything."

"Rebecca, come here, please." Naomi motioned to the teller nearest us.

"Yes, ma'am." Rebecca's face showed eager gratitude for Mrs. Waterman Talbot even knowing her name.

"Do you smell anything odd here at Tanya's desk?" Naomi continued to inhale delicately. Soon, Rebecca was sniffing, too.

"Really, I don't smell anything," I said. *Except your overdose of perfume.* Naomi doused herself in heavy quantities of some ridiculously expensive French scent and bragged about it as though I would have known Chanel from dime-store toilet water. All I knew was it gave me a headache.

After they sniffed and made a big deal about it, Naomi finally proclaimed, "Well, your desk must need to be cleaned. It's all I can think of." She threw up her hands and laughed. "Sorry to bother you, Rebecca. I know you were busy."

I'm busy, too. And my damn desk is spotless.

"Your desk may need a good scrubbing, Tanya." Naomi glared at me with a twisted smile.

"But…" I was about to argue when the bank president approached.

"What's going on over here?" He gave Naomi a concerned glance and put his hand on her shoulder.

"Oh, Richard. I have too sensitive a nose. Something smells peculiar and I worry at what customers will think." Naomi pinched her nose.

My face turned every shade of crimson. I'd gone from offended, to angry, and now plain humiliated. "I don't smell anything, sir." I knew Naomi was trying to upset me and make me look bad. It was working.

"Well, Tanya, if Mrs. Waterman Talbot wants you to clean your area, it's what you'll do." He gave Naomi a wink. "Beautiful outfit you have on today, Naomi." He eyed her from top to bottom, lingering on her long legs and high-heeled sandals.

"Now, Richard, you behave." She batted her lashes, then turned to me. 'Tanya, if you're too busy, I can clean it after work today." Naomi offered a pathetic look.

Right. She'd clean it after work. What a load of bull.

"Don't be silly, Naomi. You're management. Tanya will take care of it." *Stupid president of the bank, standing there trying to impress Naomi.*

"Well, if it's okay with Tanya, of course. I don't want to cause her extra work." Naomi's fake guilt and pout fooled him, but not me. I couldn't hide my disgust. I glared at Naomi, shrugged, and nodded. What choice did I have?

"You're a trouper, Tanya." She gave Richard a winning smile. "I'd better get busy. I have *so* much work to do today." Naomi wiggled off to her office.

Richard watched her, then turned to me. He nodded at my desk and left with his head high in the air.

I swallowed hard and thought about how much my husband and I needed the money from this job. It was better than waitressing or working at the factory. But being Naomi's secretary and what it entailed was lower than I thought I'd ever have to stoop.

Marrying Rusty Gunderson a year after high school was still one of the best things I'd ever done.

He was adorable and sweet and everything I'd always wanted... except he didn't have a dime to his name and probably never would. But being in love counted for a lot, and I would always be in love with Rusty.

Back in the storage room, I found the Clorox and a sponge and filled a bucket with hot water, then I trudged back to my perfectly clean and un-smelly desk.

I began to scrub. Naomi stood, shut the door to her office, and closed the blinds. Now the entire view of me cleaning was out of sight, out of mind. Apparently, such menial labor affected her thought process.

A half hour later, the desk had been scrubbed down and every drawer cleaned out and washed. Now I could finally settle in to work.

Enter Darby Pederson—Naomi's most frequent visitor. Everyone suspected he came around for more than financial advice.

Naomi swung open the door to her office and allowed him full view of her tight skirt and long legs. "Darby, are you here to see me?" She tilted her head and gave him a dirty little grin. His smile bloomed into a goofy grin, and his face went from ruddy to downright crimson.

"Hey, Naomi. Do you have a little time for me?"

"I always have time for you, Darby." Naomi crooked her finger and lured him into her office. She was about to close her door when she leaned out and sniffed. "Tanya, what in the world did you clean your desk with?" Naomi brought a handkerchief to her nose and breathed through the cotton and lace.

"Clorox... on my hands and knees... Why?"

"Oh heavens. Clorox is such a strong smell. I'd say it's almost worse than it was before. Makes my eyes water. You should have used Pine-Sol." Naomi shook her head and frowned. "From now on, Tanya, maybe don't let your area get so dirty in the first place."

She shut her door and I was left listening to giggles and hushed conversation coming from inside her office. Luckily, the blinds were still closed, so at least I didn't have to watch her shameless flirting.

Within five minutes, the couple emerged from her office, Naomi with the handkerchief covering her nose so she wouldn't offend her delicate nostrils with the smell of Clorox, and Darby with a look of great anticipation in his eyes. "Tanya, I'm going with Darby to check out some property he's looking into purchasing. I'll be back later."

"You have a one p.m. appointment," I reminded her.

"Of course, Tanya. I know. I'll be back." Naomi waved me off with a roll of her eyes.

Right. Like Naomi was ever on time or good for her word. She'd stumble in at one fifteen and I would have already spent fifteen minutes reassuring a grumpy client. It had happened many times before.

The morning continued in the same dismal way. It was one of those days. Right about the time

I wanted to take lunch, the school called to tell me my son had been in a pushing match on the playground.

When I returned from visiting with the principal, another loan officer demanded the papers I'd been preparing for him. They weren't ready, of course, because I had wasted so much time cleaning my desk.

And of course, the one p.m. client arrived on time, but not Naomi. And yes, I ended up fetching him coffee and visiting with him to help pass the time until Naomi finally swished in at twenty after. She did what she always did. Acted as though her life was so, so busy and she was so, so important. Somehow, the client managed to forgive her within seconds but gave me a look as though I had somehow wasted his time.

It was almost two before I even had an opportunity to pull my lunch out of the bottom drawer of the desk. I unwrapped the egg-salad sandwich after Naomi's client left. She had walked him to the front door and when she returned, she stopped in front of my desk and sniffed again.

I stopped chewing and stared at her, waiting for whatever hell was going to rain down next.

"Egg salad? Oh for heaven's sake. I'll bet I was smelling your nasty egg salad, Tanya." She shook her head and laughed as she disappeared into her office, shutting the door behind her.

I stared at the sandwich, and the longer I sat staring, the more infuriated I became. About the time I thought I was going to crack, my phone rang.

"Tanya, I need you to pick me up at work. The car broke down, and I have a dentist appointment," my husband yelled over the sounds of heavy equipment at the plant.

"What's wrong with the car? We brought it home from the repair shop last week." We'd spent more than we could afford to have it fixed after it broke down the last time. We desperately needed a new vehicle but couldn't afford one.

"I know. I think it's the plugs." I could hear impatience in Rusty's voice. He wanted to take care of his family. He was doing the best he could.

I sighed. "What time's your appointment?"

"In ten minutes. I'm sorry, hon. I don't have any choice."

My Rusty. I knew how hard he tried. "I'll be there as soon as I can."

I hung up the phone and took a deep breath and went to Naomi's office door. I knocked. No answer. I really didn't have time for this. I opened the door and poked my head in, and Naomi looked up with a glare.

"I have to go pick up my husband and take him to the dentist. His car broke down and he needs a ride." This wasn't a big deal. I tapped on the doorway with nervous fingers, waiting for Naomi's reply.

Naomi sighed. "Tanya, have a seat." She stood and pointed to the chair across from her desk.

I stared at the chair then back at Naomi. "Can I please go get my husband? He'll be late for his dentist appointment. Surely we can talk later."

Naomi's face turned sour—hard eyes and a set jaw. "*I'll* decide when we talk. Now is best for me, so have a seat." Her voice didn't allow for argument.

I sighed heavily and thought to myself, *I need this job, I need this job, I need this job.*

Sitting down, I folded my hands in my lap and hoped like hell this would be over quick.

"I'm so disappointed in you, Tanya." Naomi paced behind her desk, her hands clasped behind her back. "You started today with a foul-smelling desk. I heard you were late with some reports. Rebecca told me you had to go to school for something to do with a child of yours misbehaving? Then I catch you eating smelly old egg salad at your desk. Now this, Tanya? You have to shuttle your husband around like he's a child? Really. You don't seem to have your life in order, and I think it's affecting your work. I know it's affecting *my* work. I mean, I simply must have an efficient and clean secretary representing my office."

Naomi stopped and turned to stare at me with a look of pity. "Are you sure this job isn't too much for you? Maybe going back to being a teller would be best. I know Rebecca would love to move up and she's such a crackerjack. She has the smarts to do so well."

Heat crept up my neck to my face. It wouldn't have surprised me if I burst into flames. So this is what Naomi's game was about today. She wants to demote me. But I needed to keep this job. It paid better than being a teller, and it had taken years to work my way up.

"Naomi, I'm just having an off day. Please, I really have to go. Can we talk about this later?"

"Now see? There you go putting your work last and making excuses again. Don't you value this position?" Naomi smiled a pathetic smile and offered a look filled with false concern, worried eyebrows, and downturned mouth.

"Of course, of course. But I have to go get my husband so he's not late for his dental appointment. He's had a bad toothache."

Naomi paused. "Well, that's really not my problem, now is it?"

A cold hard stare reminded me who I was dealing with.

"My only responsibility to you is to give you a job. And my only concern is for you to do your work properly." Her face no longer hid superiority and arrogance. "So if I want to talk for another thirty minutes, that's what we'll do, Tanya. Because I'm the boss. Remember? Your boss. And it's not my fault you married a loser who can't afford a decent car."

I jumped out of the chair, my hands in tight balls and my jaw clenched. "You have no right to speak about my Rusty like that. And you can't fool me. You're trying to make me look bad so you can fire me, you... you..." I stopped myself. I had to keep my mouth shut. I couldn't lose my job.

"What's that, Tanya? You have something you want to say to me? Like it would matter. You hold no power over me." Naomi leaned over her desk, her cleavage showing, a wicked smile on her face.

"But you can get it off your chest if you feel like it."

I stood up straight and let it go. "You mean-spirited... tramp."

Damn, that felt good. But I might as well have jumped off the roof. I brought my hand up and slapped it over my mouth. *What have I done?* But it was like Pandora's box and kept coming out. "I know you've been gunning for me ever since you took this job. And I've had it." I paused, out of breath and apparently out of my mind. Naomi would make me pay for this. There would be no doubt about it. "Now, I'm leaving whether you like it or not."

"Are you sure you want to do that, Tanya? I've asked you not to leave." Naomi pulled a legal pad out of the top drawer and plopped it on her desk, then picked up a pen.

I put my hands on my hips. I was so furious and so confused I didn't know what else to do *but* storm out. "Yes. I'm leaving."

Naomi leaned over and wrote the word *Insubordination* on the yellow paper in large, dark blue letters. "Go on then, Tanya. You do what you have to do, and I'll do the same."

I never mentioned a word of it to Rusty. No need to trouble him.

As I sat in the outer office of the dentist, waiting while he had his tooth filled, I knew what I'd be going back to. While I was gone, Naomi would make sure the bank president and other loan officers, right down to every teller, knew what a troublemaker I was. All I could do was walk back in with my head held high and try to fight for my job.

In the meantime, I wondered how we'd ever pay our bills.

12

Gloria found herself becoming angry as she listened to Tanya's story. "What a..." She held back her thought.

"Bitch?" Debbie offered.

Gloria nodded.

She was starting to see the bigger picture. Naomi was one of those self-absorbed women and everything had to revolve around her. Naomi clearly didn't consider anyone else's feelings to be important. Other people seemed to be nothing more than a means to her ends.

Something occurred to Gloria. "How in the world did this pushy, narcissistic woman behave as a mother?" She gulped at the thought of Naomi being her birth mother. She couldn't imagine anything worse.

"This is where my part of the story comes in," Josie said, a sad memory in her eyes. "And I'm afraid it's an unsavory tale and the ending isn't a happy one."

Gloria cracked her knuckles and readied her hand to write notes in her yellow pad. Everything to do with Naomi seemed unsavory to her.

Josie's Teacher's Conference—1962

As a seventh grade teacher, I had to be well prepared for teacher's conferences. I shuffled through the graded papers on my table and waited for the next parent to sit down, worry in their eyes as they asked me how their child was doing in school. I was a strict teacher but loved my kids. Most of them were well behaved and most of the parents were doing their best. Yet I worried about some.

I checked my class roster. Only four more students left for the day and Doug Talbot Jr. was one of them.

The auditorium buzzed with the sounds of parents and students visiting with teachers. The principal greeted people by the doorway of the gym. The women of the PTA ran a cookie and punch table along one wall, and the booster club sold tickets for a stadium blanket at the raffle table. The room filled with the usual sights, sounds, and smells of a teacher's conference: sweaty children, tired parents, and dozens of conversations rising up into the rafters where they would fade away.

In our small town, conferences were held in the school gym. Each teacher sat at a table, and the parents made their rounds. I saw Tanya walking toward my desk and I gave her a wave. She had her youngest in tow and gripped his little hand in her own. "Hey, Josie," she said, tugging the three-year-old along.

"Hi, Tanya. Glad you stopped to visit. I have time to kill between parent visits." I reached down into a bag to pull out a Tootsie Roll for the little fella. "Here you go, Marty."

Marty's eyes lit up and his hand shot out and grabbed the candy.

"Marty, what do you say?" Tanya took the candy from him and peeled the wrapper off the treat.

"I like candy!" he yelled.

Tanya shook her head. "Thank you. We say thank you."

Marty nodded and stuffed the chocolaty caramel candy into his mouth. A drip of brown goo leaked from the corner of his lips.

"How's it going?" Tanya asked as she wiped Marty's face with a tissue.

"Not bad. I only have four more appointments. Junior Talbot's parents are one of them." I sighed and rested my chin in my hand.

"Does his father bring him or does the hag come?"

"What's a hag, Mommy?" Marty gnawed on his Tootsie Roll and swung his feet back and forth.

"It's a bad word. Don't say it." Tanya wiped his face again.

"You said it." Marty opened his mouth wide to show his mother the chewed-up candy.

"Oh! Close your mouth." Tanya covered his mouth and shook her head. She and I laughed.

"Hard to say. If Doug comes, everything will go well. If Naomi comes, it will be a whole different ballgame." Nervous, I straightened the papers again and tapped them on the desk. I didn't quite know how to handle Naomi. I don't think anyone really did.

The truth was, I had always been a little shy. It wasn't my style to argue or make waves. It wasn't the way I was raised. My grandmother always said, "A smart woman can get what she needs without causing a fuss." And it was true. Usually, I was able to get what I needed without much trouble. Most parents could be calmed with quiet, controlled words. I could almost always reason with, or at least understand the motivation of, the parents of children in my class. But not Naomi. Naomi made her own rules and tested all my limits.

"So, is Rusty here?" I asked Tanya, trying to change the subject.

"Yeah. He's visiting with coach about softball for the summer. The kids had good reports and are out on the playground. I thought I'd stop and say hi before we left."

Marty started to squirm in his seat. "More candy." He tried to stand on the chair.

"I think it's time for us to go. Candyman here has had enough sitting for this afternoon." She stood and picked up her sticky son.

He buried his head in her shoulder, smashing tootsie roll drool into her shirt. "Go home. Go home. Go home." Marty chanted as he wiggled.

"Hush," Tanya told the child.

"How's work been going?" I asked over Marty's noise.

"Oh, all right, I guess. I'd rather be a teller than what's-her-name's secretary, even though it doesn't pay as well. But I shouldn't complain. It's a better job than some." Tanya put the squirming boy down but kept a tight grip on his wrist. He strained against her, still chanting, "Go home, go home, go home."

"I will say this…" Tanya leaned closer down and whispered, "I think Rebecca wishes she was still a teller instead of being the hag's secretary." Tanya giggled.

"Hag, hag, hag!" Marty shouted.

I caught sight of Naomi coming up fast behind Tanya, and I stiffened.

"Tanya, you must be so proud of your son. Quite a vocabulary he has." Naomi stood with her arms crossed, a judgmental stare in her eyes and a smirk on her face.

Tanya spun to the voice behind her. She glanced down at Marty's face, sticky with Tootsie Roll, as he yelled, "Go home, hag. Go home, hag!"

Naomi rolled her eyes and cut a wide swath around them to get to my table. "Josie, I know it's fun to visit with friends, but I do hope you can make time to actually meet with a parent." Naomi sneered.

I inhaled deeply. "Of course, Naomi. Have a seat." I pointed at the chair in front of my table and waved good-bye to Tanya. She waved back, but it looked more like she was shooing flies.

"Talk to you later," she mouthed to me, then turned to hurry away.

"Oh, Tanya," Naomi called out before she escaped.

She stopped. Her shoulders sagged as she turned back to Naomi.

"I'll need you to run an errand for me before you go back to the bank." Naomi reached into her purse and pulled out an envelope. "I have the payment for the bill at the hardware store. Drop this off to them."

No please. No thank you. Just an order.

Poor Tanya. Working with Naomi must be a nightmare. I reminded myself I had my own nightmare to deal with, and she was sitting right in front of me.

Tanya trudged over and plucked the envelope from Naomi's hands. She said nothing, but I'm sure it was because the only thing she could think of to say would have been something foulmouthed.

Naomi settled into the chair and crossed her legs. "So, I see you still run with Tanya like you did in high school. I assume you still hang out with the whole gang—Betty, Debbie... Mari too?"

I smiled. "Yes, I'm proud to say we've all stayed pretty close." I wasn't about to let Naomi knock me from my footing. "Now, where is Doug Junior? He should be here for our visit."

"Why on earth would he need to be here? Just tell me his grades so I can be on my way. I'm a busy woman, late for an appointment as it is." Naomi brushed her skirt as though it were dirty from being in a public school. She looked around with haughty eyes at the other parents and children.

"Well, in seventh grade the children are supposed to come to conference with their parents. Is he coming?" I glanced around the auditorium. Doug Junior was nowhere to be seen.

Naomi rolled her eyes. "Well, he's obviously not here, and I don't know that his whereabouts is any of your business. I'm the parent. I'm the one who's important. I'm the one paying the taxes that pay your wages. Let's get on with it." She scooted her chair closer to the table and reached for the papers on my desk.

I snatched them up.

"Doug Junior is a smart boy," I began, the papers tight in my hands. "His grades are above average, yet not the highest in his class. He could be achieving higher scores, but I wouldn't say there is anything for us to be concerned with in that regard."

"Great." Naomi began to stand.

"Wait." I selected a paper from the bottom of the pile.

Naomi rolled her eyes and sat back down. "If his grades are fine, what more is there to discuss?"

"I wanted to show you this. It's a poem Doug wrote in class." I handed her the paper. "He's so quiet and solitary. I guess I worry about him. Is everything okay... at home?" I held my breath. I felt like I had to ask but doubted I'd get an answer so much as start a war.

Naomi glanced at the lines on the page, shrugged, and tossed the paper back onto my table. "So? It's a poem. You gave it an A. What's the problem? He's quiet? Good. He's in school. He's supposed to be quiet. You want him running around and yelling? What kind of teacher are you?"

I stared at Naomi, then looked down at the paper. "But Naomi... did you read this? I began to read the young man's poem aloud.

I'm alone again.
Homework's done. Night's begun.

In my quiet room.
Four walls make my space. My place.
No one else.
I'm all alone.

Don't make a mess.
Don't disappoint.
Don't raise my voice.
Alone.

I looked up into Naomi's eyes, hoping the mother would hear the loneliness in her son's words. I handed the poem back to her. "Don't you want to keep this?" I asked.

She gripped the paper in a tight fist. Anger boiled behind her eyes.

"So it didn't rhyme. My kid's not good at poetry. Give him a B. And for your information, he likes being alone. What of it?"

Naomi clearly didn't have time to bother with a son. I sat back and crossed my arms over my chest. "I guess I worry if Doug Junior is happy. This poem sounds like a cry for help, Naomi."

Naomi threw back her head and laughed from deep in her throat. "Happy? Cry for help? So you're a psychologist now? Give me a break." She stood and glared down at me. "Josie, seriously. Doug Junior has more money in his trust fund than you make in a year. He has everything most kids can only dream of. The only thing possibly troubling him is having a bad teacher."

She stood up, turned, and stormed away.

Part of me wanted to rush after Naomi, grab her by the arm, and give her a scolding. But I couldn't actually see myself doing such a thing. I couldn't even imagine what I would say if I did. That Naomi was a bad mother? Was it my job to declare parents good or bad? No. It was only my job to teach their children. I rubbed my fingers across my forehead, trying to push the headache away.

But if I didn't do something, who would? If someone didn't reach out to the poor young man... who knows what would become of him?

I jumped up and ran out of the auditorium and into the hallway to find Naomi. The hall seemed so long as I ran up and down, searching, but she was nowhere to be seen.

I ran out the front door and scanned the parking lot for her car. The bright red Buick Wildcat caught my eye. There sat Doug Junior. Naomi held the poem in her fist and shook it at her son as she yelled.

I couldn't tell what she said, but I could see Doug Junior's hopeless eyes. He stared out the window as Tanya and Rusty followed their three children to an old beat-up truck. They were all holding hands and laughing. Doug Junior looked as though he'd trade places with them any day of the week.

I watched Naomi yell at her son and the sadness in Doug Junior's expression. Someone had to help him, and I was that someone. When I returned to the school building, I went directly to the principal.

"Mr. Berry, I need to speak with you." I interrupted his visit with another teacher. He looked at me with a raised eyebrow. "I'm sorry I interrupted. It's urgent." I pleaded with my eyes.

He and I walked away from the front door of the gym and to a quiet alcove. "What is it, Miss Townsend?" Principal Berry wore a taut smile.

I straightened my spine. "Mr. Berry, we have a problem." I paused. A flash of reality hit me. It was no secret Doug Talbot played golf with the principal, and Naomi played bridge with his wife. Flying into accusations about the Talbots wouldn't be acceptable. I had to say what was on my mind in a professional way. "I'm concerned about parents not bringing their children to conference. I believe if we allow one parent to do it, others will follow. It interferes with good communication about the education of their children." I held my breath and waited to see Mr. Berry's reaction.

"Well, I can't disagree. Did many parents come without their children?" He glanced toward the entry of the auditorium as if searching for the culprits.

"Only one, actually. I visited with the mother about the need to have her child there, and she was... belligerent."

"Belligerent? Who are we talking about?"

I took a deep breath. "Naomi Talbot. She left Doug Junior in the car. I know because I walked outside after the session and saw him there. I'm... concerned about the boy and his family life. I think he may be... neglected."

Principal Berry cleared his throat and crossed his arms. "I see." His eyes grew vacant. "Well, this is thin ice we're skating on. The Talbots have always been so generous to the school. You know they donated a good sum toward the new uniforms for the football team. They're pillars of the community, Miss Townsend. We can't accuse them of anything without foundation. Neglect. You're making a strong claim. What do you base it on?" Mr. Berry narrowed his eyes.

"Well, sir, he's written a poem and it makes me think he's... lonely. I don't think his mother spends much time with him... or encourages him."

Mr. Berry's expression became more disinterested.

I began to talk faster. "I guess I worry as he's such a quiet boy... a loner, even." I still didn't see the reaction in Mr. Berry's eyes I had hoped for. I had to sway him.

"And I saw Naomi yell at him in the car. I'm so concerned about the child, Mr. Berry." I twisted my hands together.

The principal's face dropped and he smiled ever so slightly. I knew I had babbled on like a little girl tattling on a playmate. The more I talked, the more I could see the principal dismiss everything I said.

"I see." His words sounded hollow. "You know, Miss Townsend, my mother yelled at me on occasion. My father didn't think much when he took a switch to my hide, either. I think I turned out all right."

His smirk unnerved me.

"But Naomi trivialized Doug's poem. She didn't even show any concern for her son. And when she yelled at him... he looked so... so... sad."

Principal Berry chuckled. "Well, I assure you, every time my father bent me across his knee I also felt incredibly sad. Some boys need more discipline than others. You know this, Miss Townsend. But, if it will make you feel better, I can visit with Naomi if you'd like."

I nodded. *He's thinks I'm a raving lunatic.*

Mr. Berry added, "My wife and I are their dinner guests tomorrow evening. I'll chat with them."

I visualized the Berrys and the Talbots. They would laugh about my silly ideas over a cup of coffee and as their spoons clinked against fine crystal while eating sorbet.

As the principal walked back to the door of the gym, I knew in my gut nothing would be accomplished if I relied on his visit with the Talbots. Something else would need to be done. Monday morning I would visit with the school nurse, Mrs. Georgia Clearwater.

First thing Monday morning, I knocked on the door of the nurse's office. Mrs. Clearwater, the horror of every child under eighth grade, opened the door.

Nurse Clearwater stood as straight as a board and gleamed in sterile white from head to toe, the only color on the woman her piercing blue eyes. If I could get her behind my cause, she'd personally scare the bejeezus out of Naomi Talbot.

"What do you need, Miss Townsend?" the nurse barked. She wasn't about to give out any smiles.

I didn't expect any.

"I need a moment of your time." I began to step forward to make my way into the nurse's office, but she stepped in front of me and blocked the entry.

"What's this about? I have a busy morning. No time for chitchat."

Georgia Clearwater was always busy. She moved like a freight train through the hallways, her white shoes squeaking on the shiny linoleum. When she arrived at the door of a classroom, children froze solid and began to pray.

"I have a concern about one of our students, and I need your advice." I met her cold stare and dug deep for courage.

Mrs. Clearwater stared into my eyes without blinking. She stepped aside enough to let me pass. "I can give you," she said and glanced down at her watch, "five minutes. I give polio shots today."

I entered and closed the door behind me, then felt like I'd been committed to a hospital room. Every pile of papers in the sanitized room sat neatly stacked, every pen and pencil in rows.

Mrs. Clearwater looked at her watch and began to tap her sensible white shoe.

"Well, I'm worried about Doug Talbot Jr. I believe he's being neglected at home. I know he spends a great deal of time alone in his room and unsupervised."

The statement hung between us in the quiet room. It seemed like minutes before the nurse's expression cracked and she snorted.

She shook her head and sneered at me.

"Mrs. Clearwater, I've brought a serious matter to your attention and you look at me as though I've suggested something ridiculous? I'm confused." I crossed my arms over my chest.

The nurse straightened up and gave me a threatening glare. "Oh, you're confused, are you, Miss Townsend? Well, let me help you see things from a different perspective. A more mature perspective, perhaps. Maybe then you'll understand."

The nurse went to her desk and sat down, then pulled a thick file from a drawer. She laid it open on her desk, selected the top paper, and began to read. "Bruce Gardner. Second grade. Came to school this winter without a coat. Said his family couldn't afford one. I know it's because his dad spends most of his paycheck at the tracks. I gave Bruce a coat." Without looking up she pointed to the clothing rack, which contained a variety of sizes of jackets, pants, and shirts.

She licked her finger and picked up the next paper. "Evelyn Pieper, fifth grade. Bruises on her arms which look like finger marks. Her mom's nervous as a cat, and I've seen her jerk the child around. Talked to the mom about it. She denied everything."

Lick. Next paper. "Grady Handratty. Eighth grade. Weighs one hundred pounds soaking wet and is at least five foot eight. An unnaturally skinny boy in my opinion. I know darn well he only gets one meal a day and it's right here in our lunch room. He probably spends the weekend hungry."

Lick. The next paper. "Oh. Here's a sad one. This is about little Penny Lexington. Kindergarten. She throws up almost every day. The child is so nervous she shakes and gets headaches and a stiff neck. She's in the office every noon to ask the secretary if she can call home to check on her mama. I saw her mother in the grocery store last week. The woman sported a black eye and a cut lip. Said she fell down the stairs. I know damn well the child has a nightly front-row seat to a boxing match where her mother always loses. That's a hard thing to watch, Miss Townsend... when you're only five." Mrs. Clearwater stood and walked over to me, squared off, and stared right through me.

I fought the knot in my throat and the tears in my eyes. I knew all those kids. I knew the truth. So many children fell through the cracks.

"You don't think I know what's going on with all these children." Her voice had a hard, cold edge. She continued to glare at me. Then she raised her voice enough to make me jump. "You don't think I've confronted all these parents over the years? Talked to principals and teachers and even the damn Department of Public Welfare until I'm blue in the face, Miss Townsend?"

I backed up until my back pressed against the door. Mrs. Clearwater loomed closer with each move I made backward. Heat rose to my face and a pit formed in my stomach.

"I have done everything I can for these children, and I assure you, Doug Talbot Jr. is the least of my worries. Neglected? Quite probably. But abused? Not fed? Cold in the winter? Those things take precedence over a little rich boy who spends too much time alone in his room. Forgive me if I don't go scold little miss hot pants, Naomi Talbot. Besides, she has the school board and administration wound so tight around her finger, there's nothing an old school nurse like me could say to sway her anyway."

Mrs. Clearwater stepped back and shook her head, then marched back to her desk. She put away the file and sat down in her creaking oak chair with her back to me. Her angry words hung heavy in the air.

I'd been dismissed. The weight of ugly knowledge perched securely on my shoulders. No wonder Mrs. Clearwater never smiled.

As I trudged back to my class, I realized the nurse was right. There were bigger problems than the loneliness of a little rich boy. Maybe Naomi did know her own child. It could just be his personality.

And even when children truly were in harm's way, the state rarely took them from their homes. The lesser of two evils... the roll of the dice of foster care versus a child in a home he'd always known.

My watch showed seven forty-five. The kids would charge into the school any second. About to turn the knob of my door, I heard the voice of Principal Berry behind me. He stood outside his office, four doors down from my room.

"Miss Townsend. Would you come into my office, please?"

I glanced down at my watch again, then looked up to see the first bus arrive. I hurried to Mr. Berry's door and rounded the corner, only to find Naomi Waterman Talbot in a chair by Mr. Berry's desk. The glare in her eyes told me everything I needed to know. Talking to Mr. Berry had been a huge mistake.

Mr. Berry took a seat behind his desk. A conceited smile tugged at the corners of his mouth.

Naomi sat, her legs crossed at the knee and her hands resting casually on the arms of her chair. Her face gleamed in triumph like a cat with one paw on a half-dead mouse.

As I took the seat Mr. Berry pointed to, Douglas Junior walked past me and stood beside his mother. He had the look you see on so many rich kids' faces. Apathetic. Superior. Bored.

"Mr. Berry, children are arriving in the classroom. Is this the best time?" I sat on the edge of the chair.

"I've arranged for an aide to watch your class until you get there."

Great. He thought of everything.

My back stiffened and I met Naomi's eyes.

She licked her lips.

Dear God. She's going to eat me alive.

Naomi reached out and took her son's limp fingers into her own. "Douglas. Tell Miss Townsend what you wanted to say."

Douglas looked half asleep. Not an uncommon look for kids first thing in the morning, yet this seemed to be something else. Something like defeat.

"I like being alone," he mumbled. "My mom is a good mom." He showed absolutely no enthusiasm. The opposite, even. His expression was one of absolute indifference. The words had been fed to him like pureed carrots from a baby-food jar and he had given up struggling against the meal long ago. I could feel every ounce of his hopelessness.

"Well, there you have it, Miss Townsend. You can put your worries to rest." Mr. Berry's voice drew my attention from Douglas's blank stare. The principal's palms were up and his eyebrow rose as if to say *apparently you are crazy after all.*

What a spineless man, willing to set up a farce like this before he would confront Naomi Talbot. He couldn't risk the loss of Naomi's friendship and what it might do to his and his wife's social standing. It made my skin crawl. Naomi I expected as much from, but it would have been nice to think the principal of the school cared about the kids and his teachers.

Naomi shifted in her chair, then looked up at her son with what sufficed for a motherly smile. "Douglas, you can go back to your classroom now."

The boy rolled his eyes, then shuffled out of the office, head down. He seemed exhausted from the performance.

"So, are you satisfied, Josie? Is this what you were looking for? Or are your moral panties still in a twist?" Naomi's smart remarks made me want to leap from my chair and strangle her.

"I'm sure Miss Townsend is ready to put this issue behind her," Principal Berry answered for me. "You can go to your classroom, Miss Townsend. We're finished here."

I stared at Naomi with her false eyelashes and smug expression. The principal looked as though he was proud of himself. After all, he'd resolved this nasty situation without scarring his rank in the golf league.

Wouldn't want to offend friends. Wouldn't want to piss off such fine members of the community, would you, Mr. Berry? But me... your tried-and-true teacher who works hard for the children in your school... Sure, throw me under the bus. What an ass.

I stood to leave, under the same spell as Douglas Junior, but then turned back. "No, I'm not satisfied. I'm not satisfied at all." I put my hands on my hips. "I don't believe a word of what Douglas said, but you'll be pleased to know I realize there isn't much I can do about it, and I will butt out. But I will be keeping my eye on your son. And I will always be ready if he asks for my help."

Naomi stood and so did Mr. Berry. He watched her for his cue, but as Naomi readied to unleash her wrath, Doug Senior appeared in the doorway, his eyes wide and his face pale.

"Doug. What in the world is the matter with you? You look terrible." Naomi didn't act worried about her husband so much as irritated by him interrupting the meeting.

"You have to come with me, Naomi," he said from the doorway. He held on to its frame as if to brace himself for a storm.

Naomi waved him off like a bothersome fly. "I'm busy right now. It will have to wait."

I could tell by the pallor of Doug's face something had to be terribly wrong. Why couldn't Naomi see it? Was she so self-absorbed?

"I have to tell you something important. You have to come with me." Doug's voice reminded me of his son's. He went through the motions, tried to behave, but he knew he'd lost the war a long time ago.

"For crying out loud, Doug, spit it out." Naomi's voice reeked of impatience as she tapped her foot and glared at her husband.

Doug didn't wrestle with the decision long. He gave her what she wanted. "Your father is dead." He cringed as though he expected to be hit.

The announcement dropped Naomi into her chair as if she'd been physically hit. Every ounce of color drained from her face, leaving only the stains of garish makeup. Her mouth hung open for a moment before she closed it and swallowed hard.

"It can't be true. I saw him last night. He's fine." Naomi's words sounded absolute, but her eyes filled with tears.

Until that moment, I had never seen Naomi display any emotion other than hate. I thought back to Doug and Naomi's wedding day and how her father had babied her. Daddy's little girl, I suspected.

"He had a heart attack. He's gone, Naomi." Doug's voice was hollow.

"What can I do, Doug?" the principal asked.

Doug shook his head.

"Should I go get Douglas Junior?" I asked.

Doug began to reach out to lay his hand on my shoulder. He nodded, but before he could form words, Naomi barked, "Of course not. Leave him in class." Naomi stood and straightened her skirt. "Do not breathe a word of this to our son," Naomi told Mr. Berry while ignoring me.

"Whatever you want, Naomi... Doug?"

I could see Doug did not agree with his wife, but he also looked as though he knew better than to argue. The young man I'd once known had turned into a compliant and weak lackey to his wife.

Naomi turned to Mr. Berry. Her mouth moved as though she would speak, but instead, she broke down. She supported herself on his desk, and her shoulders sagged and shook as she sobbed.

I brought my handkerchief out and offered it to Naomi, but she pushed it away. Doug stepped forward to put his hand on his wife's shoulder. She stiffened. Doug drew back.

"I'm sorry. I..." Naomi shook her head in apology at Mr. Berry, then turned to run from the office. Doug followed.

I walked out into the hallway and watched them hurry from the building. I had never thought I'd see the day I felt sympathy for Naomi Talbot, but it had come.

Friday morning, I walked up the long concrete stairs to St. Anthony's Catholic Church. Since Doug Junior had been a student in my class, I felt it important to go to his grandfather's funeral. I sure as hell wouldn't have been there otherwise.

As I neared the top step, I halted at the sight of Naomi as she spoke with a priest in the vestibule. I had never seen her look so human. She wore her hair combed simply and tucked behind her ears, her outfit consisting of a navy suit and low-heeled shoes. The most noticeable part of her appearance—she looked completely unremarkable. So unlike Naomi not to stand out in the crowd. Her drooped shoulders shook and even from a distance, I could tell she had been crying. She wore her exhaustion like a heavy coat.

My heart broke for her. She exuded pain I had felt myself. My grandmother's passing never strayed far from my memory. Nana had been everything to me—the only parent I'd ever known. No one knew better than I how hard it is to lose the ones we love. As I watched her suffer, I understood no matter how at odds we were, we shared the common bond of humanity.

As I paused on the steps, Tanya arrived at my side.

"What are *you* doing here?" I asked.

"They closed the bank so we could all come to the funeral." She sneered. "Kind of hard to get out of it."

I suspected being here made Tanya's skin crawl.

"She looks terrible," Tanya said as she stared at Naomi. Tanya's lips were drawn tight—no empathy in her eyes. She had to work with Naomi every day and I knew the bitter taste she swallowed.

"I actually feel sorry for her today. Naomi and her father had a close relationship."

"I suppose. You remember the wedding? The way her daddy ran to her side when she needed him?"

"I do remember. I wonder if this loss might change her... make her more human?"

"Ha. I doubt that." Tanya snorted.

I loved Tanya's honesty, but today, just today, I felt the need to give Naomi the benefit of the doubt. "Well, for now we should probably put our differences aside. It seems as though she's in genuine pain."

True, I had only known the ugly side of the woman, but surely there was a little girl in mourning who loved and would miss her father.

We entered the church, passed Naomi, and went into the sanctuary. Taking a seat at the rear, we read the memorial card. Mr. Preston Waterman. Survived by his wife, Edith Kern Waterman, daughter, Naomi Waterman Talbot, son-in-law, Doug Talbot, and grandson, Douglas Talbot Jr. This must have been all the family Mr. Waterman had. Seemed small.

I glanced around. Business associates of his. Wealthy widows—probably friends of Mrs. Waterman. The society types. Employees and a smattering of their kin made up the rest of the crowd. I saw other teachers and faculty, and of course everyone from the bank. Yet the huge cathedral-style room could have easily held several hundred. The sparse crowd of around a hundred or so people gave the massive sanctuary a deserted appearance.

Doug Talbot sat in the front pew with his son and his mother-in-law. They stared forward with solemn, composed faces. I found it interesting to see Doug sitting with Naomi's mother instead of standing by his wife.

The church bells rang and Naomi walked up the side aisle of the church to take her place in the front row. She sat a good foot away from her husband and he did not put his arm around her.

After the funeral, people filed out of the church in silence, shook hands with the family—Mrs. Waterman, stone-faced, Doug, thanking people for coming, and Doug Junior, downcast. Naomi didn't offer a hand or comments to anyone. Tears streamed down her nude face, a handkerchief covering her mouth as she quietly sobbed.

People moved past her, looking down, away from her pain.

As we crept along in the line, Tanya leaned over to me and whispered in my ear, "It's all a show. She wants everyone to look at her. I don't buy it."

I elbowed her. I didn't want to believe it. Not today.

When I shook Doug's hand, his thank-you sounded sincere.

"I'm sorry about your grandfather, Douglas." I put my hand on Douglas Junior's shoulder. The young man avoided my eyes and wore the same apathetic look he'd had in the principal's office.

Are you even in there?

Neither of us bothered to offer Naomi condolences.

We left through the large open doors of the church and stood at the top of the steps as the remaining people filed out. Cars lined up behind the hearse in a sobering row.

"I don't think I'll go to the cemetery, Tanya," I said.

"I won't either, Josie," Tanya agreed. "I've done my duty. Besides, I'm having caffeine withdrawal. I need a cup of joe."

Then we heard raised voices in the church. The last of the people had left the building. Only the family remained.

"You have to go to the cemetery." We heard Mrs. Waterman's stern voice. Naomi had inherited her authoritative tone from her mother.

"I do not intend to wait one more minute. I'm going straight to the attorney's office. I plan to get this will straightened out immediately." Naomi no longer sounded weepy but spoke in the voice I knew too well—one filled with anger and power. "You have no right to control Daddy's money. I know he would have wanted me to have my share and to have it now."

"I'm afraid it simply isn't true, Naomi." Mrs. Waterman's voice sounded tired. "Your father left me in charge of all our assets. I'll decide when you inherit and how much, not you. This is exactly how we wanted it to be, and for this exact reason— because of your greed."

"We'll see about that, Mother. If I have to claim you incompetent, that's what I'll do. But no one will deny me what is rightfully mine." Naomi's voice echoed with hate.

"Naomi, be reasonable. This is your father's funeral. Please..."

"Shut up, Doug. You have nothing to say about any of this. Go mourn with the people if that's what you want... fuss over my mother if you think it makes you look good, but I'm my father's only child and I will have my inheritance now. There's no way in hell I'm going to wait until *she* dies."

Tanya and I listened as we held our breath. What a thing to worry about on the day of her father's funeral. So much anger and hate. It sounded as though Mrs. Waterman would have to deal with Naomi contesting her husband's estate.

Naomi stormed out the doors of the church and down to her red sports car. Doug didn't follow her to the car, but watched from just beyond the church doors as she got behind the wheel, revved the engine, and sped away.

We stepped back behind a tall ivory pillar to avoid the private moment. Mrs. Waterman came out and stood by Doug, with Junior by her side, acting as indifferent as he always seemed to be. Mrs. Waterman rubbed his shoulder, then hooked her hand in the crook of her son-in-law's elbow.

"Come along. The lead car is waiting for us." Mrs. Waterman's cold, tired words were more of an order than a suggestion. Doug seemed used to being told what to do, and Douglas Junior tagged along beside them.

I exhaled when the small troubled family left the steps of the church. "I can't believe I was feeling sorry for Naomi." I shook my head.

Tanya huffed. "Not me. I know exactly who she is. And right now, the person I feel sorry for is her poor mother. It will take a slew of lawyers to keep Naomi from her father's money."

13

Gloria visited the women at Meadowbrook every Tuesday and Thursday like a nun going to church on Sunday. Josie's story alone took two weeks to tell. Time spent with these old gals had racked up several months of her life, but they were months she thought of fondly.

Every day, she ran the paper, researching news stories and editing the *Rosewood Press*. In the evenings, she went for her run and thought through everything the old women told her. As the months went on, the runs lasted longer and went farther as she took time to sort the information out.

The time had finally come to sit down and visit with Mabel. Gloria shouldn't have put it off so long. She knew she needed to gather more opinions about the incident in '74, but now she'd gotten to know the women, and something in her felt defensive of them. She didn't want to hear bad opinions. Then she would have to question the truth of their story, and she would rather believe them to be innocent. But it was time for due diligence, whether she liked it or not.

Mabel sat by the road, extra aluminum chair ready and waiting. Her flabby arms waved and that big smile gleamed from a block away.

"Hey, Mabel." Gloria jogged up, panting and sweaty. "Want some company?"

"Of course I do. Sit, sit." Mabel adjusted the chair and Gloria accepted it. "You want something to drink? I'll go make some tea." Mabel started to get up.

Gloria shook her head. "I'm fine. I'll hydrate when I get home."

Mabel laughed. "Hydrate. You young kids." She rolled her eyes and shook her head. "So, what's new? You have a boyfriend yet? Remember, I'd be happy to talk to my nephew Ronnie. He's a real catch, you know. Works at the bank over in Pilger. You'd like him."

Gloria knew Mabel worried about her. Said she was too skinny. Worked too hard. And running would give her a heart attack. But Gloria's lack of a wedding ring was what she suspected kept the old gal up at night.

"Actually, Mabel, I do have something new in my life and I wanted to talk to you about it."

The old woman became deathly serious. It looked like she was revving up her mothering engines. "Tell me all about it, dear." Her lips pursed and her eyes widened as she patted Gloria's arm.

"Well, actually, I hope you'll have something to tell me. I've done a little investigating into an incident that happened back in 1974."

Gloria barely finished her sentence.

"The Thorns of Rosewood?" Mabel blurted out.

"Yes. Wow. I didn't expect you to remember it." Gloria raised an eyebrow.

The look on Mabel's face soured. "My memory is fine, dear."

"I didn't mean your memory was bad... I... Well, it was a long time ago."

"Oh, we all remember. It was a big deal. Yes, yes. What do you want to know? I know the story like it was yesterday."

Gloria decided to leave out telling Mabel about talking to the women at Meadowbrook. The ladies had made it clear to her they didn't want to be found and didn't want their story to come out until they were dead and buried. Gloria wouldn't betray them. Plus, she didn't want to sway Mabel's ideas.

"Well. I've read all the old papers and the facts reported. What I want to know is what did you think about the whole thing? You know, the missing-person case, the accusations, the four women denying any involvement. Those kinds of things."

Mabel's eyes widened. "What *I* thought about the whole thing?" She glowed and her hand fluttered at her chest. "Goodness. Well." She stammered. "Let me think. I want to get this right."

Mabel at a loss for words—this was something new.

"Why don't you start with if you think the four women did any harm to Naomi Talbot. Did they get away with murder?"

Mabel stared at Gloria, then straightened up, a look of determination on her face. "I absolutely do not think they killed Naomi Talbot." She set her mouth in a tight frown. "And let me tell you why."

Gloria leaned in so she wouldn't miss a word.

"I remember when Naomi Waterman came to town." Mabel shook her head. "She was mean from day one. I was an underclassman to those four women—a freshman when they were seniors. Everyone in school knew all about how Naomi stole Doug Talbot from Mari Brent. And you know what? I've lived here my whole life. I watched Naomi turn into the town's queen bossy-pants. And age only made her meaner. That dumb Doug Talbot. Judge or not, he had no control over the woman. She ran around like a..." Mabel paused and leaned forward to whisper, "...like a dog in heat." She raised her eyebrows. "But that's not how my dad would have said it. He'd have used the *b* word for female dog." She covered her mouth.

"Go on."

"She was pretty much mean to everyone. Even her rich friends. No one liked her, but it didn't stop her from reaching the top of society of Rosewood." Mabel huffed. "For whatever that's worth."

Gloria couldn't argue with Mabel. Of course, she'd never argue with Mabel about anything anyway.

"You want to know what I really think?"

Gloria nodded and held her breath.

"I think someone killed Naomi, all right. But not those women. I think they were goats. Framed. I don't think it was them at all." Mabel stared deep into Gloria's eyes.

"Well, who *do* you think killed Naomi Waterman Talbot?"

Then Mabel did something Gloria never thought she'd see. She shut up.

"I won't say. It's best to let sleeping dogs lie. Now, I'm tired. Goin' into the house. Give me my chair." Mabel stood up and folded up her chair, then motioned Gloria to get her butt out of the other one.

Shocked by the abrupt end to their conversation, Gloria stood. "Mabel, you can't leave me hanging." She folded the chair and handed it to the old woman.

"I can and I will. Now, go on home. You'd better not snoop around about all this. Some things are best left alone." Mabel waved and started to leave, then turned to add, "And don't forget I've got Ronnie on speed dial if you ever decide you're interested."

Gloria wouldn't be.

She turned to go home, more curious than ever about what really happened to Naomi Waterman Talbot.

14

Another Tuesday and Gloria walked through the sunroom doors to meet with the women. She saw these women through new eyes now. Mabel's. Her neighbor had claimed these women to be innocent. It was an opinion Gloria shared. Still, the reporter in her knew only facts mattered.

"So, how are you ladies this afternoon?" Gloria took a seat and Josie shoved the plate of cookies in front of her. Peanut butter. A smile stretched across her face.

Betty looked at her watch. "We're fine, dear, but we want to get started if it's all the same to you. *The Bachelor* starts tonight and we're going to need to get a nap in before supper so we can stay awake to watch it.

The Bachelor?

Why it surprised her, she had no idea. These women had done nothing but surprise her from the beginning. Gloria pulled out her legal pad and said, "By all means. Let's light a fire under this."

Betty at the Law Office—1974

I stood over the sink and washed my hands, then looked into the mirror. A little more hairspray on my bangs and I was good to go. Still didn't have any gray. I turned and looked over my shoulder to examine my rear end. Not bad for forty. Now if I could find the right man, if such a thing existed. I dried my hands on a paper towel, tossed it in the basket, and went back to my desk at Meyer Law Office.

As I aged, the more I wondered if being alone was such a bad thing. It's not like I had ever wanted to have kids. And at forty, most of the men I dated came with kids or grandkids, anyway.

I had been dating the guy who delivered office supplies. I checked the clock. Almost noon. He might stop by after lunch to deliver three reams of paper, a box of number-two pencils... and to flirt with me. He really wasn't my type, but he'd been willing to move heavy furniture and do plumbing and it's why I'd agreed to date him in the first place. Now all my furniture sat where it needed to be, and I had a newly installed showerhead and garbage disposal. Sadly for Office Supply Guy, he no longer held much appeal.

I glanced back at the closed door to my boss, Hank Meyer's, office. I shook my head. Naomi Talbot made weekly visits to Hank. I knew what they were doing in there. Pity. He had such a nice wife at home, but he couldn't keep it in his pants.

This affair had surprised me. Rumors still had it Naomi and Darby Pederson's age-old tryst continued. At first, I assumed her visits to the law office were legitimate. Why I had given the shrew the benefit of the doubt was beyond me. It took a few visits before I realized what was really happening in the back office when Mr. Meyer told me to hold all his calls.

The door opened and Naomi came out, primping her hair and adjusting her skirt. No shame. I tried not to stare as she passed my desk and left the office. None of my business, I told myself. Still… what a sad marriage Doug Talbot existed in. Maybe he had it coming.

About ten minutes later, the bell above the entry to the office tinkled and Mari peeked her head around the door. "Knock, knock."

"Hey, Mari. What brings you here? Not legal issues, I hope." I worked for an attorney who made a decent living handling mostly divorce cases. I knew Mari didn't have a perfect marriage, but divorce would never be an option she would consider. She was a stand-by-your-man kinda gal.

"No, no, Betty. Everything's fine." Mari sighed. But her eyes didn't agree with her words.

I knew better than anyone Mari had never gotten over Doug Talbot. Her marriage was content and happy—safe even—but there wasn't a flame like she and Doug once had. Mari respected Stan. He treated her like a queen. He'd hand her the moon if he could arrange it. But I suspected Mari had never been *in love* with Stan. She'd lost her heart to Doug Talbot all those years ago and had it broken. Everyone had hoped Mari would forget about Doug, but I knew she'd only managed to put thoughts of him to the back of her mind.

"I stopped by to see if you wanted to go to lunch." Mari offered me a hopeful look.

"Sounds great. Let me tell Hank I'm leaving."

After I let him know, I returned to the front room, picked up my handbag from behind my desk, and joined Mari as we headed out the door. "City Diner?" I asked.

"Oh, perfect. The Wednesday special is chicken à la king." Mari's joys included the smallest things.

We walked down the block to the small café, chatted about what we'd each done so far that day and what yet needed doing. We entered the busy restaurant, and I looked around for a place to sit. Two spots were open—one by the kitchen and the other by Naomi Talbot, who sat alone at a large table. We went to the table by the kitchen. No conversation was needed to make the decision.

Mari leaned across the table. "Wonder why Naomi is here all alone?"

Mari's question was still hanging in the air like the aroma of greasy French fries when several women came through the door. Naomi raised her hand and waved.

"Ah. The Fourth of July planning committee." I nodded toward them.

For the last seven years, these women—wives of prominent men who worked around town— gathered to plan a community Fourth of July party on the courthouse lawn in the town square. Each office in the courthouse would be given responsibilities, and games would be organized as well as contests and prizes. The evening would culminate in a patriotic program put on by select girls in the community… most of whom were their daughters, of course.

These women called it a gala event.

The people who worked at the courthouse called it doing slave labor for society women.

The community called it free food.

Mari cleared her throat and drew my attention back to her.

"I have news, Betty." A worried smile tugged at her mouth.

"Oh? What? Something good, I hope." I took a drink of my water.

"I've been offered a job," Mari answered, raised her eyebrows, and waited for my response. It looked like she was holding her breath.

"Really? It's been like sixteen years since you worked outside the home, right? This is big news. Is Stan on board with this?"

"Yes. Actually, Stan suggested I look for work." Mari looked down and wrung her hands. "Money is tight now that Diane's in college. We need the extra income."

I reached out and put my hand on hers. "Money is tight for all of us. I'm proud of Stan for letting you work outside the home. I know he takes pride in taking care of you. I never would have guessed he'd embrace women's lib."

Mari and Stan Gestling had four children, the youngest now in sixth grade, the next in eighth, then tenth, and the oldest a freshman in college—like stairsteps. Expensive stairsteps. Mari had been a wonderful mother and Stan had done a fine job providing. He was old school, like so many other men in our small town. A woman's place was in the home. I'd even heard him say as much. If Stan

Gestling had agreed Mari could take a job, I knew they needed the money.

"You know, Diane won a nice scholarship, but there are a lot of expenses those funds don't cover. Plus, Greg needs braces." Mari shook her head as she made excuses. "Stan doesn't want to dip into savings if we don't have to."

Mari stirred her coffee with a spoon, laid the utensil gently on the saucer and took a cautious sip. "Betty, you're not going to believe who offered me the job." Her eyes darted over to Naomi.

My eyes followed her glance. "Well, it's a small town. There are only a few places to work. The bank, the factory, a few restaurants... the courthouse." I ticked off the main places a job might be had in Rosewood, Nebraska.

Mari swallowed hard and looked up at me as she nodded. A worried look haunted her eyes. "The last place. The courthouse. I'm going to work for the clerk of the district court."

I nodded, then understanding overtook me. I almost spit out my water. I forced it down my throat and my mouth dropped open and I rushed to cover it with my hand. "No. Not..." I held my question as I gasped, but I already knew the answer.

"Yes. I'll be working with Judge Doug Talbot." Mari looked away and across the room at Naomi. "I sure hope I've done the right thing." Her words were almost inaudible. By the way she chewed at the corner of her fingernail, I could see she wasn't sure at all.

I didn't know what to say, but I probably shouldn't have gasped and stared openmouthed at

Naomi. Mari pushed the chicken à la king around on her plate and tried to act casual.

"Doug had something to do with hiring you?" I leaned forward and whispered the question.

"No. I don't think so. I was in the courthouse to renew my driver's license when the clerk of the district court came by."

"Connie?" I asked. In small towns, everyone knows everyone. Just the way it is.

She nodded. "She stopped to say hi, and we chatted. Out of the blue, she asked if I'd ever thought of taking a job outside the home. I told her I was looking for work and before I knew it, I had the position." Mari beamed.

I could see self-worth in her eyes. Mari had held a clerical spot at the courthouse in the county clerk's office before she got married and had children. The office had hated to see her leave. Heaven knows, Mari juggled a myriad of tasks taking care of her kids and home. She was capable of anything.

"Mari, it's wonderful, but..." I let my words fall away as I bit my bottom lip.

"You're wondering if I'll be okay working with Doug." She finished the sentence for me.

"Well... I don't know where things stand with you two. And what about her?" I tilted my head in Naomi's direction. "Aren't you worried about what she'll do?"

"Oh, Betty. I'm sure Naomi Talbot would never give me a second thought. She's far too busy running the world." Mari laughed, but it sounded hollow.

"Well, that's true. Still…" I hoped Mari was right, but Naomi hadn't given a second thought to ruining Mari's life back when she stole Doug. What would stop her now?

"I'm sure I'll only see him on court days. Connie is the person he deals with most, and she's who I'll be working with. I think it will be fine. Besides, Doug and I were ages ago. I don't think of him that way anymore. I love Stan. You know I do."

Mari preached the words like gospel, but they didn't bear complete resemblance to the truth. I knew, though, she would never betray Stan. It wasn't in her nature.

"Well, I know you'll do great in your new job, and I'm happy you found something so quickly. It'll be good to have the extra income."

I glanced over to Naomi. She glowed in her role as supreme leader while the other women hurried to take notes. Maybe Mari wouldn't have to deal with Naomi on a daily basis at work, but I suspected Naomi would grind Mari under her heel at some point. Probably at the courthouse Fourth of July event. And probably for the fun of it. I had a bad feeling. Trouble was about to begin for my old friend.

The weekend came and went and Monday morning came along as it always did.

Hank Meyer was in court. I had a stack of papers to file and three full tapes of his notes to type up. The phone rang. Glad for the distraction, I snatched it up. "Meyer Law Office, how may I help you?"

"Oh, Betty, thank God you answered. I need help, all right," Mari said with a worried voice.

"What's going on?" My eyes darted to the calendar and I remembered it was her first day of work. Wow. It hadn't taken long for a crisis to arise.

"I don't know what I was thinking when I took this job. I must have been kidding myself." Her voice wavered and she spoke in hushed tones.

"Tell me what happened."

"It was completely innocent. I don't know how I set her off," Mari began.

"Naomi?" I'd known that bitch would sideline her, but I didn't think it would be right out of the gate.

"Yes, Naomi. Doug... I mean Judge Talbot, stopped by my desk to welcome me to my new job. He was only being nice. It wouldn't have been right for him to ignore a new girl in the office. I mean, there are only three of us. Of course, it was right when Naomi walked in."

"What happened?" I asked. I could imagine Naomi throwing a tantrum.

"I can't talk right now, but maybe we could meet for lunch?" Mari sounded distressed as she whispered into the phone.

"Of course. The diner again?" I asked.

"No. Come to my house. I'll make us sandwiches. I don't want Naomi or anyone else to overhear us. Rumors fly fast." I could imagine Mari with her hand cupped over her mouth as she looked over her shoulder like a frightened prisoner worried about the cruel guard.

She was right about rumors. In my forties and still single, the town had rumored me to be pregnant many times and from many different men. I feared eating a bowl of ice cream lest I'd gain weight and start a new line of gossip.

"I'll be there."

"Thank you." Relief warmed Mari's tone.

Poor thing. Now what fresh hell did Naomi have in store for her? I couldn't let that woman mess up Mari's life again. She'd done enough damage when she stole Doug out from under her in the first place. Plus, she'd harassed all of us over the years. It was time for someone to draw a line in the sand and deal with this bitch head-on. If not, she'd continue to pop up like an ugly zit. I had always managed to avoid Naomi, but maybe the time had come for me to step up and stop the problem instead of waiting to clean up after my friends were already upset. Josie, Tanya, Debbie, Mari... they'd all had some kind of run-in with Naomi over the years. I knew I would eventually deal with the scourge. I was smarter than her, but smart didn't always trump evil. She'd stoop to lies, so if I planned to step in the ring, I'd better be ready to fight. But I had a little magic bullet... and I'd need it if I had to go head-to-head with Naomi Waterman Talbot.

Noon. I drove to Mari's house. Simple—a two-story farmhouse with a screened-in porch. They lived a couple of miles out in the country. Stan farmed part time and also worked as the school janitor. They couldn't afford much, but Mari did the best she could with what she had, and her house was always clean with a kitchen full of good food. It's the way Mari was. Always doing everything the best she could.

I knocked on the screen door. A gray cat circled my ankles.

"Come in. I hope bologna is okay," Mari said from inside.

I went into the kitchen, halted by the disarray on the counters. Dishes were piled in the sink, mail strewn across the table, and the trash can overflowed. This didn't seem at all like Mari. I looked at the table. White paper plates waited for us with sad little bologna sandwiches and a few carrot sticks. What was going on?

My eyes wandered to Mari. *She* looked wonderful—her face was made up and her hair looked great. Not at all normal for her to do herself up. Such a pretty dress, too. She must have bought it special. She even had on nail polish. Making herself pretty for her new boss?

"Coffee?" Mari asked.

"Sure," I answered and took a seat. "Now, what happened?"

Mari brought two cups and a pot of coffee to the table. She sat down but pushed her plate away and began to tear a paper napkin into little pieces. Not the kind of nervous habit I was used to seeing Mari do. Tanya, sure. Mari, no.

"Well, Naomi waltzed into the office and spotted Doug by my desk. From across the room she said, 'Mari. What in the world are *you* doing here?'" Mari imitated Naomi and tried to act haughty. She didn't pull it off. "She made it sound as though she thought I was too inept to have a job."

Mari stood up to throw away the pile of napkin pieces she'd created. "Doug told her Connie had hired me. Naomi said, 'I wasn't aware Mari had any skills.' Doug tried to lead her away from my desk, but Naomi told him to go on about his work because she wanted to talk to me. Then Doug went into his office, like a little boy who'd been told to go to the corner."

I shook my head. What in the heck was wrong with him, anyway? "Naomi wanted to talk to you? About what?" I took the last bite of the pathetic little sandwich. Not even any mayonnaise. The Mari I knew would have normally gone to at least the trouble of mayonnaise. She really was distracted.

Mari waved a carrot stick in the air as she talked. "Oh, she went on to tell me about how the Clerk of the District Court's office always headed up the food and drink tables for the Fourth of July celebration on the square. Several times she asked if I could handle it... acted like I might not be up for the task. She even yelled across the room to Connie to ask her if she thought it would be too much for me." Mari rolled her eyes and tossed the carrot stick onto the plate. One bite of a sandwich and half a carrot stick. Poor kid had no appetite. This was worse than I had imagined.

"This is all classic Naomi. She's trying to upset you... and I can see she did. Was there more?"

"Yes." Mari wrung her hands and stood up, then took her plate to the front door and tossed the food outside for the cat to eat. She came back, threw the paper plate in the trashcan, then paced around the kitchen. "When Naomi finished going over what she expected from our office, it seemed as though she was about to leave, but she turned back and said, 'Say, didn't you used to date Doug or something back in high school?'"

I shook my head. What a piece of work. "So, what did you say?"

"Betty, I told her it was so long ago I could barely remember." Mari crossed her arms over her chest.

"And what did she say?"

"She said good. Then she stared at me with the coldest eyes. It gave me the creeps. She looked like she wanted to kill me. It really shook me up."

"I don't blame you. And you shouldn't trust Naomi. I think she's capable of almost anything." I stood up and went to put my arm around Mari's shoulders.

"Do you think I've made a huge mistake? Should I quit the job?" Mari's eyes filled with tears.

"What? No. Absolutely not. But if I were you, I'd avoid Doug at all costs."

Mari nodded and looked like she was about to cry.

"I hate to tell you this, but I think Naomi will try to use this celebration as an opportunity to get to you. I'm worried, Mari. I'm going to come on the Fourth to keep an eye on you. I'll make sure the others are there, too. You're going to need your friends."

"Thank you. I don't know what I'd do without you."

I nodded. "Well, don't worry. We'll take care of you." I hoped I could protect Mari from Naomi. She was poison poured into a tight pair of hip-huggers.

Mari smiled, but as we stood arm in arm by the sink, I began to do some serious worrying of my own.

Back at the office, I pushed away my piles of work. Mari's situation and everything which had happened over the years had my brain spinning.

In the sixties, Naomi started her affair with Darby Pederson. Tanya had been the one who noticed it first. As far as I—and the rest of the town for that matter—knew, the affair still continued. Tanya said Darby still came to the bank every week to visit Naomi. Other people over the years had seen them together... in a dark parking lot, behind a building in an alley, that kind of seedy thing. Even I'd seen Naomi drive down a country road near Darby's house.

What Naomi saw in Darby mystified me. He was a gap-toothed redneck with an arrogant nature and too much money. Everyone wished his wife would leave him, but she stayed loyal. She'd even caught him and Naomi right in their own bed. Of course, when Darby's wife went to tell Doug about it, Naomi denied everything. Doug either ignored it, forgave it, or didn't care. Darby's wife even had phone records. But she forgave him in time, all the same.

How Doug dealt with his scandalous wife was one thing, but how her lover, Darby, would deal with being cheated on was another. Darby hadn't only been Naomi's side dish. He was completely infatuated with her. When she wasn't with him, he was driving past her house, past her work, and he called her on the phone and sent her letters. Tanya had seen it, and so had many other people in town. Everyone talked about it. It was common knowledge.

What everyone didn't know was Naomi must have become bored with Darby as of late because she'd begun to visit the law offices more often for closed-door sessions with Hank Meyer.

I would watch Naomi leave his office with sleepy eyes, smeared lipstick, and disheveled clothing. The woman didn't even try to hide it. It didn't take a rocket scientist to figure out she and Hank were polishing the top of his desk. Did Doug know? Maybe he didn't gave a rat's ass.

The real question was did Darby know?

And it wasn't even the best part. In my boss's office one week earlier, I had opened a drawer of his desk to look for a pen and had instead found a pair of women's underwear. And *that* was the magic bullet I hoped would stop Naomi Talbot in her tracks.

But I had a lot to learn about playing dirty. Naomi, on the other hand, was an old pro.

The Fourth came along, hotter than seven hundred hells. People still managed to drag their free-meal-asses to the celebration in the town square. Sweat glistened on every brow and sunburns glowed on children's faces. The fire department opened a hydrant across the blocked-off street and children relieved their scorched skin. Squeals echoed in the air, but the joy of the kids' noise didn't make the adults any less irritable. Yet when I walked up to the food and drink tables, Mari had a smile on her flushed face in spite of the heat.

"Everything looks wonderful, Mari, including you." I scanned the table filled with Rice Krispies bars and brownies, big bowls of chips, roasters filled with barbeque pork, and baked beans… a fine Fourth of July spread. "You pulled a feast together. Great job." Children with rosy cheeks ran up, grabbed handfuls of chips and bars, and left, giggling.

Mari beamed with pride, but something caught her eye over my shoulder and her smile faded into a nervous twitch.

Judge Talbot walked up. "Hi, Betty," he acknowledged me briefly, then turned his attention to Mari. "This looks great, Mari. You knocked the ball out of the park."

I watched their gazes lock, and I began to look for Naomi. Was Doug's goal to get Mari in trouble?

I didn't have to look long. Naomi marched up with long, angry steps and a look on her face that could scare the habit off a nun. I cleared my throat as a warning.

"Well. I see old friends have gathered 'round the food table." Naomi didn't hold back her irritation.

Doug's face converted into an expression I couldn't quite identify. But he put on a smile, looked across the crowd, and waved. "Ah, there's Bob Swanson. I need to talk to him. Excuse me, ladies." He hurried away. Lucky bastard. He got to leave and we were stuck with his nasty wife.

Mari busied herself, stirring the food and straightening things on the table.

"The food seems adequate." Naomi glanced over the arrangement with haughty eyes. "But the table is a disappointment. You didn't dress the front of it with patriotic streamers or anything. Did you see Kathy's face-painting table? It's impressive. Too bad you didn't make the extra effort she did." Naomi glared.

Mari blanched. "I did it the way Connie asked. I guess I never even thought about decorations."

"Obviously." Naomi sneered.

I stood tall and glared at Naomi as I spoke up for my friend. "The food is wonderful, and Mari has done a lot of work to organize and take care of it."

Naomi looked as though she would bring out her claws, but I disregarded her and tried to start a new conversation. "Mari, have you heard anything about Darby Pederson's rental building? I heard he's looking into selling it." When Mari shook her head and shrugged her shoulders, I stared at Naomi. "Have you heard anything? I know you visit with Darby often." I offered a wicked smile.

Naomi glared, then refocused the conversation to Mari. "Next year I'll have to make sure to remind you to decorate the tables properly. It's the little things that are so important." She shot me a poison-laced glare, turned, and stormed away. She marched over to Doug, pulled him aside, and began waving her hands in the air.

"Oh, dear. I got Doug in trouble." Mari watched Doug and Naomi with a worried expression.

"You did no such thing. He's the one who came here. And Naomi makes problems where she wants to make them."

Doug turned and walked across the street to the five-and-dime. "Wonder what that was about?" I mumbled.

"What was what about?" Tanya said over my shoulder.

"Oh, Tanya, I'm glad you could come." Mari clapped her hands together.

"Well, I wouldn't want you to be here working all alone. Where's Connie or the other gal in your office?" She looked around.

"They were here all morning, setting up. I took over after the lunch rush. They'll be back around five," Mari assured us.

"Well, I'll stick around and keep you company. So, Betty, what were you talking about when I walked up?"

"Oh, Naomi. She tried to start something with Mari, so I brought up Darby and she stormed off to yell at Doug." I shook my head.

"I saw Doug scurry across the street to the dime store. Hard to believe a man in his position still has to kowtow to that biddy." Tanya huffed.

"Say, is Debbie or Josie going to come?" I asked. "We should all sit together to watch the fireworks later."

"There's Debbie now." Tanya pointed.

Debbie swaggered over, a large canvas purse slung over her shoulder.

"Hey, girls. What's shakin'?" Debbie asked as she arrived.

Good old Debbie. Nothing much had changed about her. Still feisty, skinny, and chewing gum— but now a tinge of sadness had replaced the fire in her eyes.

She'd married Bud right after high school— drove off on his motorcycle to Vegas for a quickie wedding. They'd lived in Nevada right up until Bud had a head-on collision with a bunch of hippies in a bright red bus on a desert highway. The hippies were high and Bud had fallen asleep behind the wheel of the eighteen-wheeler he drove. The busload of people walked away with scratches and bruises, but Bud died and Debbie lost her best friend.

She moved back to Rosewood in spite of the bad memories her mom had made here. Debbie must have needed to get out of Nevada and be around old friends.

"We were wondering if you and Josie were coming today," Mari said.

"Not sure about Josie, but I thought I'd sit outside and enjoy the heat. Reminds me of

Nevada… but with bugs and humidity." Debbie grimaced.

They all laughed until the joy was sucked out of the air when they saw Doug and Naomi marching back toward them. Doug's hands were full with a stars-and-stripes bunting, blue and red pinwheels, and a white plastic tablecloth.

"Doug, I'll let you explain to your employee what I'd like to see done." Naomi crossed her arms and looked amused as she watched.

He set the things on the ground and said, "Well, it might be nice to put a tablecloth on and other decorations up. To make it look festive, I guess." He shrugged, then looked over at his wife. Emotion burned in his eyes, but I couldn't tell if it was hate for Naomi or self-loathing.

"Yes, Mari. We decided you need some help. It's my nature to take care of these kinds of details, and you're obviously not as good at it. It's not your fault." Naomi linked her hand in the crook of Doug's elbow. He stiffened. She turned and sashayed away, triumphant, Doug moving with her without resistance.

Mari shifted from foot to foot, her face flushed red and her shoulders sagging. She stared at all the food… the large roasters and big bowls. She would have to move it, decorate the table, and put it all back.

I inhaled deeply. This was it. I'd had enough. Time to have a visit with the wicked witch of Rosewood.

"I have something I need to deliver to someone," I said, then stormed away and left Debbie and Tanya to help Mari.

I caught up with Naomi by the grandstand, checking on the girls who would put on the first show of the evening. Mothers were primping their daughter's hair and pinning up costumes. People milled around.

I came up behind Naomi and grabbed her by the upper arm. "Come with me."

Naomi jerked her arm away. "Take your hand off me. I don't take orders from you, Betty."

She began to turn away, but I said, "Naomi, I know what you're doing with Hank Meyer."

She glared. "I don't know what you're talking about."

"Oh, I think you do. And I have proof, too."

"What kind of proof could you possibly have?"

"You come with me and I'll show you."

Naomi gave a stare hot enough to melt cold butter. "Fine," she said through gritted teeth.

We walked away from the stage and went behind the grandstand. I looked around for listeners and when I saw none, I began, "Naomi, you're trying to humiliate Mari and I can't for the life of me understand why. Haven't you done enough? You don't have to worry about her. She'd never try to take Doug away from you."

"Like she could take anything away from me. That's a joke." Naomi huffed and folded her arms across her chest.

"Then cease and desist. It's pointless."

"Listen. I'm in charge of this celebration, and if I think the food table needs to represent the theme, it will. And if I have to make someone do what they should have done to begin with, it's what I'll do." Naomi offered a stiff chin.

"Okay, Naomi. Then I guess I'll have to do what I need to do. I'm sure Doug will be quite surprised to find out you spend a lot of time with Hank Meyer behind closed doors." I did it. Crossed the line. It felt good and horrifying all at the same time.

Naomi looked like her head might explode. Her face turned bright red. She pursed her lips and breathed heavily through her nose.

"That's nonsense. No one would believe it."

I smiled and opened my purse. Naomi's little black panties lay right on top of a pack of Juicy Fruit and a few wadded-up tissues. "I wonder if I should take these to Doug and tell him where I found them." I smiled as evilly as I could.

Naomi made a grab for the underwear, but I snapped the purse closed. She pulled her hand back and hissed, "Go ahead. Show them to Doug. He won't believe you. I'll tell him you've blackmailed me." Naomi laughed.

"Okay. How about I take them to Darby Pederson and tell *him* where I found them? Maybe your husband won't care, but your lover will. And I'll even bet he recognizes them."

Naomi smoldered for a moment but composed herself and took a deep breath. "You won't do it. You don't have the spine."

"I will to protect my friend. You've been bullying all of us since high school and I've had it. It has to stop." I stood tall.

For a while, Naomi paced and rubbed her chin, then she turned to me, her expression calm.

"I suppose I am being silly. You're right. Mari is no threat to me. And even though you're wrong about Meyer and me, and Darby, I wouldn't want you to spread rumors. It could be damaging. I guess I have no choice but to succumb to your blackmail."

Blackmail. The word made me feel dirty. I didn't like how Naomi had turned this around to make me look like the villain, but I'd stand up to it. People knew me and they knew Naomi, too.

"Would me going to help Mari set up make this right?" Naomi attempted to look sweet.

"It would be a good start." Could it be this easy to make her do the right thing? I doubted it.

"But you have to give me back..." Naomi pointed toward my purse.

I hesitated. If I held on to them, I could hardly hide from the ugly word of *blackmail*. Did I want that on my conscience?

I handed the panties to Naomi. As she reached to take them, I almost pulled back, but the idea of holding them over her head left such an unsavory taste in my mouth. That's not who I was.

Naomi snatched them from my fingers and stuffed the panties in her pocket, then donned a wicked smile. "What an idiot." She laughed and turned to walk away. "The day I do anything for you or your ridiculous friends will be a cold day in hell."

"You, bitch." I lunged at Naomi and grabbed for the contents of her pocket, but she turned around and slapped me hard across the mouth. I reeled back, then Naomi came in and slapped me again, harder still. My lip split open and blood dripped down onto my white blouse.

I put my hand up to my throbbing lips, pulled it away, and looked at the red stain on my fingers and the red blot on my shirt. "I can't believe you did that."

I wanted to pummel Naomi with my fists. It was my own fault. I shouldn't have resorted to blackmail to begin with. I should have known I couldn't match Naomi's wickedness. My mouth ached under my touch. I felt the blood… more than there should have been. Then I realized something dangled in my mouth. I dug into my purse and pulled out a mirror. I gasped at my reflection. Naomi had split my lip and knocked my front tooth loose. "You busted my tooth."

"You attacked me. What was I to do? I had to defend myself." Naomi smirked.

I put up my hands in defeat, then hurried away and didn't look back. If sense could ever be talked into Naomi Talbot, it would take all of us to do it. Right now, I had to get ice on my lip and some cold water on the bloodstain. I put my purse in front of my shirt to cover the red blotch and a tissue over my mouth to hide my dangling tooth. I couldn't let anyone see me. I felt so ashamed of my behavior.

I'd rolled in the mud with a pig and got plenty dirty.

15

Gloria tossed and turned for an hour before she decided to give up and get out of bed. She trudged to the kitchen. If she was going to stay up all night and think about Naomi and the others, she might as well be productive.

Sure. Why not clean my stove at one in the morning.

The more she scrubbed at the gunk-plastered bottom of the oven, the more she realized how angry she was. She sat back.

I'm pissed at Naomi. I hate the woman. Even I want to kill her at this point.

Not good. A reporter is supposed to stay detached from the story.

But these women: Betty with her brave face, Tanya always trying to be nice, Josie thinking about what was best for the boy, and even Debbie. Poor thing. Lost her Bud.

It all pissed Gloria off.

She threw the rag down on the floor and went into the bathroom. The mirror above the sink reflected a woman with bed-head and a ratty old T-shirt, clinging to the last years of her thirties. Her biological clock ticked on. She sighed, decided to brush her teeth again, and hoped the sweet taste might quell her hunger pangs.

It didn't.

In the kitchen, she found a bag of chips out of the cupboard. Plopping in the overstuffed chair in her living room, she tucked her legs under herself and proceeded to eat those salty snacks like it was her job. Damn potato chips. You really couldn't eat just one.

Naomi sounded like the human version of a Venus flytrap. *She* had not only married well, but had two men on the side. Damn black widow. She couldn't eat just one, either.

And Gloria couldn't manage to find even one man. Maybe she *should* tell Mabel to call her nephew, Ronnie. She groaned. Almost forty, she spent most of her time with old people and here she sat at one in the morning taking a break from cleaning her oven while she ate barbeque chips. Worse yet, she now entertained the idea of going on a date with a guy who, for all she knew, had a third eye. Not one of her better moments in life.

Thursday, Gloria asked, "So who's going to talk today?" Gloria crunched into a snicker doodle.

Josie raised her hand. "My turn. If it's okay." She looked around at the others.

They shrugged. "You might as well." Tanya took a sip of coffee, then reached for a cookie. The story began.

Josie Remembers the Fourth of July—1974

I walked down the sidewalk in front of the shops along Main Street. Children ran up and down the closed-off street, their faces painted and their balloons bobbing in the hot summer breeze. I looked up and saw Betty hurry into the alley between the hardware store and the pharmacy. The way she was running left me worried—her purse over her chest and a handkerchief at her mouth. When I reached the alley, I looked for her, but she was already gone.

What was that about, I wondered.

Mari, Debbie, and Tanya were on the courthouse lawn. I crossed the street.

"Hey, Josie." Tanya waved.

The others turned and said hellos.

"What happened to Betty?" I looked around at the other people on the courthouse lawn as if I'd find a clue.

"What do you mean?" Mari followed my eyes.

"I saw her running down the alley. She looked upset." We exchanged worried glances.

"We haven't seen her since we started to work on the decorating."

I noticed the patriotic bunting wrapped around the table. "Looks nice."

Debbie huffed and put her little fists on her skinny hips.

I didn't ask. My mind stayed on Betty until I caught sight of Naomi behind a tent, talking to Hank Meyer. They seemed to have their heads together over something and neither of them looked too happy. "Let me guess. Naomi has struck again?"

"Of course." Tanya threw up her hands.

They told me about the fuss over the table decorations. I listened and nodded. Nothing new. Classic Naomi is all.

"Well, she's over there behind the tent in the middle of a powwow with Hank Meyer. She doesn't look too happy."

"Hank Meyer? What's that about?" Tanya cocked her head to the side.

"She's probably having an affair with him, too." Debbie rolled her eyes.

"Oh, don't even say such a thing. Rumors start so easily." Mari, always coloring within the lines.

"Naomi better be careful. If Darby Pederson sees her with another man, he'll crack. He's already so jealous of Doug it's ridiculous." I'd heard all the rumors like everyone else in town. Most of them had at least some thread of truth to them.

"What a convoluted situation. We're all in our forties, and although we've held up well for the most part," Tanya said, pushing her hair behind her ear, "it's not as though any of us could pass for twenty-five anymore. Yet Naomi is still squeezed into a size seven and looks like she hasn't aged. It isn't fair." Tanya mixed a glare with her pout.

"Oh, don't give her so much credit. Her hair color comes from a bottle, I'm sure of it." Debbie fingered her own do. "Mine does too, so I'm not judging, but I know a dye job when I see it."

"With her kind of money, I wouldn't doubt she's had a nip and tuck here and there." I mumbled my thoughts, almost embarrassed to join in the spiteful conversation. It was hard not to jump on the pile when it came to Naomi.

"Yeah... well, I've seen a crack or two in her paint job. You only have to look at her when the light is right. No one looks too good in direct sunlight." Debbie gave me a wink.

"Ladies, this isn't the issue. Doug doesn't even seem to care about the way Naomi runs around. It isn't right." Mari shooed flies away from the food.

"Yeah, and Darby would have a fit if he saw her with another man." Tanya's eyes grew large.

"Fit? I think he'd kill him... or maybe her." Debbie raised an eyebrow as though she'd thought of a fine idea.

The statement settled into the humid air and left us with something to think about. Chills ran up my arms in spite of the heat. Naomi dying *would* solve a lot of problems.

Naomi came out into the open, Hank by her side. We observed and wondered what would happen next.

"Uh-oh. Look." Tanya pointed.

Darby Pederson had come around the building behind Naomi and Hank.

He stopped short when he saw the couple. Anger glowed on his face and even from a distance, we could see it. He put his fists on his hips and called out... Naomi turned... Hank looked startled... Darby took an aggressive stance.

I held my breath. From the corner of my eye, I saw Mari turn away.

Debbie grinned.

Tanya said, "Oh, here we go."

I couldn't hear the conversation, but Naomi talked fast, her head turning from side to side. It looked as though she was checking to see who was around... who could hear. I could imagine her string of excuses. Hank looked as though he'd joined in, trying to convince Darby of something.

The redneck's face began to loosen from its tight scowl. The man wasn't too bright. It wouldn't have taken much to sway him.

"I can't believe it. He must have bought whatever Naomi was selling." Tanya looked amazed.

"Shoot. I was hoping for a fight." Debbie shook her head in disappointment.

I suspected Betty's situation, whatever it was, had something to do with Naomi and Hank. A tainted feel hung in the air.

We turned our attention to each other. The afternoon dragged on as we helped Mari with the food stand. People came by to visit and we laughed and enjoyed the day as best we could, but I kept my eye out for Naomi. Luckily, the shrew stayed busy and left us be. A blessing I suspected wouldn't last.

The sun hid itself behind the false fronts of the businesses lining Main Street. The evening would culminate in a stage show featuring community talent on the bandstand in the park. The supper rush had gone through the food stand.

"You girls go on and get a seat. It won't take me long to close up. The gals from the office will come soon to help get everything loaded and put away."

"Are you sure, Mari?" I asked.

"Yes, yes. You go on. I'm glad for the company you all gave me this afternoon."

"Well, I would like to see the show," Tanya said.

"I would, too." I looked toward the bandstand.

"Not me. The last thing I care about is a bunch of singing and dancing brats. I didn't have kids, and I sure as hell don't intend to sit and indulge those of other people." Debbie never minced words. "I think I'll go home. My feet are killing me and I have a headache."

Mari rubbed Debbie's shoulder.

Debbie gathered up her huge purse—Lord knows what she kept in there—and lit a cigarette as she strolled in the direction of her home.

"Well then. We'll go watch the show. We'll sit toward the back, so come get us if you need help."

Mari smiled and nodded, then shooed us off. We waved and headed toward the seats.

At least a hundred people were lined up in the chairs on the grass. The crowd hummed like a hive of bees, chatting and laughing. Children fidgeted in their seats. Vendors around the courthouse lawn began to put away their wares. Every year the show ended with the town chorus singing the "Star-Spangled Banner," then people left for their homes, sticky children in hand. Like dozens of small-town events across the Midwest. No surprises. Comfortably predictable.

Tanya and I found a seat near the back of the crowd and waited for the first of the tiny dancers. Mothers fretted over costumes and fathers readied their cameras.

Naomi primped and prepped at the right of the stage. Always the master of ceremonies, the face of this celebration, year after year. *Her* picture slathered the local newspaper, *her* quotes made it into the articles, and *her* voice grated in the ears of the masses. The many volunteers who worked to create the event received a small thank-you in the paper the following week. And every year Naomi threw out the orders of what to do, then showed up to criticize and take credit. Yet there were still those who flitted about her like bees to honey, hoping to be considered important by mere proximity. They were her minions and she ordered them around like Oz monkeys.

Naomi took her place behind the mike and adjusted her fake smile. Her voice rang out from the amplifiers and echoed above the assembly. People sat up straight and fell silent, the only sound, programs fanning red faces.

I looked over at Tanya and we rolled our eyes at Naomi's blathering.

She babbled on about how wonderful *this* was, and how pleased she was with *that*. How hard she worked to organize, yet again, a perfect event. In her mind, it seemed this entire shindig focused on and occurred because of her.

"Oh, get on with it," Tanya whispered.

I grinned and looked back to check on Mari. She had the food all packed up and Connie and the other girl from the office were hauling big boxes to a truck. I put my purse on the seat next to me, assuming Mari would join us soon.

Naomi droned on, talking about how she had personally watched each of the groups of singers and dancers for the show and had given them her stamp of approval. She acted like the be-all, end-all of the town.

The crowd was fading fast, but Naomi sounded as though her oration wasn't near a close when she faltered. I noticed it, as did others in the crowd. Naomi rarely paused for breath when she had the spotlight. She stammered as she searched her note cards and then looked over everyone's heads. I glanced back to where her eyes focused and saw what had distracted her.

Judge Doug Talbot stood where the food table had been. He and Mari were laughing and chatting with starry-eyed looks on their faces.

Tanya turned around to look, then stared at me. "What in the hell is wrong with him?"

"I don't know, but I wouldn't be surprised if Naomi yelled at him over the mike."

To me, it seemed obvious Mari and Doug still had feelings for each other. The fire had been extinguished long ago, but embers still glowed. Regardless, the fool was putting Mari directly in Naomi's path of destruction.

Naomi coughed and brought attention back to herself. She found her place in the note cards and continued. I hoped there wouldn't be a scene.

At last, she introduced the first group of little girls. Chubby faces, curled hair, rosy cheeks and pink tutus, all around. The crowd aahed and oohed and chuckled at the tiny ones' attempts to plié and arabesque, but my eyes followed Naomi as she beelined from the stage over to Mari and Doug.

They remained entranced with each other and didn't realize what was about to hit them. I screamed at them in my mind: *Good Lord, people, wake up. The shrew is on her way.* But smitten oblivion had them mesmerized.

I elbowed Tanya. She turned to watch the train wreck about to happen. Her mouth hung open like a teenager at a horror flick.

"What should we do?" I asked.

Tanya shook her head and shrugged.

The sounds of clapping and cheers rang out behind us as the little dancers performed. I checked over my shoulder and saw mothers at the side of the stage, preparing the next set of little darlings.

"Oh, crap, Josie, look," Tanya said.

Naomi talked a mile a minute to Doug and Mari. Mari took steps back from the verbal assault she was receiving.

Clacking tap shoes rattled the stage and filled the air. A spirited Irish song blared from the speakers and the heels of a new set of young girls rat-a-tatted like machine-gun fire. We watched but couldn't hear Naomi as she continued to yell at Mari and Doug.

"We should do something." I stood.

Tanya stood to follow and we hurried toward the escalating argument.

Tears glistened on Mari's cheeks. Naomi's jaws ground together and her hands were balled into fists.

"What's going on here?" I asked Doug, who wouldn't make eye contact.

Naomi didn't take her eyes away from Mari. "None of your damn business, Josie," she told me.

Her voice emanated like a low growl. She licked her lips and the corner of her mouth twitched.

"Mari, are you okay?" Tanya put her arm around her shaking shoulders.

Mari had blanched white. Confrontation wilted her. "I... I..." Mari tried to say something but burst into tears. She buried her face in Tanya's shoulder.

Doug took a step toward her, his hand reaching out to comfort. I held my breath and thought, *You've got to be kidding me, Doug.*

Naomi's hand shot out, grabbed Doug by his arm, and pulled him toward her. Her face inches from his, she glared into his eyes. "Don't you dare embarrass me this way."

Doug jerked his arm away. "Embarrass you? *Me*. Embarrass *you*?" His voice shook. I could tell he was trying to control the volume of his words. His hand balled into a fist and rose to shoulder height.

Doug wouldn't hit Naomi. No. Not Doug. He wasn't that kind of man. I felt myself go rigid. The clacking shoes of tap dancers still covered the sounds of the marital row in progress.

"I could never embarrass you to the degree you've embarrassed me over the years." He flexed his fingers in and out of the fist. A threatening gesture—but Naomi didn't seem to notice.

"Shut up, Doug. Don't you dare speak to me with such an insolent tone." Naomi spoke through gritted teeth, but her eyes laughed at him.

"Why? Because you're some kind of queen who can't be questioned? Hardly."

Tanya's jaw dropped.

I blurted out a nervous laugh. Great timing. This was serious stuff. Doug was standing up to Naomi. He looked capable of killing her as a matter of fact... and if anyone could drive a man to beat his wife, it would have been this bitch. Still... he wouldn't. Would he?

"What did you say?" Naomi stepped back, unaccustomed to Doug not being a doormat. "You will not speak to me like that... especially in front of *these* people."

"Who in the hell do you think you are?" Tanya looked as though she would have rolled in the grass and pulled Naomi's hair if she threw one more insult at any of us. I might have joined her. Debbie would have dug out her crazy jackknife if she were there.

Naomi ignored Tanya.

The tapping shoes on the stage ceased, applause rose in the air, and the arguing group hushed and held their tongues until noise could cover their words.

Naomi turned to the stage to watch, still mindful of her masterpiece in progress, a false smile plastered on her face.

The sun began to set. Streetlights flickered on. A breeze blew over the sweaty crowd sitting in rows of hot metal chairs. Collective relief showed on their faces. Ten teenage girls took the boards to sing. A cappella voices floated out from the stage. They sang a haunting folk tune with flawless harmonies and the crowd fell silent and reverent. I hoped the calm would transcend to those near me.

It didn't.

Naomi turned back to Mari and spoke through clenched teeth. "I don't know what your plan is, but I will not have my husband—a judge, no less—seen flirting with the likes of you."

"But it's okay for you to…," Tanya began.

Naomi interrupted. "You want to keep your job at the bank, you should shut your mouth right now." She shot a hateful glare Tanya's direction.

Tanya's lips clamped shut and she crossed her arms over her chest in defiance.

"What about me, Naomi? What will you do to me if I state the obvious?" I asked.

Naomi offered a malevolent smile. "You don't think I know every member of the board of education? You don't think I have pull with the administration at the school? Josie, haven't we traveled down this road before?"

"So what about Doug?" Mari asked. Everyone looked at her. Mari's quiet words almost harmonized with the voices on the stage.

I held my breath.

"Doug is no concern of yours." Naomi's face had turned a shade of red, which made her harsh rouge pale in comparison.

Mari turned to Doug. She was shaking and tears welled in her eyes, but she soldiered on. "Doug, why are you silent? Why can't you say what you want?"

Naomi stepped between Doug and Mari and yelled, "Shut up!"

A second earlier, the choir of voices had been at a crescendo, but when Naomi yelled out, they'd hit a rest, a pause in the song for effect. Naomi's words rang out like a blaring horn and the crowd craned their necks to look back at her.

She turned to see the faces glaring in her direction as if to say what's the matter? Who dared to interrupt the darlings on the stage?

Naomi paled.

I covered my mouth so my laugh wouldn't escape. The song resumed with robust enthusiasm, and the crowd returned their attention to the show.

Naomi turned, her vengeance pointed at Mari.

"How dare you embarrass me like this." Her whisper pierced like a scream and she reached out her hands to grab Mari by the shoulders. Doug stepped in front of her and pushed Naomi back—not hard, but hard enough for her to be repelled and stumble on her platform shoes.

"Doug." Mari swung him around and stared into his eyes. "No." She could never abide any kind of violence.

Doug was panting in anger at Naomi, but he melted in shame at Mari's disappointed eyes.

"I'm sorry… it's just…," Doug tried. But Naomi pulled them apart and pushed them both in opposite directions.

"You're both an embarrassment. How could you do this to me?" Naomi sneered at them in disgust.

Mari stood firm. "You embarrass yourself, Naomi. Your behavior is shameful. I have stayed silent for too many years. You are a mean, angry person and you've done horrible things to me and all my friends."

Mari turned to Doug. "And God only knows what she's done to you, Doug. It must be something terrible to make you tolerate her behavior. Why do you take it? Is it for the money?" Mari shook her head and echoed the confusion we'd all shared over the years.

Doug's eyes filled with shame and tears spilled over his bottom lashes, trailing down his face. "Of course not." His voice wavered. "At least not anymore. I tolerated her for the sake of my son. Someone had to care about him." He glared at Naomi, then looked down, defeated. "For whatever good it was worth. We've lost him anyway."

I knew as well as anyone how neglected the boy had been. Maybe Doug's expression of defeat was, in truth, shame for not doing enough.

Doug's small utterance held more weight than anyone could ever know, but the story of Douglas Talbot Jr. remained a mystery. He'd been a constant source of gossip in the small town. He'd moved away to go to college and never returned. Some said he'd been in jail, others said he partied with a dangerous crowd in Los Angeles. Others yet told a story of him as a hermit, a child molester, a womanizer, a thief. No end of suspicions seemed too extreme when it came to gossip about Naomi's son. The only truth to any of the stories? He'd definitely left his family and never looked back.

"We will not discuss family matters in front of these people. I won't hear of it." Naomi grasped at the last straws of her authority, but it seemed to melt around her as she spoke.

"I suppose I shouldn't talk about what you're doing to your mother, either." Doug put his chin out defiantly, but his lips trembled.

Something held him back, but what?

The sounds of the "Star-Spangled Banner" began to ring out and the audience stood; men took off their hats and veterans saluted as little girls carried flags onto the stage. Boy Scouts lined up.

It was the grand finale and Naomi's finest hour. I watched her and waited to see what she would do.

She did what I expected her to. She hurried to the stage. This argument with her husband proved trivial. Our opinions weren't relevant. The most important thing to Naomi was how things looked and, moreover, how *she* looked. She had to bid the final adieu to the audience. Her face had to be the last thing everyone saw. They couldn't leave without knowing this grand day was provided by the great and powerful Naomi Waterman Talbot.

As the final notes of the song rang out, cheers went up to meet the starry night sky.

Naomi ran onto the stage. "Thank you, thank you. Wasn't the show spectacular!" She clapped and clapped and smiled as though she personally had sung every last note and fought each and every war the veterans represented. She had brought them all together for the good of society in this pitiable town. What would we all do without her?

I expected nothing less, yet, it still shocked me. I returned my attention to those near me. Everyone looked physically ill. Pale. Nauseous. Exhausted.

Doug shook his head and let out a sarcastic laugh under his breath. He seemed unable to meet our eyes, so he turned and walked away in silence.

What more could be said? Naomi's behavior had told the whole story. She acted like a spoiled brat, a bully, a sociopath even. She'd bullied Doug most of all. The thought of their son sprang to my mind. Dear God, what had she put her son through?

From under the streetlight, we saw Doug approach his car, get in, and slam the door. He sat there, his hands gripping the steering wheel as he stared ahead with blank eyes. What were his thoughts? What would he be driven to do? Then he pulled away. His tires squealed enough to make Mari wince.

Mari gave Tanya and me a hug. It looked as though she wanted to say something, but she shook her head and gave a halfhearted wave, then turned to go to her own vehicle. Her husband and family were waiting for her at home. She, too, sat for a long time in her car, looking caged. Trapped.

What would Naomi do to us, to Doug and Mari? I couldn't imagine her letting all this drift away like the notes of the final song. I knew she would retaliate, but to what degree?

"I'm going to follow Mari home. I think she's pretty upset, Josie," Tanya said as she watched Mari, who still sat in her car.

"That's a good idea." I rubbed Tanya's arm.

Tanya nodded. We shared the worry, but it didn't make the load lighter.

"I'll head on home, I guess. Let me know if you need anything."

We parted ways.

As I walked away from the last remnants of a celebration turned sour, I saw Naomi storming toward her car. Even in the limited light, her stride emanated pure hate.

I knew one thing without a doubt. Above all things, Naomi needed to win. She needed to be on top, and she'd do anything to get there. My gut twisted at the thought of what was yet to come.

16

The mood in the room felt off. Gloria settled back in her chair and tried to be patient. The women fidgeted in their seats and exchanged worried glances. Patience was overrated. "What's going on?" she asked.

"The next part is hard to tell." Josie looked at Tanya with dread.

"Yeah. And I have to tell it." Tanya's eyes were moist.

"Go ahead, dear. You'll do fine," Betty said, encouraging her.

Tanya swallowed hard.

Tanya Wishes She Didn't Remember—1974

Naomi sped off in her car, her hands tight on the wheel. She looked pissed.

Not good. My gut clenched. It looked as though Naomi planned to make someone pay hell, and I suspected it would be Doug or Mari... or maybe both.

I'd promised to make sure Mari returned home safe and sound and that's what I would do. But first I would swing past the Talbot house... make sure I knew where the enemy had landed.

My mind focused on the events of the night. The last murmurs of the Fourth of July celebration now hummed in the background. I turned to go to my car, but a tug on my elbow brought me into the moment. My old classmate, Boyd Odvody, grinned at me from ear to ear.

"Hey there, Tanya. I haven't seen you since the last class reunion. You look great." He had a hold on my elbow. "We have some catching up to do."

Oh, God. Not Boyd and his hill-folk accent. He'll talk forever.

"Hey, Boyd. Uh... good to see you." I reclaimed my arm. I had to get away from him. Now wasn't the time to trip down memory lane.

Boyd's voice droned on while I struggled to figure out how to make a break for it. He didn't even take a breath. What in the hell was he even talking about? There wasn't time for me to be polite.

"Boyd, I'm sorry. Wish I had time to catch up, but I have to go." I waved and ran off while he blathered on.

Across the courthouse lawn I went, jumped into my car, and headed toward the Talbot house on the edge of town.

Seven minutes later, I eased down their street. Naomi's car wasn't in the driveway and no lights were on in the house. Doug must have been gone, as well, or he was sitting in the dark house. Unlikely.

Where were they?

I headed out on County Road D toward Mari's house, fretting all the way. The sick feeling in my stomach continued to build. It felt like I was playing hide-and-seek in a dark house and someone was about to pop out and grab me.

Up ahead, at least a half mile from Mari's house, I saw two cars parked on the side of the road. I slowed. My headlights locked on the vehicles.

The cars belonged to Doug and Mari.

I inched past them. They sat in the front seat of Doug's car. He held her and it looked like they were both crying. They didn't look at me... just stared ahead. I felt like a Peeping Tom.

Shocked, I drove on. If Naomi came along, she'd eat them alive. The big problem was, I didn't know Naomi's whereabouts, and I felt responsible for Mari getting home safely. After that fight, Naomi would be capable of anything.

But, what was I supposed to do? Stop and knock on the window? Should I warn them about Naomi not being home?

No. This wasn't my business.

I turned at the next corner, went around the section, and drove back into town. Something in my gut didn't sit right, though. The closer to my house I got, the more I knew this was my business. I had said I would make sure Mari made it home, and I hadn't done so. I had to go back and deal with this.

I drove back to D Road, and as I crept along, I tried to convince myself I had to stop and talk to them. A nasty headache had settled in, and my temples throbbed.

A few miles out of town, headlights appeared down the gravel road, coming my direction... coming on fast.

Very fast.

The car sped by, gravel spitting out from under the tires. I gripped the steering wheel, worried the car meeting me would lose control. I tried to make out the driver's face.

Doug.

What the hell?

I stopped right there and craned my neck back to watch and make sure he didn't fly off the road. Should I turn around and follow him to make sure *he* didn't have an accident? Was Mari with him? A sick feeling sank in my gut. What caused him to drive away so fast?

I had to find Mari right away. I raced on, my heart hammering in my chest.

About a mile past where Doug and Mari had been parked, the dirt road clouded over with dust. Taillights in the ditch glowed red through the haze. It was Mari's car—she'd crashed. Through a clearing in the haze, I saw another set of taillights way off down the road.

I parked, scrambled from my vehicle, and ran to Mari's car. It rested on its side in the ditch; deep ruts led to it from the road. The driver's door pointed to the sky, the front of the car crushed and crinkled, grass and dirt covering the fender. The headlights shone into the field through caked-on dirt. I grabbed the rearview mirror and hoisted myself up so I could open the driver's door. The car creaked and shifted down. I lost my footing but held fast.

Blood smudged the cracked window of the driver's door. Mari slumped over in a heap on the passenger's side. My stomach leapt to my throat. The car was still running, its engine revving loud. It took all my strength to pull open and then push up the door.

"Mari!" I screamed as I reached for my friend. My fingers stretched until I grasped her upper arm. Then I pulled at her unconscious form as I teetered on the edge of the car and struggled to get a good grip. Blood oozed the side of her face, her blond hair matted to her head. My stomach lurched, but I continued to pull. I worked until I could wrap my arms around her waist. Tugging hard backward, we tumbled down from the car, Mari landing on top of me in the ditch.

I worked her up to the edge of the road, and there, I cradled my friend's head in my lap. I put an ear to her mouth and tried to listen for breath, but the car revved too loud for me to hear. I put my ear to her chest and heard a heartbeat. Still alive.

I shook her. "Mari! Wake up!"

Her eyes fluttered but didn't open, and then her mouth began to move.

I put my ear close. I could barely make out what she said, but the one word I did hear was clear enough. I sat up and looked in disbelief into Mari's half-open eyes, then I looked down the road to where I'd seen the other taillights.

Mari's only word had been "Naomi."

17

Silence filled the room, sniffles and throat clearing the only sounds. Gloria ached for them all, including herself. Losing Mari had devastated these women, and it hurt her to watch them relive the loss.

Before she could make even one comment, though, Debbie took over the story.

Debbie's Anger Builds—1974

"Mari's dead." Tanya's words sounded so hollow and meaningless. They were an ugly noise in my ears.

All of us gals had rushed to the hospital. Now we huddled under the cold harsh lights of the hallway outside the ER. Weeping, we held each other for support.

But not me. Crying was for the weak. I'd put away such nonsense when I was young. It had never gotten me anywhere. Anger, I understood. A fire built inside me that wouldn't easily be put out.

The wail of family members echoed down the hall. Stan, the kids, Mari's parents, cousins, aunts, uncles… the hospital was filled with sorrowful relatives. I could almost feel them buckle under complete shock. The sterile walls of the building burst with the sounds of agony. The children's cries... more painful to me than my own loss... a sound I have never forgotten.

I moved, caught up in the group as we gripped each other to keep from falling down, a mass of comfort and sorrow on wobbly knees, baptizing the hallway with tears.

In the visitors' room, we sat in dumbfounded silence. The noises of the hospital screamed in my ears, the hum of florescent lights and beeps from machines. I sat rigid on a cold vinyl chair and clicked my lighter... enough rage building in me to burn the whole place down.

"What the hell happened?" I bounced my knee and shook, rattling like a pot ready to boil.

Tanya looked as though the memory haunted her. She searched my eyes for comfort. She'd have to look elsewhere. I wanted answers.

"Tell us, Tanya. Tell us now," I barked.

Tanya began to sob. She held out her arms and stared at them like they were the instruments of murder. She began to shake. "She died in my arms." Tanya wailed and covered her face. She told us everything. It spilled out like knives of hard details and raw emotions.

Betty pulled Tanya close and held her head against her shoulder like a mother. Then she said what we all were thinking. "Naomi ran her off the road. That's what happened. That's whose taillights Tanya saw, I'd bet on it."

"Of course it's what happened." I stood up, my eyes filled with rage, not tears. "And we are going to figure out how to make the bitch pay."

18

Gloria felt overwhelmed. The women must have killed Naomi, revenge their motive. These women she'd come to enjoy visiting, one of whom was, more than likely, her birth mother.

She had to get out, get some fresh air. Go home and think everything through. She needed a new perspective. Any perspective. All she could think was Naomi had coming whatever she got... and it wasn't good to think that way. She couldn't allow herself to be so one-sided or vicious. Was Naomi really so deserving of the hate festering in Gloria's heart?

At the diner over a hot beef sandwich, Gloria wondered who could give her more information. Maybe Delbert from the old-man table. She could ask to meet with him privately. Or, maybe with enough prodding, Mabel would cough up more information. But gossip wasn't what she needed right now. She needed clear eyes to find out if she was seeing things straight.

Tildy slammed a ticket down on the table with her usual flair.

Gloria jumped. "Jeez."

"What?" Tildy took no guff from anyone.

"Nothing." The waitress was probably exhausted and had been on her feet all day.

Gloria fished money from her purse and went back to searching the room to see if there was anyone she could quiz about Naomi Talbot. No one.

It was for the best. She had to drop a deposit off at the bank and get back to work. Might as well move on with her day. She wasn't solving the world's problems sitting here eating diner food.

Thoughts of Naomi and Mari and Tanya swam in Gloria's brain. She slung her purse over her shoulder, then opened it and started digging around as she hustled through the front door of the bank. She didn't even notice the man on the other side until she almost knocked him over.

"Whoa!" he said.

She looked up into a face she hadn't expected. A smiling face. Actually, a laughing face.

"You okay?" He stared into her eyes with his baby blues.

She gulped and made a few mental notes. Nice head of hair, mostly blond, some gray at the temples. Maybe forty. Dark suit and a light blue tie. In decent shape. Tall. Confident.

Then she realized she was staring at him with her mouth hanging open.

"I'm Ron Camden." He held out his hand.

Trimmed nails. No wedding ring.

Gloria shook his hand and smiled back, then got a grip on herself. "Gloria Larson. Sorry. I don't always mow people down." Her laugh sounded dorky. *Great.* "Wait a minute. Ron Camden? Ronnie Camden? Do you know a woman here in town, Mabel…"

"My aunt. Yes. She calls me Ronnie. You know her?"

"You could say that." Gloria assessed the man in an entirely new way now. He looked good on the surface, but if this was the much-lauded Ronnie, she had to be suspicious.

He laughed, then shrugged. "How do you know my aunt?"

"Oh, she lives down the street from me. She's mentioned you a few times."

"Wait a minute." Ronnie took a step back. "You're not the editor of the *Rosewood Press*, are you?" He cast her a sideways glance.

"I am." She glanced askance back at him.

Ron laughed. Heartily. "Well then, I've heard all about you. Aunt Mabel's been trying to convince me she knows a gal who's perfect for me."

Now it looked as though he was assessing her. Gloria didn't like it.

They stared at one another for a moment, each lost in their own process of measuring each other.

"Well, I have to keep moving. Sorry I literally ran into you." Gloria's mind was already on other things.

"Yeah, I have to get going, too. Nice to meet you, though." Ron's eyes seemed to be focused on other things already. He scooted around her and they passed like cars on the road. A brush of traded paint and they were on their way.

Gloria turned to watch him. He climbed into a black Lexus. For a moment, she wanted to go out, stand at his window and say something more. She shook her head. *What was she thinking? It didn't even make any sense.*

Moving on into the bank, she gave her deposit to the teller, chatted for a moment, then turned to leave. At the entryway, she saw the Lexus still parked in front of the bank. Her breath stopped.

Should she go talk to him?

Before she could even make the decision, Ron jumped out of the car and ran back to the bank. He opened the door and offered her a big smile.

"Hey, this is going to sound really weird, but… you want to have lunch next week? I have another meeting here at the bank next Thursday. My treat. Out at the First Stop. We can put Aunt Mabel's theory to the test."

A smile tugged at the corner of her mouth. Something in her brain said to go for it. What the hell. "It's a date."

He grinned. "See you there at noon, next Thursday."

Gloria watched him run back to his car. Now all she had to do was try to remember how to behave in the company of a man. It had been quite a while.

Her inner reporter kicked back in. Maybe she could run her ideas about the Thorns of Rosewood past good old Ronnie. He might be just the unemotional perspective she needed.

19

On her way to Meadowbrook, Gloria thought about what she'd wear to her lunch date with Ronnie. Should she call him Ron or Ronnie? So many things to think about. She didn't normally worry about how she dressed. Jeans and a shirt was her calling card. Khakis and a shirt if she thought the interview was more important. Slacks and a blouse if she had to go somewhere dressy. No one would have ever called Gloria Larson a fashion queen, but next Thursday she wanted to look right. Not anxious, but like she cared at least a little.

She couldn't wait to tell the women she had a date.

"Good for you!" Tanya clapped her hands together when she heard Gloria's news.

"It's just lunch. I'm sure I'm making too much of it." Gloria felt her cheeks turning red.

"Be cool. But if he doesn't take the bait, no big deal." Betty shrugged. "Guys are a dime a dozen."

"Be yourself. It will win him over." Josie patted Gloria's arm.

"Time's wasting, girls. We're old. We could die soon. Someone better get back to telling this story before we all keel over." Debbie pulled a cigarette out and lit up.

So much for Gloria's shining moment. But the story was what she'd come for. It looked like Betty had positioned herself to talk. At this point, Gloria could read these characters like a book.

Betty Talks to Hank—1974

My nerves were on edge. The four days between Mari's death and her funeral seemed to evaporate into the humidity of the Nebraska summer.

Josie checked on Tanya every day and let me know how things were going. From what Josie told me, Tanya was holding up, but just barely.

I had my hands full with Debbie. I knew all of us friends were closer than sisters, but for some reason, Debbie's rage seemed all-consuming.

I went in to work Monday to find the Closed sign hanging on the door. Hank was always at the office a solid hour before I arrived. He hadn't even called me, which set off alarm bells in my brain. Could he be in grief, too? Hell, the whole town was—Mari had been well loved, but still. Hank?

Besides, my workaholic boss would never fail to come in without giving me notice. Something must have happened to him. I wondered if the something might be a someone… like Judge Doug Talbot. Time to pay Naomi's husband a visit. The courthouse sat right across the street, so I walked over.

When I entered the Office of the District Court, everyone looked up with worried eyes. Connie wore a haggard expression. They'd have to hire someone to replace Mari—not that Mari could ever be replaced.

I glanced over to the Judge's office. His door was shut.

"Is Judge Talbot available?" I asked.

Connie shook her head but otherwise didn't respond. Her eyes veered over my shoulder and widened. I turned around and found myself face-to-face with someone I hadn't seen in years. At first I didn't quite recognize him, but somewhere in his eyes, I saw a child I had once known.

"Douglas?" I stepped back and stared at Junior. He looked plenty worse for wear. Long, dirty hair and bell-bottom jeans with frayed hems and holes at the knees. His T-shirt clung to his chest, displaying a Hamm's Beer logo, and judging by the reek, he had partaken of it or something akin.

Junior didn't answer. He edged past me, bumping my shoulder as he passed, and went into his father's office without knocking. Before he disappeared behind the closed door, I noticed his right hand was bandaged around the knuckles.

I turned to question Connie, but before I could ask anything, she offered a whisper and put up three fingers. "Third time this morning he's been here, Betty. He doesn't talk. Just goes into his dad's office."

"What's going on? Where did he come from?" I whispered back.

"We don't have a clue, but the Judge is plenty upset. It's going to be a long day."

I decided to get the hell out of there. The world had clearly spun off its axis. Mari was dead, Doug

Junior had returned from hell knows where, and my workaholic boss hadn't come in to work today. I needed to go check on Hank Meyer.

Hank's wife was pulling away as I drove up to their house. The scowl on her face told me the woman was doing more than just going shopping. I parked in the driveway, walked up to the door, and knocked. I rang the bell, knocked several times more, and was about to leave when the door creaked open. Hank stood in the shadows. He had a hat and sunglasses on and his hand covered his mouth.

"Hank? Is everything okay?" I asked.

"Fine," he said as he began to shut the door.

I'd worked for Hank Meyer for years and kept his secrets to boot. He wasn't about to get off so easily.

"Hank... what is going on?" I put my hand on the door and pushed it back open.

He allowed me in but turned his back to me.

"Hank?" I tried to move in front of him, but he continued to turn away from me. "Hank." I put my hands on my hips. "Tell me what in the hell is wrong, right this minute."

He turned to face me, moved his hand away from his mouth, and revealed purple, swollen lips. He took off his sunglasses to expose two eyes almost swollen shut and a cut along his temple. He looked down in embarrassment, then raised his eyes to mine.

"I had hoped the whole town wouldn't find out about this." He tried to smile but winced in pain.

I opened my mouth to ask the obvious but waited instead.

He took a deep sigh. "You know about Naomi and me." He crossed his arms over his chest.

I nodded.

"Well, now Naomi's husband and son do, too." He pointed at his smashed-up face. "And so does my wife, unfortunately." Hank motioned toward the driveway where I had seen Mrs. Hank. I had been right. She wasn't off to buy a new pair of shoes.

Hank went into the living room and collapsed into an overstuffed chair.

I followed him but remained standing. "I saw your wife leaving. She looked upset."

"Leaving me for good, she said." Hank leaned his elbow on the arm of the chair and rubbed his forehead, then winced in pain again.

"Can you blame her?" I spoke my mind. I would have liked to think he was a broken man, but what I saw was a man caught. Not guilt as much as irritation about the mess he now had to deal with. "So you decided not to go into the office today?"

"I can't be seen like this. You go in. Open up and take the phone calls. Cancel everything for the next several days. I have to do damage control here. Let things blow over. I should have called you, but..." He swept his hand around the room as if I could see and hear the arguments that had occurred over the last twenty-four hours.

Before I left him to deal with his sordid affairs, I asked, "So who kicked your ass, Hank?"

His eyes went dark. "The son. Doug Junior. Bastard blindsided me in the street last night when I got out of my car. Didn't even give me a fighting chance. It was like he was psycho or something. I guess the rumors about him are true. He must have been high as a kite. He screamed on and on about his mom... I was terrified."

You had it coming, you scumbag was what I thought.

Watching him cry like a little girl on the ground was what I imagined.

"Weird" is what I said.

The color left his face. "If Judge Talbot hadn't shown up, I could be dead. He pulled the kid off me."

I felt no empathy for the coward in front of me. If Naomi's son beat the living hell out of his mother's lover, more power to him. I suspected Doug stopped the process because he was worried about legal issues, not about Hank Meyer's safety.

"I'll keep the office fires at a slow burn while you recuperate." I left the room and the pathetic home wrecker behind. I had things to do, like ordering flowers for Mari's funeral and checking in on Debbie. The office could stay closed for another hour or two. What would he do... fire me? I suspected with what I knew, I had job security for the rest of my natural life.

20

As Gloria listened to Betty talk about Naomi's cheating, she couldn't help but wonder why she was so excited about having a date. Would she be cheating on Ronnie in ten years? Or would he be cheating on her?

"What are you thinking about, Gloria?" Betty asked.

"Marriage," Gloria answered.

Maybe I should cancel the date. I don't even know the guy's phone number. I could ask Mabel, but the idea of involving her gives me more anxiety. She'll want to know why I want his number. She'll try to talk me out of it.

Debbie yelled and snapped her fingers in Gloria's face. "Gloria!"

"What?" She jolted.

"Pay attention. I'm going to tell you about the funeral now."

Debbie Deals With Death—1974

Mari's family gathered in the cemetery. I sat in silence behind the steering wheel, staring through my windshield at them. The car's motor ran quietly, cold air gusting from the vents. The little tree air freshener fluttered in the breeze. A tear rolled down my cheek, but I caught it before it touched my chapped lips. I sure as hell didn't want anyone to see me cry. I opened the door and a rush of heat and humidity pushed at me. I straightened, then walked through the grass, making my way around the tombstones.

"We're gathered here to lay to rest…" I shut out the minister's voice. He had said a lot during Mari's funeral, but none of it gave me comfort. He didn't know how Mari really died.

Searching the sea of faces, I found Josie's. She looked up as though my glance had physically touched her. Our eyes connected and a fresh tear streaked down her face. I looked away.

Tanya stood at Josie's side. She blew her nose, her shoulders shuddered, and pain wracked her expression. It looked like she hadn't slept since the night Mari died. She kept shaking her head and covering her face with both hands.

Betty came and stood by me. "Look at poor Tanya," she whispered.

"Yeah. She's a mess." I forgot to whisper and an old woman in front of us turned and scolded me with a glare. I made a face at her, crossed my arms, and stayed quiet until the burial ceremony finished.

As family and friends dispersed, the four of us gathered at the edge of the cemetery. Josie folded and refolded her handkerchief, which was trimmed in little purple flowers, every sigh deep and filled with sorrow.

Betty rubbed her shoulder. "You okay, Josie?"

Josie nodded, but her sobs became louder and she clutched at Betty's hand.

"Oh, here we go again." Tanya began to wail at the sound of Josie's outburst. She shook her head. "If you cry, it makes me cry… you know that."

"I know. I can't help it." Josie sobbed and she and Tanya held on to each other.

Betty wrapped her long arms around both of them, and I watched, blowing smoke into the air and sweating in the hundred-degree heat. It felt so weird to be a group of four instead of five.

"Any of you going to the dinner at the church?" I asked.

"No. I can't take any more of this." Josie shook her head emphatically and Tanya echoed the sentiment.

Betty wiped her hair from her sweating forehead. "I'm not up for it, either."

We stared in silence as the people trailed away from the cemetery. The cars made a long line, going to the funeral dinner in the Presbyterian Church basement.

"How 'bout we go to my place and have a few drinks? It'll calm our nerves." I flicked my cigarette and the ash floated away on a slight breeze that blew past.

We nodded and went to our cars. Then we drove out of the cemetery, turned the opposite direction of the masses, and made our own funeral procession to my little house on the edge of town.

At my place, the women filed in and sat down in steel-and-vinyl chairs around my gray Formica table. From the cupboard, I brought down a bottle of whiskey and grabbed four juice glasses.

Tanya objected first. "Oh, wait a minute, now. I can't drink that."

"I'd rather have a beer." Josie made a face.

Betty didn't argue.

I set down the hooch with a thud in the center of the table, poured a healthy shot for each of us, shoved a glass toward each woman, then held up my own. "We're going to drink to Mari." I stared at Josie and Tanya until they conceded.

They both gazed at the amber liquid and picked up their glasses with hesitant fingers, their faces filled with dread. I gave them a nod of approval.

"Here's to Mari Brent. She was our friend. We loved her. May God rest her soul." I put the glass to my lips and tilted my head, knocking back the generous shot of Tennessee Whiskey. It burned, but not as badly as my anger.

Tanya drank, shook her head, and clutched her throat. Josie coughed. I poured another shot and pushed the glasses back to their owners.

"No," Tanya whined, but Josie grabbed her glass, jaw set.

"Raise your glasses one more time, girls. This time we drink to Naomi Talbot."

At the sound of Naomi's name, Tanya pushed back her chair and jumped up. "No, Debbie, I will not drink to her. I won't do it."

I had never seen such fury in Tanya's eyes. "Good, Tanya. You *should* be mad. That's what we need. And you're right. I'd never make a toast to that whore. But I do want to make a promise."

Tanya's eyes lit with understanding.

We stood and held our glasses of alcohol with trembling fingers, then clinked them together.

I began, "Naomi Talbot will not get away with murder."

The women's faces turned dark red and their knuckles went white. They nodded, keeping their eyes on me as I continued.

"We will be fierce. We will make her confess. And she will pay for what she's done. We will stop at nothing to get revenge." I knocked back the whiskey, poured another glass, and drained it too, then staggered out through the screen door. It banged shut behind me. I sat down heavily on the front step and finally allowed myself to cry.

Choking back sobs, I thought about my troubled childhood. My drunken mom hadn't cared if I had decent shoes or money for school lunch. She hadn't helped me with homework or tucked me in at night. But Mari and her mother had helped me for years, and they did it so quietly that no one ever knew. No one knew how many meals I ate at Mari's house or how she made sure to bring an extra sandwich in her sack lunch for school field trips. Bags of clothes showed up on the front steps... these same steps I was sitting on. Mari and her mother gave me so much, but Mari's acceptance gave me a group of friends. Because of her, I had decent women who kept me on the straight and narrow.

I dropped my face into my hands and soaked my fingers with tears.

The screen door opened quietly. Betty sat down on the steps beside me. She put her arm around my shoulders and waited in silence.

I straightened up, swiped away the tears with the back of my hand, and stared straight ahead. "Did you know Mari used to help me with my homework so I could pass?" I had never told a soul.

"No, but it sounds like something she would have done." Betty's low voice comforted me.

"She never judged me, you know. She was like snow and I was dirt, but she always made me feel equal."

"Mari always played fair." Betty hugged me close. "And you weren't dirt, Debbie. We all love you and always have."

"Thank you, but Mari… she really changed my life. I owe her." I took a deep breath.

I was done crying. My anger had settled back in to stay.

Betty's grip on my shoulder tightened. "You're right—what you said in there. Naomi has to pay for what she's done."

I stared into Betty's eyes and gritted my teeth. "If it's the last thing I do, I will make Naomi confess. No way is she going to get away with murder." And I meant it. Naomi Talbot was lucky that's all I had in mind.

21

Gloria sat mesmerized, listening. Debbie slumped in her chair, her wrinkles seeming deeper than they'd looked before. Funny how people can remember every ill done to them like it was yesterday, but yet forget the simple joys. Debbie could obviously still become agitated by the mere memory of losing Mari.

Betty cleared her throat. "I think I'll tell the next part."

Gloria nodded and flipped the page of her notebook.

Betty Takes the Lead—1974

"You have to talk to the police, Tanya. You have to tell them what Mari said and what you saw. If you don't, Naomi gets away with this."

I tried to keep my wits about me. Debbie and I had returned to the table in her kitchen. The shots of whiskey were making my head float, but they had done Debbie in. She was sleeping at the table, head pillowed on her arms.

I made coffee.

Josie dug a bottle of Tylenol out of her purse and we all put out our hands like children asking for candy. "It's true, Tanya. Betty's right. You have to do it. We'll go with you." Josie went to the sink to wash down her pills with water. She pushed the bottle of whiskey sitting on the counter as far away from her as she could.

Tanya rocked back and forth in the chair, holding herself. "I know I have to do it, but darn it, I'm scared to death. If the police don't arrest Naomi, I'll be on the witch's hit list."

"Over my dead body!" Debbie shouted.

I started and so did the others. Debbie had been dozing in a quiet stupor since I brought her in from the front step. But the mention of Naomi's name brought her out of her whiskey-induced daze. I put my hand on her shoulder. Her eyes closed and she nodded back off to sleep.

"We'll all go together tomorrow. We don't have a choice. This has to be reported and Naomi is obviously not going to step forward. She's had enough time." I didn't leave room for argument.

The next morning, I picked everyone up around eight. Debbie sat in the back seat, a dark pair of sunglasses covering her bloodshot eyes. She stared out the side window of the car. I knew not to try to start a conversation with her when she was hungover. Josie climbed in the back with Debbie. It was the one thing she held in common with her mom—she was an argumentative drunk and a bear when suffering a hangover. Tanya took shotgun.

"You ready?" I asked Tanya.

"No, Betty, I am not ready." Tanya looked like she was about to cry and her voice wavered.

"Stop it." Debbie barked from the back seat. "No more crying. Don't waste tears on the she-devil."

I watched Tanya bite back her fear and nod her head.

At the Rosewood Police Station, I bent down and whispered to the dispatcher, "We need to visit with someone about a murder."

The large woman behind the desk raised her eyebrow, a mole above her left eye dancing on her broad expanse of forehead. "Excuse me?" she blared, as though to tell me there would be no secret keeping under her watch.

I was in no mood to take crap from anyone.

"You heard me. Get the police chief. We won't talk to anyone but him." I crossed my arms over my chest and kept my eyes locked on Mrs. I'm-So-Important Dispatcher Lady.

The woman gave a *well, aren't you special* eye roll and shuffled away.

What seemed like an eternity later, the police chief appeared in the front room, the same front room we'd all stood in so many years ago, bailing Debbie out of jail. The same chief who put Debbie in the jail—only looser in the jowls and rounder in the belly. His graying hair poked out from under his hat as he looked from face to face.

I stepped forward. "We need to talk to you in private." I glanced at the dispatcher and gave her a hard stare.

The dispatcher returned a snide smile.

He nodded and motioned us to follow him. We all settled around a table in a small room down the hall.

"So what's this all about, Ms. Striker?" He gazed at me with sleepy eyes and fought a yawn.

"Our friend wants to report a murder." I nudged Tanya.

Tanya's eyes grew round as donuts, and Josie's filled with worry. No one knew what Debbie's eyes looked like behind her dark glasses.

There was a long pause without breathing or blinking.

The police chief leaned back in his chair and crossed his ankles, his black shoes squeaking against each other. "Well, report away." He looked to be waiting for the punch line of a joke, a small upturn of his lips at the corner of his mouth. I half expected him to pull out a toothpick and start removing the lunch from between his teeth. The man wiped away the smirk forming on his face.

Tanya cleared her throat and looked to us for help. Josie shrugged, and Debbie seemed to be staring at the chief—it was hard to tell with her glasses.

"Go on, Tanya. Just tell him," I said.

Through chattering teeth and with a wavering voice, Tanya managed to stutter out the basic details of how she suspected Naomi had run Mari off the road. I chimed in about my run-in with her at the Fourth of July celebration and how Naomi had knocked out my tooth. I smiled to show the chief the hole where my tooth had once lived. Josie helped by nodding and backing up our stories, but Debbie sat in silence.

"And the last word Mari said was 'Naomi,'" Tanya said, then looked like she would burst into tears.

Debbie turned to glare at her. Tanya stared at her own reflection in the surface of Debbie's glasses and bit her lip.

The chief stood up and put his hands on his hips. "So let me get this straight. You all have been having some kind of petty little fight with Naomi Waterman Talbot, way back since high school."

He pointed at me. "Ms. Striker seems to be blackmailing Naomi with some panties and a threat of spreading a rumor about her having a fling with your boss." He raised his eyebrows and grinned, then shook his head.

I began to speak, but he put his hand out, stopping me. "Let me finish."

"And Miss Townsend, you saw everything and were worried about Mari but went on home, leaving it to this one." He jerked his thumb at Tanya.

Josie grimaced.

"And Mrs. Coleman. You're hiding behind dark glasses and haven't said a word. What are you even here for?" He shifted his weight to his back foot.

Debbie took off her glasses, revealing bloodshot eyes. She looked like she might burst into flames. "Well, ain't that the million-dollar question, Chief. Moral support, I guess. It sure as heck isn't because I think *you're* going to help us. I, for one, know damn well you're not going to do anything about this. You're going to tiptoe all around this issue like one more sheep in the flock, protecting the rich and making the average person pay all the debts of society. Like the idiots in power always do."

"Well. You're full of big talk, aren't you?" He leaned down and stared at her over the table, a smile inching across his mouth.

Debbie shrugged. "You asked. I answered."

The two locked in a staring match. I suspected the police chief remembered Debbie's drunken mom. Debbie most likely had her own bad memories of the chief, too—being dragged off to jail at Naomi's wedding came to mind. Either way, this wasn't getting us anywhere.

"What do you plan to do?" I broke the silence.

He settled back down in his chair and crossed his arms over his chest, leaned his head back, stared at the ceiling for a moment, then sighed. "Well, you do realize you're accusing the judge's wife of murder. That's a serious charge, and aside from her word"—he nodded in Tanya's direction—"you have no proof."

Tanya fidgeted in her chair. I saw the color draining from her face.

"The best I can do is visit with the judge and ask him why he was speeding away from the scene and ask Naomi what she knows about Mari's death." The chief stared at Tanya. "Regardless, if you want anything more to happen, we'll have to see what the county attorney has to say about it. Would you be willing to testify in a court of law?"

I could see Tanya try to swallow down the lump in her throat as she shook her head. The reality must have hit her. The chief was going to tell Naomi that Tanya had accused her of murder. Tanya's eyes filled with panic, and I could almost hear her thoughts scream out in horror. The mere idea of sitting on a witness stand in front of people and pointing her finger at Naomi—it was too much for her. She couldn't answer the chief's question. She couldn't even speak.

The chief must have seen it too. He leaned across the table toward Tanya and spoke to her like she was simple. "I guess beyond that, I'll need some kind of proof to magically appear. If not, I can't just throw her in the pokey because you girls don't get along."

Debbie stood up. Her chair screeched across the floor and she stormed out of the room.

"Well, she certainly has a bee up her—" the chief started to say.

I cut him off. "How many times did you give Debbie's mother a ride home from the bar?"

He considered the question. "Quite a few, I suppose."

"And you knew she had a child. Well, Debbie was that child. What did you do to help Debbie? Huh?" I glared at him.

He didn't answer, but the sudden flush creeping up his neck told me I'd hit a nerve.

"I have a feeling our friend doesn't have a lot of faith in the law—or at least in your brand of it." I lost a little faith that day as well.

Tanya looked as though she didn't understand what had gone wrong. "You're going to arrest Naomi, aren't you?" she pleaded.

"You have to do something about what we've told you." Josie echoed Tanya's concern.

"I said I'd visit with Naomi and the judge, but you all have to understand I need more proof. Unless Mrs. Talbot confesses... I got nuthin'." He raised his palms to the air.

We stared at the chief for a moment. Then we rose and trailed out of the office, past the snotty dispatcher, and out to my car. I held Tanya's hand. We walked like a funeral procession all over again, but this time, the funeral might be Tanya's.

22

"You must have been terrified." Gloria said to Tanya.

"I was, and with good reason. Naomi was about to roll over me like a tidal wave."

Tanya at the Bank—1974

From the moment we left the police station, it felt like I'd been tied to the tracks and left to wait for the Naomi train to run me down. Dumped in the desert and the bitch buzzard was circling. Damn her. She literally murdered someone and I, the witness, ended up terrified and filled with guilt.

Naomi didn't have any concern about paying for her crime. She always got what she wanted, no matter who she had to bulldoze. She'd probably bribe the police chief if he did go to talk to her. But I worried most about who would protect me from Naomi's wrath after she finished with him.

On Monday, I pulled my car into a space behind the bank. I took a deep breath and went into work. Time to find out if the chief had talked to Naomi and, if he had, what she would say and do to me now.

Keeping my head down, I entered the employee entrance and went to my teller window. I put my purse under the counter, then worked up the courage to look around the bank at the others.

It was ominously quiet. No other tellers stood at their stations. No chatter between loan officers. No one sitting at their desks.

Did the world end and I didn't get the memo?

I looked up and what I saw sank like a stone to the bottom of my stomach. The entire staff was crowded in Naomi's office—every teller, every loan officer, the vice president, and president, all swarmed around her desk, listening.

I stared, my mouth going dry. I knew what was going on in there. Naomi was telling a tale to turn everyone against me. What else could it be? Someone would have contacted me if they'd planned a special meeting this morning. Besides, special meetings were held in the conference room, not in the she-demon's office.

As I stared, heads turned to look my direction. My face burned and the hair on the back of my neck rose. The door to Naomi's office opened and they all poured out. Not one person said good morning to me. Not one person offered me a smile or as much as a glance. The president of the bank came and stood in front of me. I met his eyes and held my breath.

"Tanya." He nodded. "Please follow me." He turned and went back to Naomi's office.

On shaking legs, I followed the bank president. Heads turned to watch, gawking at my misfortune.

When I entered the office, he shut the door behind me. A vacuum of disapproval hung heavy in the room.

"Have a seat." He pointed to a chair.

Naomi, the vice president, and the president stood high above me, looking down on me like an ant under a magnifying glass about to get scorched by the sun. I squirmed in the chair. Naomi had a sickening look of satisfaction on her face.

"Last night, Doug and I were visited by the police chief." Naomi glared at me. "He told us you have accused me of causing, then leaving, the scene of Mari's car crash. You can imagine how upset this made us."

Naomi picked up a photo of her and Doug, he in a tux and she in a gown. Some kind of political fundraiser at the governor's mansion. Naomi set the picture back down and smiled at the photo.

"Of course, the accusation is laughable." She smirked at me, and both the president and vice president shook their heads as though they were dealing with the prank of a naughty child. "There's no proof, and Tanya... seriously." Naomi pursed her lips and gave me a sideways glance. "I would never do such a horrible thing."

My mind raced. Now was when I needed my friends. Now was the moment I should have thought of before I ever said a word to the police chief. I wanted to bolt from the room and run away, but I remained, paralyzed with fear, destined to be humiliated by Naomi Talbot.

The president of the bank sat down on the edge of Naomi's desk and laced his fingers together. "Of course, you must realize we can't ignore this."

"No. No. Not acceptable." The fool vice president muttered in agreement with his boss.

Of course not, I thought. *We can ignore Naomi for as much as murdering Mari, but me reporting it... no, no... not acceptable... we mustn't ignore that.*

"We have to let you go. This kind of slander is bad for the bank and the community. We have to think of the bigger picture." The president sounded so authoritative, his low voice filling the room.

Naomi stood up and put her hand on the vice president, then the president's shoulders, a show of unity. She attempted to look rueful, but I could see the smile tugging at the corner of her mouth. "You'll need to clear out anything you have here and leave immediately, Tanya. We'll escort you out."

Escort me out? Like a common criminal?

They stared at me while their words sank into my brain. My hands lay numb in my lap. My leaden feet planted to the floor... *in* the floor, like cement. My brain throbbed with the echo of the words I still couldn't understand.

Escort me out.

Their stares bored into me, burning through the fog around my brain. I heaved myself up from the chair, my weight in worry and humiliation almost too much to carry, but I pushed myself from the room and to my station where a box sat waiting, all my things already dumped inside. The sight of the bare bulletin board and blank wall space blurred.

Everyone still staring at me.

Frowns and glares of disapproval.

I picked up the box. So light. So many years working here for this bank and every item that represented me—pictures of family, my word-of-the-day calendar, and the cartoons I'd cut out from the paper and pinned to the wall behind the counter. A troll doll. A Mother's Day card. A small wooden cross. My entire world outside this bank, stuffed in a little box—my existence beyond counting money.

Ten minutes later I was sitting in my car, fighting back tears. Naomi and the two men stood at the back door of the bank, watching me, waiting for me to drive away. As though I would burst back in and rob the place or something. They made me turn in my key. Shoved papers in front of me to sign, agreeing to whatever the blurry words said.

Finally, I gave in, started the car, and drove down the alley. Even a half a block away when I reached the stop sign, I could still see them in my rearview mirror.

They were comforting Naomi.

And right there and then, I stopped crying. I hated Naomi. Truly hated her.

And I wanted to make her hurt as badly as I hurt at that moment.

23

Gloria didn't think for one minute Tanya had it in her to hurt anyone. But she didn't blame her for thinking about it. She knew what she'd be asking Ronnie about on their lunch date tomorrow—banking procedures.

Without giving names or more information than necessary, Gloria told Ronnie about the way Tanya had been fired. "It seems so harsh to escort a long-term employee out of the bank, doesn't it? Was the woman employer pulling a power move, or is this protocol?" Gloria stabbed at her chef salad.

Ronnie paused a little too long for Gloria's liking, and she realized she had monopolized the conversation. "Sorry. This is a date. We should talk about something else."

He smiled at her, his chin resting in the palm of his hand.

Oh no. I have something between my teeth. She glanced down. No food stains on her blouse. He was still grinning at her. "What?"

"I'm enjoying your enthusiasm. I've never dated a newspaper editor. I had no idea how excited a story can make a person."

Gloria felt her cheeks flushing red. "Are you making fun of me?"

"Not at all." Ronnie put his hands up in defense. "Quite the contrary. I'm genuinely intrigued."

She tilted her head to the side then realized she probably looked like a dog who had heard a high-pitched noise. "Well. Thanks, I guess."

He chuckled, shook his head, then took a big bite out of his cheeseburger. No insecurities there. Men. They had it so easy. He probably ate cheeseburgers every day and didn't even have to run to keep his weight off.

He swallowed the bite and his Adam's apple bobbed in his throat. "Let's see. Protocol or power mongering. That was the question, right?" He took a drink of his cola and wiped his mouth with a paper napkin. "I'd say in today's world, it would be protocol. In 1974, I really don't know. But honestly, I think even when bank rules demand it, it could be done after hours or with more discretion. I'd say what she did to her employee was harsh."

"So you think I'm on to something then? This is part of a story I'm working on. A book, actually." Her eyes darted up to catch his reaction. His eyebrows rose, but thoughtfully, not like he was judging her.

Gloria knew she was acting goofy but couldn't stop herself. It was the novelty of being on a date, in public, no less, and the truth was it felt great to tell someone she planned to write a book. This was actually the first time she'd said it out loud to another person. She would write a book, and this man sitting across from her knew it.

Oh, God. This man sitting across from her knew she planned to write a book.

The realization clanged like a gong in her head.

She pushed her salad away, no longer feeling hungry. "You must think I'm crazy. Who am I to write a book? Especially nowadays. Everyone and their dog writes a book. What makes me so special?" Gloria dropped her forehead into the palm of her hand.

"Whoa. Slow down. Your instincts are solid. The one scene you described was interesting, so I can only imagine there's a lot more to the story." He reached across the table and took her hand, the one holding up her head. He pulled it down onto the table and held it there.

She looked up into eyes of understanding—gorgeous blue eyes—and an incredibly adorable crooked smile. He squeezed her fingers, then rubbed them gently with his thumb. She melted.

After he paid for lunch, they walked out to their cars. The awkward moment after a date. The locals were all staring at them. It was one in the afternoon and broad daylight. Cars were pulling in and out and hurrying past on the highway. She searched her brain for words but couldn't find any.

He saved her. "I'm really enjoying getting to know you, Gloria. Thanks for sharing your story." His hands casually rested in the pockets of his trousers. The sun hit his face, highlighting the dimple in his chin.

"I hope I didn't bore you." She fumbled for the keys in her purse.

"Absolutely not."

When she looked up, he was staring at her mouth as though he was about to lean over and give her a kiss. She froze. *Not in a truck-stop parking lot in broad daylight. No, no, no, no.*

A wind blew hair across her face. He reached out to brush it from her eyes. The warmth of his fingers lit a fire across her cheek. He stepped closer.

"As a matter of fact, I'd really like to hear more about the story, and a lot more about you." His gaze searched her eyes, holding her in the moment.

"I'd like it very much." She moistened her lips. *Oh, what the heck. If you want to kiss me, who am I to stand in the way?*

"Tomorrow night open for you?" he asked— his low voice sending a shiver up the back of her neck.

She nodded. They still hadn't broken the connection with their eyes. Now she was trying to will him to kiss her. *Kiss me. Kiss me now.*

"Be at your house at seven?" His fingers reached out and took her hand. Vibrations ran up her arm.

"Mmmhmmm." She smiled like a mesmerized dork.

But he was smiling, too. "You know what I'd really like to do right now?"

She swallowed an amazingly large lump in her throat. "What?" she squeaked.

"Kiss you." He squeezed her hand. "But I'm not going to."

Her heart fell and her face did too. *So close.*

"Because, you know, it's broad daylight and everything, and I think it wouldn't take long for it to become the hottest news in town." He nodded his head toward the diner.

Gloria looked over and saw a small group of folks—Delbert being one of them. She already knew she'd be answering questions during coffee at the old-man table next week.

Their hands fell apart and the world returned to normal, but a bit of magic lingered.

From her car she watched Ronnie drive away. It occurred to her she hadn't felt this good in a long time and she was enjoying it.

Her attention returned to the people standing outside the diner, specifically Delbert. He was the one who hadn't been as wholehearted in his opinion the women were innocent of foul play. Foul play or not, this was going to be a great book.

No matter how caught up she might get in potential romance, a decent story would always be her first love.

24

Jumbled thoughts clouded Gloria's mind as she drove to Meadowbrook. Her cell phone rang, jarring her out of her reverie. She checked—it was her mother.

She had too much on her mind and didn't want to answer all the questions her mother was sure to have, so she decided not to take the call and let it go to voice mail.

Gloria loved her mother, but talking with her about these women felt like she was cheating on her mother with a bunch of other potential mothers. Maybe that was exactly what she *was* doing. She knew she was going to have to talk to her mother soon. It had been a while. What must she think? Gloria knew she was worrying about her. Maybe she'd call her tonight. But in the meantime, her thoughts strayed back to today's interview with the women.

On her last visit, Tanya had told about how she'd been fired and escorted from the bank like a common criminal. It sounded, based on Gloria's conversation with Ronnie, like Naomi had played too rough. No big surprise there.

Gloria tried to imagine the humiliation Tanya must have felt. How she was able to hold her head up in a small town after such a thing was a mystery.

But could the humiliation drive Tanya to murder?

She also thought about Ronnie. Tomorrow night they'd have their second date. The idea made the hairs on her arms stand up in a good way.

"Look what the cat dragged in," Debbie announced when Gloria entered the sunroom. Then she blew a smoke ring.

"Hello to you, too." Gloria pulled up her chair.

"You look different," Josie noted as she looked her over. "Did you change your hair?"

"Her hair is the same. It's her smile. It looks a little naughty." Debbie raised an eyebrow.

"Well, you'd know naughty." Josie crossed her arms.

"My guess is she had her date with the fellow she told us about." Betty smiled.

Gloria didn't figure she'd get out of it, so she went ahead and told them all about Ronnie. The ladies nodded with approval as they listened with curiosity in their eyes. "So, anyway, enough about me. Tell me more of your story."

Tanya cleared her throat. "Well then. Let's get started."

Tanya Needs a Drink—1974

After being escorted out of the bank, I drove around the block and down the street. Like a magnet, I was drawn to Sully's Bar. At 9:22 in the morning, the signs in the dark front window blinked. Miller High Life. Pabst Blue Ribbon. Open. Open. Open.

With my head leaned back on the headrest, I stared at the ripped cloth ceiling, then looked up and down the block. Where in the hell would I get a job in this town? The grocery store? Maybe at the Pizza Hut that recently opened out on the highway? Or the factory?

I poked my finger through the rip in the cloth and touched the rusty metal above. No way could we afford a new car now.

The Post Toasties I'd had for breakfast did a dance up my esophagus. I clutched the door handle of the car, thinking I would throw up, but I held it down. Then I thought about having to go home and tell Rusty and pushed the door open, leaned out, and retched into the gutter. *Damn weak stomach.*

Stepping far over the mess I'd made, I left the car and went to stand in the shade under Sully's awning. My stomach began to settle, but a breeze would have helped. The Open sign still blinked at me. I looked left, then right, checking to see if I knew anyone on the street. No one. So I went into the air-conditioned darkness for a drink to calm my nerves.

One old man sat at the far end of the bar. He and Sully glanced my way. They appeared blinded by the light from the doorway, but I could see them clear enough. They looked like permanent fixtures—part of the decor.

At first I hesitated, then figured what the hell. The day couldn't get any worse. I had six hours to kill before Rusty came home from work. I might as well hide here where no one would suspect where I'd be. It would give me time to think.

I chose a table by the wall, across from the bar. There was no place to sit that I couldn't be seen from the front door. Not that anyone I knew would come in.

Sully came over and stared at me for a moment, a quizzical expression on his face. "Tanya." He nodded.

I couldn't make eye contact. My hand wiped at the table and I swallowed hard. Sully's kid had been in my daughter's class through school. I'd waited on Sully at the bank many times. He was a scruffy fellow with a protruding belly. The top three buttons of his shirt should have been hooked, but they weren't, and his chest hairs and gold chain were on full display. I glanced up and caught the one-sided grin he wore.

"Day off from the bank?" He chuckled.

I should leave. I should absolutely leave.

"Just teasin'. What can I getcha?" Sully shifted his ample weight from one foot to the other.

"Whiskey." I didn't even recognize my own voice. It sounded like some desperate, frightened bum.

"Really?" Sully asked. "Straight?" His voice cracked in surprise.

"Uh… whatever… or you can mix it with something. You decide," I muttered. The one time I'd drank whiskey had been at Debbie's. It was the only time I'd had anything stronger than beer. I never even drank beer to speak of. I just knew I needed something strong. Something to kill the embarrassment, the humiliation, the shame, and whatever other unsavory crap would happen to me that day. I was tired of behaving like a good girl and being penalized for it.

Sully shuffled off. I hoped he'd come back soon with the drink.

He pulled down levers, poured things in a glass, brought it over, and set it down in front of me. "Whiskey and Coke." He smiled. "You'll like it."

The dark brown liquid and ice shined in the short glass. I picked it up and took a sip. Cola with a biting taste of whiskey... the taste I remembered, but better. I downed the entire glass.

"I'll have two more." I pushed the glass to him. "Should I pay you now? How does this work?"

Sully picked up the glass in his stubby fingers with their long nails and turned to go. "I'll run a tab. Don't worry about it right now."

The warmth of the drink blanketed me. I could feel the ugly edge of the morning begin to glow.

Sully brought over two more glasses and set them down. I pulled them in front of me and ran my fingers down the condensation of their sides.

"Might want to drink those slower than the first one," he offered.

"Okay."

I didn't bother to look away from my drinks. They were my promise of relief, and if these didn't work I'd have some more.

The door of the bar opened and light pierced through the dark room. I turned and stared into the same blinding glare I had cast five minutes earlier.

A man entered, and as the door shut, my eyes adjusted. I recognized the new patron as he took a stool at the bar—Naomi's son, Doug Junior.

Sully put a drink in front of him before he even asked. He must be what they called *a regular*. He looked like he'd been up all night. Maybe this was his breakfast.

The rumors about him floated through my fuzzy head. I'd drunk half of another glass of whiskey and cola and the world around me became a soft-edged and slightly shaky movie reel.

Douglas Junior never so much as looked at the rest of us in the bar. I studied him in silence and wondered if he hated his mother as much as I did. I couldn't imagine anyone liking Naomi—even her own blood. I even considered asking him. Instead, I finished the second glass of whiskey and cola and pushed it away. Sully came by and scooped it up.

"Want another?"

I nodded and sucked at the little straw in my third drink.

"Slow down. I mean it. You'll be sick." Sully warned me with a low grumble of a voice.

"Okay," I said again, but the drinks tasted too good. I wanted to make this day disappear fast.

25

The idea of Tanya in a bar drinking her troubles away caught Gloria off guard. Yet the weight of the world had been on the woman's shoulders. The idea of such a nonconfrontational person dealing with so much hostility—Gloria could see how it could drive someone over the edge. Not to mention the financial burden looming over her.

Betty rubbed Tanya's shoulder. "But Naomi was only warming up. It was as though after the chief of police visited with her, she sat down and plotted war against all of us. Tanya was the first battle, but Josie and I were next in line to come under fire." Betty sighed.

Betty Hears the Rumor—1974

Hank came to work in a rare mood, his eye still sporting a hint of greenish purple. Then Naomi showed up for a visit. Then all hell broke loose. I could never have even imagined what was about to go down.

The two stood in the hallway whispering. Naomi glanced over her shoulder at me for effect. I heard snippets. "Tanya" one moment. More whispers. "Chief" the next moment. More whispers.

Then the word *lesbian* hit the air and I straightened in my chair and raised an eyebrow.

That was odd.

More whispers ensued, then the couple disappeared into Hank's office.

I thought I'd better figure out what was going on. I called the bank to talk to Tanya. "Hi, may I talk to Tanya Gunderson?"

The woman on the other end of the line stammered. "Uh, she's not here." The voice sounded wobbly, then I could hear the mouthpiece being covered and muffled voices. "Who's calling?" the voice came back to ask.

"Betty over at Meyer's Law Office." I waited. Usually the mention of a call from a law office received quick attention. Not today.

More muffled discussion.

"She's not here." The voice came back, but with no new information.

I was about to question why they were behaving so clandestinely when I heard someone pick up. Either Hank or someone else at the bank was now listening in.

"Thank you," I said and hung up. I drummed my fingers on the desk.

What's going on here?

The door to Hank's office clicked open and Naomi appeared from the shadows of the hallway. Normally she sauntered right past my desk, but this time she stopped to talk to me.

"You're friends with Tanya Gunderson, aren't you?" Naomi pulled a mirror and lipstick from her purse and began to apply a fresh coat of paint.

"You know I am, Naomi." I glared at the woman.

"Too bad I had to let her go this morning. You know, one can't have slanderers in their employ." She smiled and locked eyes with me.

I refused to show emotion. It's what she wanted.

"Say, it occurs to me. You hang out with Tanya, Debbie, and Josie. Now, Tanya is married and Debbie once was, but Josie. Hmmm. She never has been, and nor have you. Interesting." She tapped her finger on her chin as if pondering life's mysteries.

"What are you getting at, Naomi? Spit it out." I'd had enough of this game.

"Oh nothing. Just the rumor mill is grinding away. I'm sure you'll hear about it soon enough. Never mind. I don't want to upset you." Then she whisked out of the office.

What in the hell is going on in this town?

I'd stood to go to Hank's office so I could get to the bottom of things when the front door flew open. Josie burst in, her eyes swollen from crying and her face wet with tears.

I hurried over to her. "What's wrong?" I couldn't imagine what could drive Josie to such sobbing, but since Mari had been killed, it seemed the worst wasn't out of the question.

"My contract has been terminated!" Josie wailed as she wiped at her eyes with her handkerchief.

I put my arm around her and rubbed her shoulder as she cried.

From behind me, I heard Hank say, "Dear God, not in the front office."

We parted and stared at him, dumbfounded.

"If you girls want to do that kind of thing in public, you need to move to a big city. Folks around here aren't going to tolerate it."

"What in the hell are you talking about, Hank?" I was at the end of my rope. Tanya fired. Josie crying. Naomi talking about rumors... such ugly rumors... they had to be about... "Shit." I saw the signs in Hank's raised eyebrow.

I turned back to Josie, my hands still on her shoulders. I pulled my hand away and asked, "Why were you fired?"

Through heavy sobs, Josie wailed, "Sexual misconduct. They think I'm a lesbian!"

"Oh, good Lord. Of all things. This is ridiculous." I slapped my palm to my head. *Filthy lying bitch, Naomi.*

"You can't blame the school board," Hank said. "She interacts with children, after all."

Josie cried louder. I had thought it couldn't be possible. "Hank, I don't know what rumors you've listened to, but they aren't true. Shame on you for believing them."

"Well, from where I'm standing they look pretty believable." He crossed his arms.

All of those years working together and he was so quick to believe a rumor. It sickened me. "That's it. I'm out of here. My friends need me, and if I stay here another minute, I'm going to take your head off."

I left Josie's side and went to grab my purse. If Hank responded, I didn't care. We left the law office and I slammed the door behind us.

I wrapped my arm around Josie's shoulder and led her to the car. As we walked down the sidewalk, I saw people stare, even whisper. *Had this town lost it's ever-lovin' mind?* Then I noticed Tanya's car in front of Sully's.

"Wait here," I told Josie. I wanted a stiff drink right about then, but what were the odds Tanya would actually be in the bar? I opened the door and peered in. There she sat, and it looked like she'd been there for a while.

26

Gloria suspected that in 1974 accusing someone of being a lesbian was like calling them a unicorn—an unreal concept in a small town of the time. And losing a job over it... what a blow it had to have been.

Could it be a reason for a woman to give a child up for adoption? Moreover, could it be a reason to murder someone? Gloria didn't get much time to ponder the concept.

Debbie stubbed out her cigarette, took a sip of water, then said, "I'll take it from here."

Debbie Gets a Letter—1974

I walked out to the end of my driveway. It was going to be one of those days, I could tell. The bird shit splattered on the top of the mailbox confirmed it.

On my walk back to the house, I rifled through the bills and saw the copy of *Playboy*. Bud's subscription. I'd never had the heart to cancel it. It was one more thing to remind me of him. I dropped it in the trashcan by the front door and said what I always used to say to Bud when I found one of his naughty magazines. "Buddy... what am I going to do with you?" I shook my head with sad nostalgia.

The rest of the mail I threw on the kitchen table and out from the middle slid a handwritten envelope. A twinge in my gut drew me to it. I plopped down into the chair and sliced it open with my knife.

You're a white-trash rat and your mother was a drunk. You and your friends have gone too far. And you will have to pay.

No signature.

Coward.

I tossed it onto the table. I knew exactly who sent it. Time to go talk to Betty. We had to figure out what to do about this thorn in our side.

When I pulled in front of the law office, I noticed Josie and Tanya's cars also parked on the block. I got out and began to walk toward the door to Meyer's Law Office, but my attention was drawn back to their cars. Josie and Tanya should be at work, so why would they be parked here?

I walked along the sidewalk, peering inside the windows of the storefronts along the way. I didn't see Josie or Tanya in the pharmacy or the hardware store. The next place was Sully's.

Surely not Sully's.

I opened the door and my jaw dropped. The girls all turned to look, then waved me in.

"Well, now I've seen everything." I approached the table. No one looked happy, or sober. "How much of this pity party have I missed?"

"About an hour," Betty slurred then waved her hand at Sully to bring another round.

Tanya's arm draped across the table and her head rested on top of it.

"What's up with her?" I pointed.

"She was fired this morning." Betty pushed out a chair and I took it.

Sully arrived with drinks and asked what I wanted.

"Just a Coke."

"She'll have a Jack and Coke," Betty said.

"Whoa, it's morning, ladies. What the hell's going on here?"

Sully waited.

Betty leaned in. "You made us drink when Mari died. Now *you* drink. Tanya's been fired, Josie lost her contract at the school, and I'm going to quit my damn job because Naomi has spread the rumor around town that Josie and I are lesbians and my boss apparently believes it." Betty sat back and crossed her arms, then challenged me with a glare. "Those good enough reasons for ya?"

I looked up at Sully. "Make it a Jack and Seven and you may as well bring three. Looks like I have some catching up to do."

27

Before Gloria could even make a comment, Tanya picked up the story where Debbie left off. The clock read five o'clock, and these women didn't seem to want to stop. Normally this is when she'd take off for home, but she'd listen to one more segment before she left.

Tanya Wishes Naomi Dead—1974

We gobbled up greasy burgers and fries around one in the afternoon and switched to soft drinks about the same time. Coffee followed, badly needed. On my third cup of coffee, reality began to set in. Around four thirty in the afternoon, we pulled ourselves together. A strange mixture of whiskey, cola, coffee, cigarette smoke, and grease hung in the air and on our breath.

"Oh, heaven help me. I have to go home and tell Rusty. He's going to blow his top." I hoped I would be able to keep down the contents of my stomach, but it seemed unlikely.

"I can't imagine he'll yell at you," Josie offered and patted her hand on my arm.

"Oh, he's not going to be mad at me. He's going to want to tear up the street, racing to kick ass at Talbot's house." I laid my head down onto my folded arms.

Josie nodded. "Oh dear. I hadn't thought of that." She cradled her coffee cup under her nose and hid behind it.

"Let him." Debbie stewed over her coffee. "It's high time someone taught Naomi a lesson." Cigarette smoke clouded the air.

Betty stood up and walked away, then turned abruptly and came back. "Why in the hell are we hoping some man is going to fix this for us? Seriously. We thought Doug would do something, but all these years he hasn't. We hoped the chief of police would do something, but we were kidding ourselves. Now we think Rusty's going to solve the problem? He won't. He can't. Only we know the havoc she's wreaked. We're the ones who need to face her." Betty thumped her fist on the table. "We have to stand up to her if we ever want to get past this."

"It's that or move away." Josie's voice sounded weak, but her look was determined. "Come on, girls. Let's move away. This town will always have Naomi in it. We'll always hate her, and she'll always try to ruin our lives. Until she dies, we're stuck with this situation. Our only hope is to leave."

"Until she dies." I stirred my coffee, poured more sugar in the cup, and tested the words. "So maybe she needs to die." I couldn't look up. I waited and wondered what they would say.

Debbie pointed. "Now see, I like the way Tanya is thinking. Finally we have a solution that makes sense."

Betty didn't say anything for a moment. "That's a joke, of course. I know Tanya doesn't mean it and neither do you, Debbie. Still, we need to go confront Naomi. We need to end this. And we need to do it tonight." She sounded dead serious.

No one said a word, but we all nodded in agreement. Deep down, I believed my first sentiment. I hadn't been joking. Naomi didn't deserve to live, and no one would miss her anyway. But how to get rid of her was a question I'd keep to myself.

28

It looked as though Josie wanted to take up the story next, and without a doubt, Gloria wanted to hear it. But Linda Weldon came into the sun room and broke up the session.

"It's getting late, ladies." Linda came up to the table. "Dinner in ten minutes. Can't let you miss a good meal."

Josie glanced to the clock on the wall, and Tanya checked her smart phone.

"It is getting late. The rest of the story can wait. We'd better stick to our schedule." Tanya patted Linda on her hand. "You take such good care of us." She gave her a smile.

Gloria sighed. It had been long day and her own stomach growled. If she wanted to get a jog in before dark, she'd better be on her way.

"Ladies, Linda's right. It's five thirty and I'd better let you all have your dinner." Gloria stood up.

Josie's face fell. "Well, okay. Maybe you should come early on Tuesday, because this is where the story gets good."

Josie—always the problem solver.

"Good idea. I'll be here around one thirty. See you next week."

Gloria chuckled as she thought about those old women all sitting in the bar, drinking away their problems. Of course they were younger women then, but still. Debbie, she could see, but the rest—the image remained hard to conjure.

It made her think back to her college years and her friend Leslie and the parties and hangovers they had back in the day. *Wonder what Leslie has been up to lately?* When her friend had moved away to New York, Gloria gave up on trying to find another friend to replace her. The hole she'd left was too big to fill. It was hard to be so attached to people and then lose them. And Leslie had a big life up there in the city. She probably wouldn't even want to talk to tiny potatoes like Gloria.

She had barely walked in the door of her house when her landline started ringing. Caller ID said it was Karen Larson. Her hand hovered over the phone. It had been a couple of weeks since they'd chatted. Oh, an e-mail here and there let her folks know she was alive, but a real chat—she couldn't. Somehow it felt wrong. Her mother would ask her how the interviews were going. Gloria knew it made her mother uncomfortable. It made her uncomfortable, too.

Too many rings. She had to pick up.

"Hi, Mom. Just walked in the door. How are you?" Gloria shook her head. *Too chatty. Too perky.*

"Sweetie. I haven't heard your voice in so long. How are you?"

"Fine, fine. Just busy. Sorry I haven't called you. I have a lot on my plate right now." Gloria went to the bedroom and started changing into more comfortable clothes, the phone cradled between her shoulder and cheek.

The call continued. Her mother kindly avoided asking anything too inquiring. Just surface stuff. All the same, Gloria was relieved when the call ended. She needed to get this story, and she needed to find out which one of these women was her birth mother. It was like a hunger pang she had to feed. She didn't want to hurt her mother, but she would have to understand. And in a deep place in her subconscious, Gloria knew no matter what, her real mother, the one who raised her, would be patient and let her do what she had to do and still love her unconditionally when it was all said and done.

That's what real mothers do.

Gloria had a dinner of salad and a tuna sandwich. Gourmet cooking would never be her idea of a good time. But running was another story. She couldn't wait to work up a sweat and feel her muscles as she pounded the pavement.

A wave here and a shouted hello there, and she soon found herself on a country road headed out of town. The leaves had changed color. Crisp air pushed her to run even harder, and as her heart beat in her ears, she thought about Ronnie and decided thoughts about the Thorns of Rosewood could wait for next week.

She had no idea what she and Ronnie would be doing the next night. She hadn't had the presence of mind to ask him, so how to dress remained a question. But the idea of a surprise was great fun.

Before she knew it, she'd made her way around the section and headed back into town. Thinking always made the run go faster. Soon, Mabel's little house and Mabel herself came into view. Gloria didn't even wait for an invitation. She plopped down into the aluminum lawn chair beside the old woman, panting and happy as hell.

"Well, don't you look pleased with yourself?" Mabel wore a big smile. "I hear you're going to have your second date with my Ronnie." The old gal rubbed her hands together.

"I most certainly am. It's why I stopped. I wanted to thank you for telling him about me. So far I've really enjoyed his company." Gloria stood back up and started to stretch out her muscles.

"Well, sweetie, you certainly must have made an impression on him. From what I hear, he has special plans for you tomorrow." Mabel looked as though she would burst with her secret.

"Tell me. Tell me now." Gloria wanted to squeal like a little girl getting a present, but she toned it back to a large grin.

"Nope. I won't spoil his fun." Mabel shook her head back and forth.

"You have got to be kidding. You can't do that to me, Mabel. I don't know how to dress. I don't know if I should eat before he comes or if I should wait. You have to throw me a bone here. You don't want me to disappoint him, do you?"

"All I'm going to tell you is don't eat first. The rest, you'll have to figure out on your own."

Gloria tossed and turned until one in the morning, the time of day she had begun to associate with house cleaning. Then she got up and proceeded to do just that.

She swept and vacuumed, dusted, and made sure the kitchen gleamed. She purposely didn't clean her bedroom because Ronnie wouldn't be seeing her bedroom for a long time. She was many things, but easy was not one of them.

After cleaning, she began to try on different clothes and concluded she hated absolutely everything in her closet.

Finally she gave up and flopped down on her bed. She'd wear what she always wore. No time to try to be something she wasn't. She was a jeans and simple shirt kind of gal, and that's exactly what she'd be tomorrow night. He'd have to get used to it or take her shopping. Either would be fine with her.

Morning came fast and the workday went even faster. She pawned off covering the high school basketball game on one reporter, but she still didn't escape the office until almost six. After hurrying home, she tried to make herself look fresh and pretty. She had no idea how in the world to accomplish such a feat in less than an hour, but working under pressure had always been a challenge she willingly accepted.

Gloria was staring at a bottle of perfume in her hand when the doorbell rang. She threw it back in the bottom drawer. Soap was her fragrance anyway.

She couldn't commit to eau de anything. The women at work who apparently bathed in perfume had turned her off scents altogether.

She took one last look in the mirror—she was as good as she was going to get. She took off out of the bathroom and started running to the front door, then forced herself to slow down.

Just breathe.

The sun lolled in the pinkish-gray sky. Not quite sunset, but getting nearer by the minute. A hint of light painted the side of Ronnie's face. It only made him better looking.

"Come in." She held the door open wide and tried to be cool.

Ronnie wore jeans and a polo. *Good. Nothing fancy.*

He walked around her kitchen like a surveyor. He peeked into the living room, turned, and said, "This is going to work fine." He grinned from ear to ear. "I have a few things I need to get from the car, but let's get this out of the way first. He walked over, cupped her face in his hands, leaned down, and kissed her.

Firm. Warm. Not lusty. Just a nice kiss.

It took her breath away.

He straightened back up and smiled. "There. I've been wanting to do that since the parking lot." His eyes twinkled, and he clapped his hands and rubbed them together. "Now the fun begins."

Off he went, out the door to his car. As she watched, he unloaded full paper bags from his trunk, then hustled back up to the house. He came in and deposited the bags on her kitchen table.

Groceries. Fresh vegetables and packaged meat, even fresh herbs. She didn't have a clue what to do with fresh herbs.

He turned to her with a broad smile. "Did I mention I really like to cook?" Out of one of the bags, he pulled a red-checkered tablecloth. "And I'm hoping you're up for a little picnic on your living room floor."

Dear God, please don't let him be a serial killer because I think I just fell in love.

Later, her stomach was full of amazing food and her lips were swollen from proper kissing. She waved good-bye from her front step, went inside, and closed the door behind her.

She hadn't felt this mixture of exhaustion and excitement since she was young. He'd even washed the dishes, leaving her house as spotless as when he'd arrived. And the best part was, she could still smell him in the air. It smelled like garlic, tomatoes, and shaving lotion. She liked it just fine.

It occurred to her that the first thing she used to do after a date was call her friend Leslie. But now that Leslie was gone, what could she to do with these emotions bouncing around in her head like bubbles? Her possibilities were limited. Her mother? *No.* Mabel? *Absolutely not.* What she needed was someone her own age—someone who could relate to the euphoria she was feeling.

She punched the digits into her cell and waited, but not too long before she heard her friend's familiar voice.

"Hey, Leslie. It's Gloria." Her words sounded tentative. Hopeful.

They chatted for over an hour.

29

Turned out that even in the midst of all the excitement of New York, Leslie still had issues similar to Gloria's. She was still finding it hard to find a guy she felt really connected with and even harder to find a group of friends she clicked with. She described her life as *routine*. Her mother even pestered her like Gloria's did.

Good to know she had company, but it meant she had to stop using small-town life as a crutch for not doing the things she wanted to do.

Gloria no longer felt like she looked up at the world from the bottom of a lake, but more like she treaded on top, maybe was even swimming toward shore. She had a guy in her life, and it seemed like it might actually turn into something. She'd made contact with a friend whom she'd been, in all truth, embarrassed to call because she thought her life didn't measure up. Hard to admit you aren't sure your life is going the right direction to someone you think is a raging success. And, best of all, she had all the makings, so far at least, for a great book. Things were looking up.

Now all she had to do was decide if she really wanted to ask those four sweet, cranky, funny old women if any of them had given birth to her. She had reached the point where she wasn't sure she wanted to know.

When she walked through the doors to the sunroom at Meadowbrook, it didn't take but a moment to draw her thoughts back to where they needed to be... attentive to these women and their plight from 1974. They appeared as enthusiastic to start telling the story again as she was to hear it.

Josie Offers to Drive—1974

I vowed to never drink again as I dug through my purse then handed my money to Sully.

He took the cash and counted it. My head throbbed and my last burp smelled like whiskey, onions, and coffee—unpleasant to say the least.

The old man at the end of the bar slept soundly, snoring, his face flat on the counter. Sounds from a ball game coming from the radio filled the air. The whole bar smelled like an ashtray and grease.

"Shouldn't you do something about him?" I asked, pointing at the old man.

Sully didn't so much as look his direction. "Nah. He'll wake up in an hour or so. He does this every day." He shrugged. "This is kinda like his home, ya know?"

I shivered at the idea of such a sad existence. Yet, here I was. How could I judge? And I was newly rumored to be the town's lesbian teacher who'd been fired for sexual misconduct. Seriously. Who *did* I think I was, anyway? My head throbbed again. I needed an aspirin.

We all moved to the front door and opened it wide. The late afternoon sun shocked me like a flashbulb from a camera. I squinted and turned my head aside. "So. What now?"

Betty drew her sunglasses from her purse and slipped them on. "Now we go confront Naomi."

Tanya shot nervous glances up and down the sidewalk, her gaze stopping at the man leaning on the hood of his car. Doug Junior. "Keep your voices down." She tilted the top of her head in his direction. The rest of us looked his way.

Junior had been in and out of the bar all day. He'd come in, have a drink while standing at the counter, talk to Sully, look at his watch, and then leave again. When he was in the bar, we'd bring our heads together and whisper or stay silent. Now I thought back over the day and hoped we hadn't slipped up and spoken too loudly.

"Junior's too stoned to hear or care what we're saying." Debbie shook her head and flicked the ash of her cigarette away.

"How can you tell?" Tanya asked.

"I just can. Besides, why else would have he kept checking his watch and leaving? He probably met with a drug dealer or something." Debbie crushed the butt under her toe on the dirty cement in front of the bar.

I wasn't sure I bought Debbie's assessment, but this didn't seem like the time to argue.

"Don't worry about it. We have other things to concern ourselves with." Betty drew their attention. "Let's take one car. Stay calm and get what information we can out of Naomi. We can't leave until she understands this vendetta has to stop. We have to make her comprehend the gloves are off and we're going to start fighting back if she doesn't rein it in."

Debbie smiled and cracked her knuckles. The sound drove a chill up my spine. Tanya's eyes burned with hate—something I never thought I'd see. Maybe years of pent-up frustration had to bubble out at some point. Maybe this proved true for all of us. I glanced from face to face, then to Doug Junior.

He still sat there. Why?

"So who's driving?" Tanya asked.

"Not you. Naomi fired you this morning, so she might call the police if you even go onto her driveway." Betty hiked the strap of her purse up on her shoulder. "We won't all fit in my little car. Debbie? Josie?"

"I'll drive." My car had more room than Debbie's. It made sense. Plus, I'd ridden with Debbie before. The woman had a lead foot.

30

Josie Learns Good Manners Don't Count With Murderers—1974

My headlights swept across Talbot's lush green lawn. A strange mixture of jealousy, hatred, and fear twisted a knot in my stomach. A large fountain gurgled and a cherub spit out water into a massive basin shaped like a clamshell.

Betty left the car first. The look of determination on her face made me both confident and terrified. Debbie and Tanya fell in behind Betty's long steps. I could almost feel the vibrations of anger in the air.

Be calm. Right. Not gonna happen.

Betty's finger jammed at the doorbell. The sheer curtains over the large bay window parted. Naomi stared at us through the glass. An image of Medusa sprang to mind. The curtain fell back and footsteps sounded.

None of us had ever been in the Talbot house, only viewed it from the road like all the other common folk. It was as I had always imagined. A winding staircase leading up to the second level. Shiny white tile floor. Large entry mirror. Dark, heavy furniture. But of all the ostentatious trappings of the home, Naomi stood out as the most blatant statement of exclusivity, hands down.

"Well. This must be my lucky day. A visit from all my favorite people." Naomi smiled stiffly, sweeping her hand toward us like a game show hostess as she rolled her eyes and tapped her foot. She wore high-heel lounge slippers with fuzzy fluff at the toe. Marabou mules, they were called. The fluff danced with each tap. She held a glass of white wine in one hand and the other hand sat firmly planted on her hip, her long red nails like drops of blood against her silken white robe.

"So this is what you look like without makeup. I've always wondered." Debbie smirked.

"We need to talk." Betty's voice was firm.

"Well. Start talking." Naomi took a casual sip of wine, one eyebrow raised.

"Inside, Naomi. We need to come inside. This is going to take longer than a few minutes." If Tanya had stuck out her tongue, it would have matched her tone.

"Please, Naomi. It's important." I hoped the magic word would make a difference.

Seconds ticked away as we waited. Naomi finished her wine in one gulp. "What the hell. I'm curious." She turned and walked into the sitting room off the entry.

We followed, and I closed the front door behind us.

Naomi's white robe fluttered around her legs as she walked to the table where a bottle of wine chilled in a bucket. She filled her glass, took another drink, then finally turned to face us. "Spit it

Gina M. Barlean

out. I won't have much patience for this, so you'd better get to your point."

Betty stepped forward. "Your antics today were way out of line, as we've come to expect from you."

"Antics? Whatever do you mean?" Naomi looked to be having fun.

"Firing Tanya. Making sure Josie's contract didn't get renewed. Sending Debbie a threatening letter."

Betty wasn't finished when Naomi interrupted her. "I suppose you think I'm behind the news about you and Josie being lesbians, too."

"We're not lesbians!" I hadn't meant to yell, but darn it, it wasn't true.

"Sure you're not, Josie." Naomi drowned her laughter in another swallow of wine.

"Don't forget how you murdered Mari." Tanya threw her hands up. "None of the rest of it matters compared to that."

"That's enough. I'm not going to stand here in my own home and be accused of murder." Naomi pointed to the front door. "You can all get out right now."

"And if we don't?" Debbie stepped past Betty and went to stand nose-to-nose with Naomi.

I took a step back. This was about to get ugly. Naomi's face blanched white, and for once, she had nothing to say.

Tanya joined Debbie. "We're not going anywhere until you give us some answers. I know you ran Mari off the road. It was the last thing she said to me before she died!" Tanya was screaming now. Her shrill yells bounced off the room's high ceiling. "You only fired me to keep my mouth shut, and it isn't going to work, I can tell you right now!"

I looked out into the foyer. Surely Doug would come in and put an end to this catfight.

Betty joined Debbie and Tanya. "Admit it, Naomi. Starting rumors and getting people fired is bad, but nothing can ever compare to what you did to Mari."

"I did no such thing. You're all yapping dogs without a stitch of proof about any of these accusations." She stepped toward Tanya. "And if Mari said my name at her end, it was probably because she was admitting defeat."

Tanya lunged at Naomi, but Betty grabbed her arm and held her back.

"Get out. Right now." Naomi stormed to the big mahogany doorway in the entry, her silk robe whipping around her legs as she went.

Debbie marched after her. "We're not leaving until we're damn good and ready, and I'd like to see you make us."

Betty and Tanya were right on Debbie's heels, and I brought up the rear, hoping we *would* have to leave. This had become a disaster. It could only get worse. *Where in the hell is Doug?*

"Debbie's right. We're not going anywhere." Betty blocked the doorway.

For a moment, Naomi had a trapped look on her face, then one of her eyebrows rose and she turned with a huff and went toward the back of the house.

Tanya reached out and grabbed her by the arm. "Where do you think you're going?"

Naomi snatched her arm away and surged on.

We followed, ending up in the sizeable living room. French doors led to a patio at the rear of the house. A wet bar stood in the corner by the doors. And an enormous painting of Naomi hung over the fireplace. I stared at it, my mouth hanging open, trying to comprehend the colossal ego it took to have such a thing made.

She spun around to face us. "You all have quite the imagination. Some might even call your accusations crazy." Naomi made circles with her finger by her temple. "Seriously. Why would I waste my time on any of you? You're nothing to me. Less than nothing." Regardless of her confident words, she was pacing back and forth, the fluff of her marabou mules blowing in the breeze created by her fast steps.

"Well, you'd better take us seriously right now, Naomi, because we are prepared to settle this stupid vendetta you have against us, no matter what it takes." Betty broadened her stance and put her fists on her hips.

"Oh good heavens. You must be joking." Naomi rolled her eyes. "Do you all even know who you are? What people think of you?" Naomi began to explain it to us. She pointed at Tanya. "You're nothing more than a whiney little nobody. A little pissant married to a blue-collar worker." She wheeled to face Debbie. "You... a washed-up, white-trash punk whose mom was the town drunk." "Betty... you're a lesbian slut from what the rumors tell us. And Josie"—she jerked her thumb at me—"is nothing more than Betty's mousy, lesbian sex partner."

Debbie stepped forward and grabbed Naomi's arm, digging her fingers into skin. "Take it back, you bitch."

Naomi tore away. "Get off me, lowlife." She wiped at her arm as though Debbie's touch had left filth. "Now get out or I'm calling my husband." Naomi grabbed the phone sitting on an end table and shook the receiver at us.

Doug isn't here.

"Go ahead, Naomi. Call him. I'll bet Doug would be interested in all your escapades. Surely the poor man will come to his senses eventually. He can't possibly love you. You're too cold for even your own mother to love." Betty spit out the fiery words, and it didn't look as though she'd regret them any time soon.

Naomi threw her head back and laughed. "You fool. Doug would never cross me. You're living in the dream world you all had back in high school. Back when you thought Doug was such a great guy. Well, let me tell you. He's not so great. He's a lazy coward, and if it weren't for me, he'd have no career at all." She panted in anger.

"Maybe happiness means more than a career, Naomi. Have you ever thought of that?" Tanya's chin jutted forward in defiance.

"Oh, what would you know? You and your ridiculous Rusty and those scroungy children you raised. You think you're happy, but you're too stupid to know the difference."

Tanya's hands shot up and she rushed forward at Naomi as if she would choke the life out of her. Debbie pulled Tanya away. "No. If anyone's going to lay hands on this woman, it's going to be me."

Naomi ran around the couch to get away from Debbie and Tanya—surprisingly quick for someone in marabou mules.

"And if I put my hands on you, it's going to be to drag your fancy ass to the police station to confess." Debbie inched toward her.

"Confess to what? Knowing you're all a bunch of losers? Confess to being twice the woman any of you could even dream of being?" She laughed, her eyes glowing with self-adoration. This seemed like the final round of a game she had been waiting to play for a long time.

Debbie drew the jackknife from her pocket.

I gasped. "Debbie, no."

Naomi's smile grew wild at the sight of the old weapon. "Don't worry, Josie. She doesn't have what it takes to use it." Naomi picked up a tall, heavy crystal vase. "Go ahead. Come on. I'll take you all on." She kicked off her shoes and they flew through the air and tumbled behind her.

I stood frozen, watching, shaking in fear of what would happen next.

Betty and Tanya were at Debbie's side, ready to fight. They mimicked Naomi, standing with their hands raised, clenching into fists and unclenching, feet spread shoulder width, and crouched to move into action.

Had everyone lost their minds? "Maybe we need to all take a step back. Settle down before we do something we'll regret." Things had to stop or there'd be no turning back.

"Oh shut up, Josie. Go back to your little house and pet your cats. If you don't have the spine for this, you shouldn't have come." Naomi's eyes darted from the three women to me.

Is that what people thought of me? Had being nice made me harmless? I stepped up to stand by my friends. "You really don't know anything about me, Naomi. I don't even own a cat."

Tanya reached out and grabbed my hand in solidarity. I gripped Tanya's hand tightly, needing the support.

"So what am I supposed to do now when I don't have a job, Naomi?" Tanya asked. She let go of my hand and began to creep closer to Naomi.

"You should have thought of that before you went to the police." Naomi took a step in Tanya's direction, showing no trepidation.

"And what in the hell did your stupid anonymous letter mean, Naomi?" Debbie began to move on the other side of the couch, trapping her.

"You're nuts. I never sent you a letter." Naomi gripped the vase in her hands and held it at the ready.

"And what am *I* supposed to do now? I've been teaching my entire life. One stupid rumor and a visit to the school-board members ended my career. Those kids, my friends at the school, my classroom… all gone, thanks to you. You had no right to take my livelihood away from me!" The more I talked, the angrier I became.

A noise sounded from a different room. We all stiffened and our heads snapped in the direction from where it came.

"Doug?" Naomi yelled out, hope filling her eyes. No answer, but a cat sauntered into the room. Panic flashed across Naomi's face.

"Confess already. You left Mari to die in that ditch because you were jealous. You knew Mari and Doug still loved each other. Everyone at the celebration on the Fourth could see it plain as day. And you couldn't handle it." Tanya closed the gap.

Naomi raised the vase above her head. "Fine. I'll admit it. I tried to scare the Goody Two-shoes, and she ran off the road. What of it?" Her smug expression was more than I could take.

"You admit to killing her!" Tanya pointed her finger in accusation.

"I didn't say any such thing. I only tried to threaten her. Drove fast behind her and overtook her. She ran off the road because she was a terrible driver. Not my fault." Naomi shrugged.

Tanya stepped forward. "How can you absolve yourself so easily?" Then Tanya gave Naomi a shove. Naomi fell back and tripped over the mules she'd kicked off earlier. Her arms flailed in the air, and the hand holding the vase drew back, landing square on Debbie's head.

Our gasps and screams followed the sound of shattering glass, and an "oomph" from Naomi as she landed on her back at Debbie's feet.

Debbie cringed as shards of glass fell like rain on her shoulders. She yelled out, grabbing her head as blood started to run down the side of her face like a waterfall.

"Debbie!" Betty screamed and ran to her side, but not before Naomi flipped to her stomach and grabbed Debbie's ankle, pulling her down to the floor. Naomi scrambled to hover over Debbie.

Tanya lunged and grabbed Naomi by the waist, dragging her off Debbie and trying to pin her to the floor. The area where they struggled was tight—between the rear of the couch and a large bookcase. The two women churned on the ground, and as the fight continued, Betty pulled Debbie out from behind the couch and began searching her skull for the source of bleeding.

"It's just a scratch." Debbie waved Betty away although blood continued to stream down her cheek. She pushed up from the floor to stand but wobbled, and her eyes rolled back in her head and she fell. Betty caught her before she hit the ground.

"Just a scratch, my ass. Naomi knocked Debbie unconscious." Betty dragged Debbie to a chair and propped her in it.

Tanya was still straddling Naomi, pushing her face down into the carpet. "You lying, conniving tramp. You're a murderer. Admit it!"

I could hardly believe how strong and fierce Tanya was as she fought.

Naomi kicked her bare feet on the ground, her red-tipped toes flailing up and down like a pedicured duck paddling water.

I looked back at Debbie—still out cold. Betty fanned her and slapped her face but kept glancing over her shoulder toward Naomi and Tanya as they wrestled on the floor.

Then Naomi bucked Tanya off and turned the tables, climbing on top and gaining the upper hand. She wrapped her fingers around Tanya's throat, but Naomi didn't hold back. Tanya's eyes began to bulge as Naomi squeezed with all her strength. Tanya tried to scream but only a rasp escaped. "Josie, help."

Would Naomi really choke the life right out of her? Tanya was losing color fast, kicking and fighting with less strength by the second. I had to do something. I had to make it stop. She'd killed Mari, knocked out Debbie, and it looked as though Tanya would be her next victim. I grabbed a large trophy from the bookshelf beside me, then tested its weight in my hands. I held it by both handles, raised it high above me, and swung it down as hard as I could onto Naomi's head.

The sound of the trophy meeting her skull cracked like a clap of thunder. Naomi expelled air and let out a grunt as she fell down on top of Tanya.

Tanya shoved her off and rolled away. She grasped her neck and coughed as she struggled to get to her hands and knees.

I ran to Tanya's side but kept an eye on Naomi. "Are you okay?" I pushed my glasses up on my nose with sweaty hands.

"No." Tanya rasped and coughed as she shook her head. She looked deep into my eyes. "But thank you, Josie. You saved my life." Tears welled up, but coughing didn't allow her to talk any more.

With the trophy still gripped tightly in my hand, ready if needed, I went to examine Naomi. She lay completely still. I pushed at her with the toe of my shoe. "Naomi?" Her eyes were open—rolled into the back of her head. I toed her again. "Naomi!" I yelled.

Nothing.

I let go of the trophy and it fell from my hands and bounced on the carpet. I stooped down to look closer at the unconscious woman and saw a puddle of blood forming under her head. I gasped and put my hands to my face as the room began to spin and my brain pulsed.

"You guys. I think I killed Naomi." I turned to look at my friends.

Debbie had bled all over Naomi's expensive chair, but was slowly coming around. Tanya was throwing up on the white carpet. And the only thing I knew before everything went blurry and I passed out was that I was going to fry for the murder of Naomi Waterman Talbot.

31

The tension in the room made Gloria's skin tingle. Josie unconscious, Debbie bleeding from the head, Tanya puking, and Naomi possibly dead—the vision Josie painted with her shaky words was making the women look like the common criminals lore had purported them to be.

It sounded like they'd been defending each other, though, yet manslaughter was still a crime. These little old women—these sweet relics with thick glasses and age spots. It made Gloria uncomfortable. But now was no time to interrupt, and it would never be a time to give her opinion. She was a reporter. She had to stay neutral so she could get the whole story. But her sense of ethics warred with her hate for Naomi.

Josie drank her water, then wiped at her nose with the tissue she fetched from up her sleeve. Their eyes met, and Gloria knew Josie wanted to get back to the story. Gloria readied her pen, gave a nod, and Josie began again.

Josie Comes To—1974

A dull ache drummed in my head with each heartbeat.

Hands shook my shoulders. I struggled to open my eyes. Blurred faces looked down at me. Muffled voices seeped into my brain. I tried to make my friend's faces come into focus.

Tanya leaned over me, her face flushed. "Oh, thank God. She's waking up."

My eyes trailed down to the finger marks beginning to show up as bruises on her neck. I shifted my gaze and winced at the sight of Debbie, her face swollen from the blow of the crystal vase wielded by Naomi. Caked blood matted her short dark hair.

"Nice hit," Debbie said as she pinched my cheek.

Then I remembered smacking Naomi in the head with the trophy. "What have I done?" I mumbled, pushing away Debbie's hand and shifting my weight up on my elbows.

"The world a favor." Debbie stood up, put her hands on her hips, and grinned down at me.

Betty had been kneeling by my side. She also stood, and her face switched from worried to serious. "We have to get out of here."

I looked over to see the red stain creeping from Naomi's head onto the white carpet, and the room spun again.

"Get up, Josie. We don't have time for you to be fainting." Debbie yelled down at me as I swooned. "We gotta go, and we gotta go now." Debbie started for the door.

"But we can't leave her there." Tanya helped me stand. "And there's blood all over the chair and

I threw up all over the carpet and Naomi's bleeding all over the carpet, too."

"Our fingerprints are everywhere, Betty," I mumbled as I stood on shaky legs.

"There's no time to worry about this now, Josie. We have to leave. This has all gone way too far," Debbie yelled, already near the front door.

Debbie was right. We did have to leave. We couldn't be caught here in Naomi's home with blood literally all over our hands.

So we all ran, crazed and haunted, out the door and to my car. I was too dizzy to drive, so Debbie took the wheel and drove everyone back to their respective cars in front of Sully's.

When we arrived, Debbie grabbed Tanya by her hand. "Tanya, keep your mouth shut, you hear?"

Tanya stared at Debbie like she'd lost her mind. Maybe she had. "I have to explain to Rusty where I've been. I smell like puke and bar and alcohol. I have bruises on my neck. I have to tell him what happened."

"You tell Rusty you were fired and then spent the rest of the time with us at the bar, you hear? Tell him I choked you for all I care. Just don't tell him anything about Naomi. Not yet. We can't have anyone else knowing until we decide what we're going to do. Do you understand me? Don't say anything else, no matter what." Debbie was yelling and it was scaring the hell out of all of us.

Tears welled in Tanya's eyes. She looked through the car door window at her own car. "I don't know…"

"What don't you know?" Debbie shouted.

"If I can lie to Rusty." Tears streamed down her face.

I reached out and touched her shoulder. "Just for now, okay, Tanya? Until we can figure out what to do."

Tanya nodded.

"Listen to Josie. Don't breath a word about going to the Talbots'. We have to figure this whole thing out, but not until tomorrow. Right now, we can't be caught in their house and the less people who know we were there, the better. We shouldn't be seen together either, so get out and go. We all need to think about how we can prove we were nowhere near the Talbots' house. Lock yourself in your homes and shut the hell up!" Debbie vibrated with impatience.

At first Tanya's bottom lip quivered, and I expected her to continue arguing. Then she nodded and answered in a small voice. "Okay." She took a deep breath and left the car, running to her own car as though if she didn't do it right then, she'd never have the courage again.

Then Betty and Debbie left for their cars and drove away to their own homes. To sit silently. And that's what I had to do, too. Go home, sit quietly, and wait until someone told me what to do next.

32

Gloria shook her head. "So you all just left Naomi on the floor and left all the mess behind? You took a big risk."

Debbie stubbed out her cigarette and leaned forward. "Don't interrupt," she said, then took over the story.

Debbie Cleans Up—1974

I had told everyone to get in their houses and keep their mouths shut.

"Do you have a plan, Debbie?" Betty asked me before she left.

"I'll talk to you later. That's all I can say right now." I didn't know what to do, but I knew we'd done more than enough as a group. A lot more than we should have. Anything more would require more stealth and less people.

In my own car, I hoped no one had seen me with blood all over my face. It was dark and the town was quiet, as usual. I drove away slowly, in control, to my home—trying not to draw any attention to myself.

Hot water from the showerhead pelted my face. I stood under the stream until I knew every spot of blood had been rinsed clean from my body. Steam rose around me and my head throbbed. I was so exhausted, but I had way too much to do before I could sleep.

I dressed, then drank a cup of hot coffee and smoked a cigarette while I sat at my kitchen table and tried to make sense of everything. I couldn't sit in my house and hope the situation was going to turn out all right. It wasn't. I was sure. It was going to be a huge scandal and we were going to be right in the vortex of the storm.

Three cigarettes later, I finally knew what I had to do. I had to go back to the Talbots' and deal with the body. Clean up the mess. If not me, then who? I had the least to lose.

I threw a shovel in my backseat and headed back to Naomi's. When I pulled my car around through the alley, I saw the rear of their house. It was still dark inside. It had been at least an hour since we'd left, maybe more. I remembered us turning off the lights before we scurried out like the rats we were. At least we had that much presence of mind.

I exited my car and stared at the back patio. The French doors of the big living room loomed like an invitation to a horror movie. I began to walk through the grass and toward the house and tried to prepare myself for what I had to do. Clean up the mess. Polish away the fingerprints. And drag Naomi's sorry carcass out of her house and then figure out where to bury her. It was going to be a hellishly long night.

I swallowed hard, then checked the doors. Open. Gently turning the knob, I entered the murky darkness of the house. Silence greeted me. The sound of my own breathing was as loud as a blaring horn, accompanied by my heart thumping a rhythm hard in my ears.

I couldn't see a thing, and although I would have liked to work unseen in the shadows, I didn't know this house well enough. I was going to need light. I fumbled along the wall until I found the switch, then braced myself for what I was about to see. I had a feeling it was all going to be much uglier than it had been before.

The lights blazed on and I turned to the scene. I gasped.

Naomi was gone.

The pool of blood was there. The vomit. My own blood all over the chair. But no Naomi.

My God. Where was she?

I scanned the room, terror filling my lungs. She could be anywhere. Then the worst thought of all.

She could be out driving in her car right then, trying to find us and do to us what we thought we'd done to her. I had to warn everyone, and I had to do it fast. I caught sight of the phone on the wall, grabbed it from its cradle, and punched in Betty's number.

She answered with a tentative "Hello?"

"Betty, this is Debbie." I breathed into the phone. "I'm at the Talbots'."

Betty gasped. "What in God's name are you doing there?" Her voice was almost a scream.

I didn't have time to explain. "Betty, right now all you need to know is Naomi is gone and you need to be on the lookout."

"What do mean, Naomi is gone?"

"Gone. Just gone. I don't know where. But she's not lying on the floor where we left her. She could be anywhere. She could be in her car driving straight to your house for all we know."

"Oh my God!" Betty screamed.

"Listen, Betty. Calm down. Call everyone else and let them know. Maybe you and Josie should be together. Tanya has Rusty. Keep an eye out. We don't know what's coming."

"Okay, Debbie, but what are you going to do? What if Naomi is still in the house?"

I felt my heart clench in fear. I peered through the blaring light of the living room and into the darkened recesses of the rooms lying beyond. Rooms I wasn't familiar with. I didn't know where the darkness led or what it contained. Naomi with a gun pointed at me? I squeezed my eyes shut. "I don't know yet, but I'll come to your place after I'm done here."

"Okay," she answered. "Debbie?"

"Yes."

"Be careful."

I hung up. *Careful*? We'd all gone way beyond careful. The time for taking care was gone. Now it was time to be smart.

I started working and an hour later, the bloodstains were out of the chair and carpet. The bleach I'd used was going to ruin both, but I needed the evidence gone. What did I care if Naomi's chair and carpet needed to be replaced? I ran around with a cloth and bleach and polished everything I could think of that might have our fingerprints. The trophy. Doorknobs. I hated being Naomi's housekeeper even for one moment, but this was for us, not her.

The whole time I cleaned, I kept expecting Naomi to sneak up behind me, or Doug to come home. Neither happened. Regardless, I made it through, then turned off the light, ran out to my car, and hurried over to Betty's place, smelling of chlorine and fear.

"Debbie." Betty exhaled as though she'd been holding her breath. She opened the door wide to let me in but slammed it tight and locked it as soon as I was in the house. I entered like a shadow, and they watched me as though I had a disease. I wanted to tell them to rest assured, they'd already been infected with what was ailing me.

Josie stood a few feet behind Betty. I don't know what I looked like, but they looked like absolute crap.

Finally, Josie broke the silence. "Where is she?" Her voice cracked.

"I don't know." I wasn't lying. I really didn't know. Part of me had wanted to search every room of the Talbot house, but the bigger part of me was too scared to find her. Had she stumbled to her bed and died? Or to the shower? Maybe she was lying at the bottom of a bathtub with blood rippling out in waves as water pelted her from above. Or maybe she was in her car and on her way to the police. No scenario sounded good to me.

"We won't know until someone comes knocking," Betty said as she stared at the door in horror.

I really couldn't think straight anymore. I didn't have a clue what we needed to do next, but I had to keep thinking, keep working toward a solution. "You told Tanya, right?" I asked Betty.

"Yes. She and Rusty are locked down and keeping watch," Betty mumbled. Her eyes were dazed. "Debbie, tell us what you did?"

I shrugged. "Cleaned up."

"What do you mean, cleaned up?" Josie asked as she wrung her hands.

"I cleaned everything. With bleach. The vomit, the blood. The prints."

The women stared down at their hands. "Do you think you got it all?" Josie asked, hope in her eyes.

"I tried. I don't know. Maybe I missed some things. It's hard to say." I felt a sickening lump forming in my throat. I tried to swallow it down, but it didn't want to budge.

"And Doug never came home?" Betty's fingers nervously pinched at the skin of her bottom lip.

"Never," I answered.

"Do you think the neighbors saw anything?" Josie asked.

"It's possible." I hoped not. But only time would tell. What more was there to say? Nothing. We sat in silence for a while, then we checked the doors and windows one last time to make sure they were locked. None of us wanted to be alone, so we stayed together all night. Safety in numbers. If

Naomi was out looking for us, we'd fare better as a team. We each found some kind of weapon and made ourselves as comfortable as we could in the living room. I clutched an old baseball bat, Josie hugged a tennis racket, and Betty grasped a frying pan.

I didn't feel safe at all.

In spite of our fear and worry, exhaustion overtook us. We cuddled into our throw blankets on the couch and chairs and slept like the dead until eight in the morning when someone started pounding on Betty's door.

33

Debbie Takes Control—1974

I jerked awake at the noise. Betty and Josie were staring, bleary-eyed, at the door, their mouths hanging open. It didn't look like they could move even if they wanted to.

I went to the door, then braced myself for whatever was on the other side. Cops, Doug... Naomi. I held the bat in my white-knuckled hand and opened the door a crack.

"Package for Betty Striker," the courier said with a smile far too perky for the moment.

Betty jumped up from her chair and ran to the entry. She signed for the package then peered around the doorway at the world beyond her yard. She slammed the door shut and locked it tight.

"We need to check on Tanya," I said.

Josie went to the phone. We watched as she dialed, then waited for the conversation. It sounded as though she and Rusty had survived the night without visitors. I assumed Tanya had cracked and told Rusty everything. It didn't matter. He'd know eventually and if they could trust anyone, it would be Rusty. In the light of day and after a few hours of sleep, I realized she could have never kept it from him. It was mean of me to demand it.

"Now what?" Betty asked me as though I had a clue.

I began to pace. I acted like I was thinking, but I already knew what I planned to do. I just had to think it through properly. " Well," I said, "now you need to go to work, Betty. You still have a job. If you don't show up, it will look suspicious."

Betty nodded. "What about Josie?"

"Josie and Tanya are both out of jobs right now, thanks to Naomi. Why don't you two spend the day together out at Tanya's place. You can try to keep each other calm. Don't let Rusty call the police."

Josie nodded, then shook her head vigorously. I could tell she liked the thought of being with someone and did not like the idea of cops. "I'll call Tanya back and tell her I'm coming out." She turned and ran back to the phone.

Betty searched my face. "What about you, Debbie? What are you going to do?" she asked with suspicion in her voice.

I didn't answer. She wouldn't have wanted to know, anyway. While Josie talked on the phone, I gave Betty a shrug, turned, and left for my house. The less they knew, the better.

I sat at my kitchen counter, drank coffee, and thought about my plan. No way in hell were we going to be able to keep this thing quiet. Doug would eventually—if he hadn't already—figure out Naomi had gone missing. He'd have seen the wet spots on the carpet and smelled the bleach. He wasn't an idiot. Even though I'd cleaned everything, he'd know something had happened... that someone had been there.

And what about Naomi? Maybe she was still somewhere in the house. Or maybe he's the one who came home, found her, then took her to the emergency room. Or maybe she drove off the road into a ditch somewhere like she'd left Mari. The police might have already found her. There were too many variables, and it was driving me mad not knowing.

I kept coming back to the fact we were the most likely suspects. We'd reported Naomi to the police. Tanya had been fired. Josie and Betty had a motive, too. We'd sat in a bar all afternoon. There were too many dots to connect. Even the village idiot could have eventually figured it out.

The only thing I could think to do was take the blame. I had the least to lose, and after all, I had cleaned up the mess. The longer I thought about it, the more sure I became. I'd made up my mind. I had to go talk to Doug. I'd feel him out and if I had to, I would confess—tell him I'd murdered his wife. I'd take the fall.

A half hour later, I was standing in front of the district court office. I steeled myself to carry out my plan, but I'll admit, my stomach was rolling.

My plan was to see if I could read Doug's mood. I needed to see his face, see how he was acting. He had either come home and seen the blood and mess, then gone out to find Naomi, or he'd come home to the smell of bleach and then gone out to find Naomi. Or maybe he came home to find Naomi dead somewhere in the house. I didn't know, but I couldn't wander through life waiting for it to sneak up on me.

Finally, I turned the knob and entered the office. "Hey, Connie. Is Judge Talbot in?" I tried to act casual and rifled through my purse, acting like I'd stopped by for the heck of it.

"Well, yes, but the door to his office is closed. I haven't talked to him yet this morning. Is this a legal issue?"

I almost laughed out loud at the irony. Illegal issue, more like it. "Oh, no. Just wanted to bend his ear. Had a question. Not a big deal. If he's busy…" I let my words hang and turned back to the door with a wave of my hand. I also wondered what I was actually going to say to Doug.

"Wait while I check." Connie gave me a smile. "I don't think he has much on his docket today." She rapped on the judge's door, poked her head inside, then looked back to me. "Go right on in. He said he has time for you."

"Hey thanks, Connie."

He was in his office. What did that mean?

I walked through the door on shaking legs, wondering if I was insane to be there. I heard Connie shut the door behind me with a click and there I stood, trapped in Doug Talbot's office.

Doug offered me a casual glance as he looked up from the file on his desk. He pointed at a chair. It seemed as though if he'd been searching for his wife all night, he'd look a bit more frazzled. A good sign.

"Debbie? What brings you to see me?"

I took a seat. "Oh, just wanted to chat. You look fresh and chipper this morning. You must have slept as well as I did last night. It's all this cool fall air. Been great sleeping weather, hasn't it?"

I searched his eyes and held my breath, attempting to look calm. This was the moment of truth.

"I look fresh? Really?" Doug stared at me with a solemn face. "Odd. I was up all night."

I exhaled. *Shit.* Well. What had I really expected? "Oh? Why?" Still playing nonchalant— hoping I could pull it off. But I knew I was circling the drain.

Doug looked deep into my eyes. "Actually, I'd be more interested to hear what you were doing last night. I know it wasn't sleeping." He leaned back in his chair.

My stomach clenched and I was thankful I hadn't eaten breakfast. It would be all over his desk right now if I had. I stared at him and didn't say a word. I couldn't quite decide which direction to go. I hadn't rehearsed how I'd start my confession.

He waited for what seemed an eternity but was maybe only twenty seconds. Then he leaned forward and propped his elbows on his knees. "So, tell me where you gals went after you whacked Naomi on the head with the trophy?"

There was that lump in my throat again.

"I saw the whole thing, you know. I was in the kitchen. You remember the noise before the cat walked out? That was me." He cleared his throat. "I watched and did nothing to stop it. So I'm an accomplice."

"Or a coward." I couldn't help myself. It slipped out.

"Yes. A coward, to be sure. You always have called it like you see it, Debbie." He stared at his hands as he twirled the wedding ring on his finger.

"I'll be the first suspect now, as a matter of fact," he said. "But of course, we can control what people know, can't we?" He looked up at me with a hopeful look in his eyes.

The lump in my throat doubled in size.

"Was it you who came back and cleaned up the house, Debbie? You did a great job. Not a speck of blood anywhere. I even did a little polishing. Never hurts to be too careful. And, you'll be relieved to know I checked with the neighbors first thing this morning. Mrs. Morton has horrible vision. Can't see past her front porch, even with her pop-bottle glasses. The Hunters happen to be visiting their family in Michigan; Mrs. Morton told me as much." He smiled. "Oh, and she *also* asked me how I slept last night. Said she slept like a baby. I told her I did too."

I let him do all the talking.

"Anyway. All you really need to know is I've taken care of everything. You and the others won't have to worry about Naomi anymore." Doug smiled and laced his fingers across his chest as he leaned back.

I couldn't believe any of this—yet. Was this a trick? I was afraid to speak. I didn't want to implicate myself.

"I won't say anything this weekend, at least not publicly. I'll tell Junior his mother left me. I'll give him a few thousand dollars. He'll beat it back to Colorado where his friends are. He's been bugging me for money since he's been back. It's why he's here in the first place. Out of funds."

"What about the bank? Aren't they going to miss her today?" I asked.

"They already called looking for her."

"What did you tell them?"

"I told them she wouldn't be in today."

"What reason did you give them?"

"Didn't give them a reason."

"And they didn't press you for it?"

"Debbie. I'm the judge. They kiss my ass like it's made of sugar." The corners of his mouth curled up in a devilish smile. "I plan to go in on Monday and talk to the president of the bank. I'll tell him she left me for another man. I'll act devastated. Tell them to keep it quiet. Then I'll talk to my staff here. No one will be surprised. Most everyone will be relieved she's gone, whether or not they're willing to admit it."

I inhaled. Could this really be so easy? What had he done with her? "What about Naomi?" I asked—cautious, wary, not sure I wanted to know.

"What about her?" he asked as he stared a hole through me. "You want to know if she can hurt you anymore?" His eyes softened.

I nodded. Still afraid to say too much.

"Naomi Waterman Talbot won't be hurting anyone anymore." He stood up and walked over to me. He reached to my hand and pulled me up from my chair, then enveloped me in an all-consuming hug.

I didn't know what else to do, so I leaned in and hoped his hug wouldn't end with his fingers closing around my throat.

He finally let me go and I slowly turned to leave, but at the door, I paused to ask one more question. "Why, Doug?"

He stared at his ring finger again, and I could see the muscles working in his jaw. "Because of Mari. I could tolerate about anything from Naomi, but when I heard her confess what she did to Mari…" His eyes filled with tears and he kept staring at his hands. There really wasn't anything more to say.

I left with so many unanswered questions. What had he done with her? I wanted to know. Needed to know.

Or did I?

Maybe the less I knew the better. It didn't change the fact we all had killing Naomi Talbot on our conscience.

34

Debbie Tells Her Friends—1974

I went home after my visit with Doug, unsure of what to do with this new information. I couldn't deal with it alone, so I called in the troops. They were all at my house in ten minutes flat.

"What's going on?" Tanya blurted out as she busted into my living room.

Josie was right behind her, questions all over her face. Betty sidled in with a frown, suspecting the worst.

"Doug got rid of Naomi." No reason to beat around the bush. I said it outright.

They stared at me like I'd spoken gibberish.

"Like... got rid of the body?" Betty finally found some words.

"I have no clue. I know he said he took care of her and she wouldn't bother us anymore. Said we should all keep our mouths shut and not worry about anything." I could see their confusion turning into relief.

They respectively sank into chairs and I waited for more questions. They didn't come. I saw tears in Tanya's eyes and a blank stare on Josie's face. I went ahead and filled them in. "I went to Doug's office. I was going to confess."

"Debbie!" Betty stood up. "Why would you do that?"

"I had to know what happened. I can't walk around waiting for Naomi to sneak up on me or Doug to confront me. I can't live like that. And I have the least to lose."

Betty shook her head but stared at me, waiting for more explanation.

"Anyway. He told me he was there when we, you know."

"Killed her?" Now Josie was the one standing, a horrified look on her face since she was the one who had wielded the trophy.

I nodded. Josie dropped back down in the chair and covered her face with her hands.

"So he'll be holding it over our heads for the rest of our lives?" Tanya threw up her hands.

"No, no. I don't think so. His hands are as filthy as ours. He was there when we, you know, and he didn't even try to stop us. It makes him like an accomplice or something, right? And he got rid of her. We don't even know where he put her. So even if he decides to tell the authorities where she is and point the finger at us, he still has to take half the blame."

They all nodded as understanding slowly arrived.

"So what will he tell people?" Josie asked.

"That she left him. Not much of a stretch. Everyone knew she was cheating on him."

"This is true." Betty nodded.

"So that's the story he said he'd tell. Girls"—I paused and took a deep breath—"I think we're in the clear!"

We joined in the center of the room and hugged but didn't have a clue what was about to hit us next.

35

"But the stories in the paper. Someone pointed the finger at you. If it wasn't Doug, then who accused you of murder?" Gloria asked the women.

"That good-for-nothing Darby Pederson. Thinking with his pecker," Tanya said.

Debbie leaned forward with a bitter look in her eyes. "It took Darby only three days before he knew something was wrong. Apparently, he and Naomi had a standing date and she missed it. He kept going to the bank to check on her. She was never there. He asked where she was and the folks at the bank were all hush-hush, as Doug had told them she'd left him and he didn't want people to know."

"And Darby didn't believe the story?" Gloria asked.

"No, ma'am. He did not. He ended up storming into the judge's office to confront Doug." Debbie crossed her arms.

"Doug told you that?" Gloria kept the idea of Debbie and Doug in the back of her mind. Seemed like they were talking to each other a lot. The fact that she was looking for her birth mother among these women never strayed far from her mind.

"Doug and I were close, you know. He didn't have anyone else to talk to about this mess." Debbie shrugged. "Anyway, Darby started pointing fingers at the judge, accusing him of foul play. He said he knew damn well Naomi wouldn't have left."

"So, essentially, he admitted to Doug he was the other man." Gloria tapped her pencil on the table.

"I don't think he said the words, but everyone knew anyway, including Doug. But the Judge called his bluff. Told him to get the hell out of his office or he'd turn the tables and point the finger at him. And Doug, being a judge, had a hell of a lot better reputation than old Darby Pederson."

"And it worked?" Gloria asked.

"Well, old Darby put his pea brain to thinking about it. He had it so bad for Naomi, he couldn't stand the idea of her being gone forever. He knew something bad had to have happened. So he told the police chief to talk to Doug Junior, hoping maybe he had some inside information. It turned out drinking in the bar is what landed us in trouble in the end. Junior told the chief he had overheard his mother's name a few times in our conversation throughout the day. Of course, it led the chief to question us."

"But without a body? And Darby, he really couldn't have been the one to press charges, could he?" Gloria asked.

"It wasn't really anything formal. The chief was following up on Darby's gossip," Debbie answered. "Then of course Darby started bending the ear of the newspaper editor. He also blabbed about it at the coffee shop and to anyone else who would listen. Between Darby's finger-pointing and

Junior's comments, it was enough for the chief to bring us in for questioning."

"And it was terrifying." Tanya shuddered at the memory.

"It was, but we held steady. We all kept our mouths shut, like the judge told us to do," Betty said triumphantly.

"Right. And in the middle of the questions, the judge burst into the room and saved us. He told the chief Naomi had left him like the cheating whore she was, and no one had any business dragging us poor girls through the mud like they were doing." Debbie grinned.

"Wow. And it put an end to things?" Gloria asked.

"You bet your ass it did." Debbie banged her fist on the table.

Betty chimed in. "Didn't end up changing much, though. We were still caught in a whirlwind of gossip. But, at least the police stopped badgering us, and we kept doing exactly what Doug had told us to do. We kept our mouths shut. Never said a word. And thank God, no one ever came forward."

Debbie nodded in agreement. "The chief questioned Judge Talbot because Darby insisted. But being the judge made all the difference. The whole thing was dropped like it was a hot rock. Doug maintained that he didn't care where she was and he accepted she had left him. Case closed. But of course, it didn't stop the rumors from flying or the story from living on for years. The folks in town enjoyed thinking we were Naomi's killers. People do love a good rumor, you know."

"So, what did Darby do once the police weren't willing to assist anymore?" Gloria asked.

"Oh, he fussed around, claiming he'd hire a private investigator, but nothing ever came of it," Betty said. "In the end, he went off and licked his wounds. Took to drinking a lot. His wife finally left him. His kids wouldn't have anything to do with him. Sad." Betty shrugged.

"But it was too late for us. The weeks while Darby was stirring up gossip were grueling. Every time we left our houses, reporters snapped our pictures and hounded us with questions. Damn it. Right in the frozen-food aisle at the Jack & Jill Grocery, one reporter asked me if we killed Naomi Talbot. People all around stared at me. I thought I would faint." Tanya pouted.

"Well, the articles pretty much ended after the one, *Thorns of Rosewood Go Free,*" Gloria said.

Debbie sneered. "Not the best picture of me. Yes. The reporters laid off after that. Once we couldn't be turned into monsters, the paper had nothing left to sensationalize. 'They lived happily ever after' doesn't sell newspapers." She huffed.

Gloria felt a twinge of guilt. How many times had she highlighted a story and riled up the masses? How many times had she thought more about the sales than the people in the stories?

But one thing continued to weigh heavily on Gloria's mind. She'd put it aside to focus on this story, but it was time to bring it out into the open.

36

So far, she hadn't heard any of the women talk about having a baby. Gloria had ruled out Mari and Naomi. The timeline of their deaths didn't work with her birth in '75. She had no choice, she had to broach the topic. She would have to start the conversation and see where it led.

"Well. What did you all do after things died down? Just go back to your lives?"

"We tried. Oh, we tried. It didn't take long for Hank Meyer to suggest I look for a different job. I didn't wait around to do it, either. I told him he'd better damn well give me a good reference or I'd make sure those snoopy reporters knew he'd been messing around with Naomi." Betty wagged her finger.

"Where did you find work?"

"I found a job at a law firm in Lincoln. Moved there and worked for them for quite a few years. Ended up in Ohio in the mid-eighties. Followed a man there I thought I might marry. Didn't marry him, but no matter. It led me to a job I loved and I worked there until I retired." Betty smiled.

"So you never had children, then?" Gloria held her breath.

Debbie snapped to attention at the question.

Betty's eyebrows rose. "Well, no, dear. I never did." Betty exchanged glances with Debbie.

Gloria knew it had to be one of these women. Her mother had been a woman in her forties from Rosewood. A woman accused of murder.

"What about you, Josie?" Gloria moved on.

"Me? Well. Originally, I felt lost at sea. I tumbled on the waves, not knowing which way to swim. Then my aunt in Connecticut called. Wealthy elderly woman. She wanted me to come live with her and help her out. She wasn't bedridden or an invalid, but she had poor hearing and vision and couldn't drive. She had no children of her own. She knew I was struggling, so she looked to me for help and ended up giving me a whole new life." A warm glow filled her eyes.

"So you cared for your aunt, but then what? She must have died long ago."

"Oh yes. Long ago. But the interesting thing is she left me her entire estate. I had a big beautiful house and I made friends in the neighborhood. It didn't take long at all before the neighbor down the street, a principal at a private school in the area, came to ask if I'd teach for them." She winked.

"And she's leaving out that she ended up becoming the school's administrator before it was all said and done," Tanya said proudly.

"Yes. I had a wonderful career and enjoyed my life there."

"Did you ever marry? Have kids?" Gloria probed. She saw Debbie shake her head.

"No, dear. I never did. I had a very nice relationship with the principal who lived down my street, but we were really just great friends. My life was so full. And my school children were my kids. I had hundreds of them over the years."

Gloria didn't think Josie could lie even if she wanted to. She was actually relieved. Such a lovely woman. She didn't want to think a woman like Josie could have given her away.

"And you, Tanya?"

"Me? Oh, Rusty and I moved out to Colorado. Our oldest son lives out there and we decided it would be easiest to start over. Seemed the folks in town were never going to stop looking at us with suspicious eyes. We ended up starting our own little business." She smiled at the memory.

"Business? Really? What kind?" Gloria asked.

"A little bar in this ski town up in the mountains. We loved it. Ran it for almost twenty years before I lost my Rusty." She darkened but perked back up. "But they were such good years." Her smile beamed and her eyes glistened with tears and joy.

The room grew silent for a while.

"So no more kids for you and Rusty?" Gloria had to ask, even though she had never even suspected Tanya.

"Oh, heavens no." Tanya shook her head and waved her off.

Gloria heard Debbie sigh, and so she turned her attention to the last possible woman who might have given birth to her.

She was disappointed but not really surprised. Gloria had the same impatience and quick temper Debbie had. Plus, Debbie was hard and cold enough to give away a child. But Gloria had come to love Debbie. Now, though, the thought of the woman turning her back on her own child ate at her. Turning her back on *her*. It was too much. She almost hated to ask, but she had no choice.

"And Debbie? What did you do?" Gloria tried not to clip her words, but she could feel her back stiffen. It hurt to think this woman had given her away. How could she hide her feelings of abandonment?

Debbie's glassy eyes stared into Gloria's. She inhaled deeply and pursed her lips as though she was steeling herself. Then Debbie pushed herself away from the table with shaking hands.

"I'm not feeling well." Her face paled. Grayed. She tried to lift herself from the chair but sat back down in failure, her arms shaking, fear suddenly in her eyes.

At first Gloria was suspicious. The old woman was trying to get out of being confronted. But then she realized Debbie really did have an ashen pallor and worry on her brow. Gloria had never seen Debbie act tired or sick, or anything but full of piss and vinegar. But as she thought about it, Debbie had only had half of a cigarette throughout the day. Usually she managed two smokes an hour—if not three when she felt particularly irritable. Something *wasn't* right.

"Debbie, can I take you to your room?" Gloria jumped up and went to Debbie to offer her arm. She expected to be shooed away. Heavy concern settled in when the old woman took her hand.

Gloria guided her up from the chair, waited as Debbie teetered then found her balance. The other women raised their eyebrows and the room fell silent, as though they'd inhaled all the air in a collective gasp.

Every question Gloria had was no longer important. "Let's call it a day, ladies. I'll come by again tomorrow afternoon. It'll give me time to come up with more questions. Sound good?" She knew Debbie wouldn't want to look anything less than tough as nails. Regardless of what choices Debbie had made, Gloria really did care about the old gal. She couldn't turn her affections off.

"Of course." Josie quickly stuffed her yarn into a bag and shuffled over to Debbie's side. "You okay, Debbie?" Her eyes were worried.

"I'm a little dizzy. Need a nap. Mind your own business." Debbie's words were harsh, but her voice was fragile and her face pale.

Josie threw up her hands. "Fine!" She hurried past them and rounded the corner with surprising speed for a plump old woman.

"I could use a nap myself." Tanya passed them in an equal rush, the yellow balls of her walker squeaking along the floor. "Sweet dreams, Debbie." She gave a little wave as she left the room on Josie's tail. Gloria had never seen her move so fast.

Debbie leaned heavily on Gloria's arm. It seemed as though she might fall down at any moment. Something definitely wasn't right.

"You want me to get a nurse?" Betty asked as she came to take Debbie's other arm.

"Get me to my room. I need to lie down." Debbie's jaw drew tight with strain.

Gloria put her arm around Debbie's waist to support her.

As they entered the hallway, a nurse appeared with a wheelchair and a calm smile. "Hey, Debbie. How 'bout a ride?"

The nurse pushed the wheelchair under Debbie and helped settle her in, even as Debbie's eyes filled with gratitude. "That's better now, isn't it? You ride and I'll do the work."

Debbie gripped the arms of the wheelchair with trembling hands. "That's what we pay you for," she barked, then smiled and quietly added, "thank you."

The nurse rolled her eyes and shook her head. Debbie was all bark and no bite. But the "thank you" at the end worried Gloria more than anything.

The nurse pushed Debbie past Josie and Tanya, who were clearly fretting. They had hurried to get help, Gloria suspected—always taking care of each other.

After Debbie disappeared down the hallway, Gloria turned to give the other women hugs. "I'll be back at two o'clock tomorrow," she said, then hurried out the door before they could see the worry in her eyes.

37

Ten miles out from Meadowbrook, Gloria pulled over to the side of the road. Something in her gut told her to go back. She couldn't explain it— she just felt drawn to do so. She wanted to go sit with Debbie. Even if the old woman was sleeping, Gloria could at least hold her hand.

She laughed at the notion.

It would actually be best if Debbie *was* sleeping if Gloria planned to hold her hand. She'd probably get smacked if she tried to do it when Debbie was awake.

The nurse's station sat empty when she walked back through the doors of the facility. No matter. Gloria knew where to find Debbie, and she headed to her room.

In the doorway of Debbie's room, a doctor visited with the nurse who'd helped earlier. They looked up in surprise at Gloria's entrance.

"I came back to sit with Debbie. I guess I'm worried about her. Is she okay?"

The doctor handed the chart to the nurse, nodded at Gloria, and left the room at a quick clip, flitting away like a moth to another flame.

The nurse tried to offer a look of assurance but failed miserably. "She's weak. Doc checked her and, well… she's old, you know. We never know. She's probably just tired."

Gloria sensed the nurse was holding something back. "I hope I didn't wear her out." Gloria meant it. The thought of being the cause of Debbie's exhaustion troubled her.

"Don't you think such a thing for a minute. All the women look forward to you coming. Your visits are the highlight of their week. If anything, we nurses have all been worried about the day you won't be visiting anymore."

It occurred to Gloria that with today's breakthrough the day would be soon. Maybe that was part of Debbie's problem.

"Gloria." Debbie's voice barely carried across the room. She lay in her bed, weak, her voice raspy, scarcely loud enough to be heard from the doorway.

The nurse and Gloria turned. Debbie looked so small and frail, her shaking hand reaching out toward them.

The nurse walked over. "You okay, Debbie?"

"No! I'm dying here! Of course I'm not okay!" Debbie tried to shout, then coughed. "Now get out of here and let me talk to my friend." She waved the nurse away and beckoned Gloria with a crooked finger.

"Gotta love her." The nurse smiled and shook her head as she walked past Gloria. "Push the light if you need any help," she said as she left the room.

Gloria went to the tiny old woman and took the hand held out to her. What a surprise to see Debbie initiating contact. The old gal either liked her or she was about to cast a curse.

"Strong grip for someone who says they're dying." Gloria attempted to joke.

Debbie ignored the comment. "Sit." She patted her bed. "There's some things I need to tell you."

Gloria found a space on the bed and sat down. She could feel her heartbeat dance in her chest. Debbie's tiny body barely took up any room on the bed. Her hand felt cool and smooth. The hum of the fluorescent lights created white noise.

Gloria wasn't sure she wanted to know whatever it was Debbie wanted to tell her. "Debbie, you should probably rest. This can wait until tomorrow. Why don't you let me sit here with you while you sleep?"

"That's dumb. I don't want anyone watching me sleep, for crying out loud." She waved a hand in the air. "Anyway, I'll be dead by morning." She squeezed Gloria's hand and gave it a sharp pat. "That's why I need to talk to you now."

"Oh, Debbie, you'll be here tomorrow." Gloria tried to laugh, but it didn't sound believable.

"Don't be cute. It doesn't suit you." Debbie shut her eyes. "Now, I'm getting tired, so shut up and listen. I'm going to tell you what really happened to Naomi."

Gloria held her breath—afraid to say anything to stop Debbie's revelations.

The woman took a deep breath and continued. "You need to know we didn't kill Naomi Talbot." Debbie's voice was so shaky and frail.

Gloria had to wonder if she was in her right mind.

"I see the look on your face. I'm lucid. Don't be thinking I'm crazy. Just listen up. This is important." Debbie made her voice as stern as she could. "We beat Naomi up, trashed her house, and left her for dead. Certainly, of those things we are guilty. And if Doug had cared about his wife, I'm sure we'd have all done some jail time."

"But he didn't. If you remember, Doug watched the whole fight. Saw us leave. Didn't do a thing to stop us or help Naomi. Turns out, after we left, he snuck out from his hiding place to deal with her. He thought she was dead. He told me the first thing he did was pick her up to move her to the tile floor closer to the back door. Then she started moaning. She was still alive."

Gloria put her hand up to her mouth. "So Doug killed her?"

"Hold your horses and listen. It's actually worse." Debbie shook her head. "When Naomi moaned, Doug considered choking the rest of the life out of her. He even put his hands to her throat, but she came around all of a sudden, sat straight up, and started screaming. 'Bout knocked Doug backward. Apparently, Naomi began ranting about how we'd come and beat her up and tried to kill her. She was raving and punching at the air, threatening to kill us all. Doug said she was slamming her fists on the ground repeatedly, and he'd never seen her so out of control. He said he was sure she broke both of her wrists slamming them against the tile floor."

"What did he do?" Gloria gasped.

"Well, he let her rant for a while, tried to calm her down, but she couldn't be contained. She'd gone mad. Possibly the blow to the head jarred something lose in her brain. He told her he had to take her to a hospital because he was worried about how much blood she'd lost and about the gash on her head. At first she wanted nothing to do with it, but the more he showed concern, the more she warmed to the idea. So he managed to clean up her wound, although she never stopped screaming and yelling. Then he took her to the car, where she proceeded to pass out again."

"I'll bet she had a concussion," Gloria said, interrupting her.

"I'm sure she did. One way or the other, it was advantageous because it gave Doug time to make a phone call to an old friend."

"Phone call. To whom?" Gloria asked, on the edge of her seat.

"Jack Anderson. Remember how we told you about the homecoming dance? Betty and Jack Anderson were the runners-up to Mari and Doug? Well, over the years Doug had stayed friends with Jack. Jack Anderson knew all about the trouble Doug had been having over the years with his wife. He knew what a neglectful mother she'd been to Doug Junior. He knew how she put her own mother in a nursing home and declared her incompetent so she could get her father's money. And he knew about all her dalliances over the years. For years, he'd been telling Doug she needed psychiatric care."

"But why did Doug need to call Jack? It seems like a strange time to talk things over with an old friend." Gloria shook her head in confusion.

"That's not why he called Jack, dear." Debbie smiled. "He called Jack because he needed his professional help. Jack, you see, was the director of a mental institution in Texas. The mental institution Doug took Naomi to. The one she lives in to this very day."

38

Gloria sat up straight, then jumped off the bed. "Naomi's alive!" Her words bounced off the walls. She frantically searched the old woman's eyes.

Debbie nodded her head. "Yes. She's at a psychiatric hospital in Houston, Texas. Menninger's. Has been for the past forty years."

"He kept it a secret?" Gloria could barely wrap her mind around this new information.

"It's the way Doug wanted it. Besides, whose business was it anyway? And Doug and I had our own little secrets, too. "

Gloria frowned. She knew what Debbie was alluding to. A secret baby. An unwanted child. *Her*.

She crossed her arms and played along. "Go on."

"The others told you about how they carried on with their lives. Well, I did the same, but I didn't have skills like Betty, a rich family like Josie, or a husband, like Tanya. Hell. I was so poor I could barely keep myself in Winstons. Then a strange thing happened."

"What happened, Debbie?" Gloria asked, her voice quivering with anger. *You had a baby and gave it away, didn't you?* She wanted to scream.

"Well, Doug Talbot and I fell in love, that's what happened!" She primped her hair.

"Excuse me?" It occurred to Gloria who her birth father was.

"Doug started calling on the phone. He had so much to tell me about Naomi and had to talk to someone about it. Then we started meeting out of town. Soon we had quite the hot little romance going. Eventually he rented a little apartment in Omaha. I moved down there and he'd visit on the weekends. I was a *kept woman.* Oh, those were the days, let me tell you. Then after a year or so, we decided to move away and be together."

"You got married?"

"Heavens no. We lived in sin." Debbie winked.

Gloria burned with anger and then couldn't take it anymore. She yelled at Debbie, "Tell me the truth already! Just tell me the damn dirty truth! You and Doug had a baby. You had me! And you gave me away like an old coat. How could you do such a thing?" Hot tears ran down Gloria's cheeks as she shook with waves of sobs.

Debbie's face went pale.

The nurse showed up at the doorway. "Everything okay in here?"

"Fine, fine. Go away. This is private." Debbie shooed the nurse out with a weak and trembling voice. Once she'd left, Debbie turned back to Gloria. "Sweetheart. That's not what happened at all. You're wrong."

Gloria stared at Debbie. "What do you mean?"

"I mean I did not have a baby. And neither did Doug." She reached out her hand, but Gloria refused to take it. She stood back and waited, barely any trust left in her heart.

"Gloria. I'm mean as an alley cat, there's no denying it. And Doug wasn't much of a father to his son. But darling, if we'd have become pregnant, we wouldn't have given the baby away." Wrinkles creased at her eyes and a warm smile graced the old woman's mouth.

Gloria stared at Debbie in total confusion. "If not you, then who?" Exhaustion shook her voice.

Debbie whispered, "It's Naomi who had the baby, Gloria. Naomi was your birth mother."

The room spun.

39

Gloria's mouth hung open. *Naomi?*

It was more than she could digest. She turned her back on Debbie and ran from the room. Ran down the hallway. Ran out to the car. Then she sat behind her steering wheel, panting and crying until she cried her tears dry. Then she drove home and laid awake most of the night, staring at the ceiling and crying more.

The next morning, Gloria refused to think about it. Her brain couldn't handle the concept.

She dragged her butt to the office at the newspaper by five in the morning. Print day. The *Rosewood Press* was a weekly paper, and print day was always a bit of a rat race. Everyone ran around in a hurry and loud and frantic was part of the natural process.

Of course, the chaos of print day held no surprise, but it sure was a pain in the ass after a night of little sleep and the worry on her mind. She had tossed and turned all night, fighting with the information Debbie had told her. When she finally slept, she dreamt Naomi was bleeding all over a white carpet as she gave birth to her.

At noon, she hit Send on her computer and e-mailed a copy of the paper to the main office in Omaha. She leaned back in her chair, thinking she'd take a little nap before leaving for Meadowbrook to see the women again. She had a hell of a lot more questions, and she couldn't hide from them anymore. She had to ask everything until she completely understood what had happened.

Unfortunately, her nap lasted until two o'clock.

Gloria woke with a start and sprang up from her chair. "Why didn't anyone wake me?" she yelled at no one in particular.

"I tried, but you mumbled at me to *go away*," the front office assistant answered. "You looked like you needed the sleep."

Throwing her hands up in exasperation, Gloria grabbed her keys and ran out to her car. It would be three before she arrived. The women were probably worried and Debbie... Debbie! She remembered Debbie had been sick, had said she was dying. And Gloria had run out on her. What if it really had been her final moments in life? Gloria hoped she wouldn't get a ticket on her way, because she planned to speed.

Forty-five minutes later, she swung into the parking lot of Meadowbrook and ran to the entrance. When she saw Tanya, Betty, and Josie sitting on a couch with mournful expressions, Gloria stopped cold.

"Debbie's gone?" Gloria asked, searching their eyes for the answer she dreaded.

"She's in her room," Tanya said.

"They just left her in her room after she died?" Gloria shivered at the thought.

"Died? That cranky old thing?" Tanya snorted. "Of course not. She's too mean to die." She shook her head and grunted with irritation.

Gloria's heart jumped. "Well, why isn't she out here?"

"Oh, she has a terrible case of indigestion and gas. Thought she was having a heart attack last night. She's all bound up, too. I'm here to tell you, when us old folks get irregular, it isn't pretty," Tanya said. "It can feel like dying, no joke. But, she refuses to drink any kind of juice. It's her own fault. A glass of prune juice with breakfast and she'd be right as rain." Tanya shook her head, a look of frustration on her face.

Josie commiserated. "No argument there. Remember last year when I had that bout? Oh dear. It's no laughing matter."

Gloria took a deep breath and exhaled with relief. Thank God Debbie was all right. "Well, why does everyone look so upset?"

Betty put her hand out to take Gloria's and pulled her down on the couch beside them. "Have a seat, we need to talk." The look on Betty's face gave her pause.

"Debbie told us you came back last night. Said she told you the truth." Betty looked deep into Gloria's eyes.

Gloria held back the hurt and anger. "Yes. She did."

"Well. There's more for you to know, so why don't we go to the sunroom where we can visit? This is no place for the conversation we're about to have." Betty stood, then forged off down the hall, straight-backed and all business. Gloria wondered how in the world she would hold up under yet more information.

Once they were all seated in the sunroom, Betty took the lead. "Now, we all visited with Debbie this morning. We know she told you about Naomi being your birth mother." Betty cleared her throat as though the idea tasted bad.

Gloria had never seen Betty look so flustered. The normally gracious woman fretted like, well, like Tanya. "Betty, ladies, I don't know what to do with this information." Gloria looked around into their eyes. She'd never felt so lost.

"That's what we want to help you with, sweetheart." Josie reached out her hand, and then the others did the same.

They scooted near her and rubbed her shoulders and arms. Their faces filled with empathy. Gloria could feel tears building, then cascading down her cheeks as the love poured out to her from each old woman.

From the doorway behind them, Debbie's voice turned their heads. "Guess I wasn't dying after all!"

"We knew you weren't," Josie smiled.

"Get over here. Gloria needs our help," Betty told Debbie.

Debbie shuffled over and pulled up a chair. "You need to hear the rest of the story so you can understand. Are you ready to listen today?"

Gloria shrugged and sighed heavily. "I guess."

Debbie began. "Of course, we didn't know Naomi was pregnant. We wouldn't have practically killed her if we'd known that. Doug hadn't known either." Debbie shook her head. "It wasn't until she was admitted at Menninger's and they did a full physical that we found out. Then the doctors told Doug. He went to see Naomi, and she took great delight in making sure he knew it wasn't his baby. He knew anyway, of course. He and Naomi hadn't done anything more than share a roof for years."

"So, who was the father?" Gloria threw up her hands. How could this get any worse?

"See, that's what we need you to understand, Gloria. Father is a term of respect. It can only be given to the man who raised you. This other guy is a sperm donor," Betty said as she squeezed Gloria's arm.

Gloria nodded, but all this information was too fresh. She wasn't ready to come to terms with it. "I'd still like to know who."

"Well, either Darby or Hank, we suspect. We never had them do a blood test. Didn't really think it mattered," Tanya offered.

"We?" Gloria asked.

"Yes, we. Debbie told us all about Naomi being in the mental hospital. Then she told us when they found out Naomi was pregnant. From that point on, we were on a mission. All of us and Doug made it our top priority to find a good family for the baby." Josie smiled proudly. "But very hush-hush. No one could know. It was a private adoption. Doug took care of legal issues, of course."

"What about Naomi?" Gloria asked. "Didn't she care at all?"

"Honey, Naomi was so damn crazy with rage they had to keep her in a straightjacket most of the time. Since she was pregnant, they couldn't sedate her, and Naomi refused termination. She wanted to rub Doug's nose in the fact that she was pregnant by another man. It was fine by Doug anyway. He was sure there was some reason you were joining this world." Debbie smiled with pride.

"Turns out, he was right. It's all come full circle now." Betty's face glowed at Gloria.

"Your adoptive father is my cousin twice removed, dear," Debbie offered.

Gloria shook her head. The information wasn't even sinking in at this point. Nothing made sense at all. It would take some time to process this.

"The day you came into this world and we put you in your parents' arms... it was one of the happiest days in all our lives." Betty beamed.

"You were all there?" Gloria could hardly believe what she was hearing. Her parents had known all this for so many years. Gloria's first thoughts were of their betrayal, but how could have they told her about all of this? It would have been too much for a child to know. Too much for a teenager. It was too much now. She really couldn't blame them.

"Yes, we were all there when your real mother and father first held you. Doug was there, too. It was a beautiful day." Josie gazed into Gloria's eyes.

"But then we had to stay away. It was hard, but there wasn't any way we could keep showing up in your life. It would make us all have to lie too much. We didn't want to do that. You needed a fresh start to life. And we needed to put that part of our lives behind us." Debbie's face grew stern.

Gloria understood.

"Your parents love you with all their heart. You know that, don't you, Gloria?" Debbie asked.

Yes. She knew this. She'd never wanted for love or attention. She knew she was blessed.

"Those people who raised you are the only parents you ever need to care about. Naomi was just the oven you cooked in. Sex and simple biology isn't what makes a parent. It's sleepless nights and trips to the doctor, sitting at ball games, band concerts, and teacher's conferences that make a parent. You know this, Gloria. I know you do." Debbie patted her hand.

Gloria was sobbing. Through her tears she managed to say, "My parents gave me so much— everything. They would *still* do anything for me. They love me no matter what." Tears flowed down Gloria's face and she sank back in her chair in exhaustion.

"That's exactly right! You have no reason to be upset about your birth parents. Forget them! They are nothing to you. You have a wonderful family who will always be there for you. You are blessed. And I know you had a wonderful childhood."

Gloria wiped the tears from her cheeks. She had had a wonderful childhood. Memories of birthday parties and sleepovers, vacations and

Christmases. Grandparents, aunts, uncles, and cousins. And love. She remembered always feeling loved.

"We knew what was going on in your life, too. Your mother sent me a Christmas card every year and told me about you." Debbie grinned. "I shared the information with all the others." She pointed at the women.

Gloria shook her head in amazement as it all sank in.

"We were beyond happy something so beautiful came from something so ugly."

Gloria looked up, her eyes swollen from tears, her throat tight from holding back her sobs. The women reached out to rub her shoulders and squeeze her hands again. These women. She had them to thank for finding her a wonderful life.

"Your life is far better than you imagine, Gloria," Betty said. "You have it all, you know. A new fellow in your life, a good job, a book on your horizon, and parents who love you." She paused. "And we all love you, too."

"Yes, we do," Tanya said as a big silver tear ran down her creased cheek.

"More than you can know," Josie added, her round face beaming.

"And have for a long time." Debbie reached out and enveloped Gloria in a warm hug.

On Gloria's drive back to Rosewood, one desire overshadowed every other. She wanted to call her mother. She'd put off talking to her for the last few weeks. She'd let the poor woman's calls go to voice mail and had been tight-lipped about her relationship with the old women. Now her hunger to know who her birth mother was had been quelled. She understood the information was nothing more than simple facts. A piece of knowledge she would carry with her. It didn't change anything truly important. And her parents, the people who loved and nurtured her, would always be there for her. It was what mattered most of all.

The phone rang only twice before she heard the beautiful voice she hadn't even realized she missed so much.

"Gloria? What a surprise for you to call me. Is everything okay?"

"Mom, everything is better than okay."

"Well, that's good. What did you need, dear?"

"Just to tell you how much I love you."

40

It took another year after her book was written before she had the courage to put an end to one specific chapter of her life.

Gloria knew she was blessed. Her parents were beyond important, and without any reservation the only people she would ever call or consider to be her mother and father.

Yet...

Just knowing Naomi Talbot still existed in a psychiatric ward in Houston, Texas, was more than Gloria could stand. She had to meet her. See her for herself. She had to put a face to the genetics she'd sprung from. This was the woman who for years she had wondered about. The woman who she thought would make such an impact on her life. Of course, Gloria had been wrong. Birth was the sole impact the woman had made. Yet something itched at the inside of her brain and made her want to lay eyes on Naomi once and for all.

Ronnie supported the notion. But Ronnie was always her biggest fan. They were in love and as far as Gloria could tell, they always would be.

She even managed to persuade the four old women the visit was a good idea. Debbie was the hardest to convince. But in the end she said, "Some people need to stare at a train wreck. Can't blame you. You're only human."

It was when Gloria's mother said, "Yes. You should go. See her for yourself. You're strong enough, now," that Gloria knew it was the right thing to do.

And she didn't do it alone. Ronnie was right by her side. Like he always was.

The thirteen-hour drive down to Houston was the most painful road trip Gloria had ever taken. Ronnie tried to keep it light, but Gloria couldn't stop reviewing all the things she knew about Naomi—such horrible things.

She'd called down to Menninger's and made arrangements to visit Naomi. The staff had told her that although Naomi remained aggressive and unstable, it would be safe for her to visit. It was an odd thing to be assured one's birth mother would probably not attack her.

Ronnie and Gloria held hands as they walked down the hallway to a common area. The nurse had told them Naomi sat by a window most every day.

Just staring out at a sallow tree.

Gloria spotted her right away. Still some red to her white hair. Terribly obese now. Rolls of fat hanging over the sides of her wheelchair. A long scar running down the side of her forehead. Maybe from being smacked by a trophy or some kind of lobotomy, but Gloria didn't ask to confirm. It didn't matter.

She and Ronnie stood about ten feet away, watching Naomi as she angrily mumbled to herself and occasionally tapped on the windowpane.

"Guess we should be glad you're a runner. You probably won't ever get fat. Will you?" Ronnie nudged Gloria and she gave him "the look" as he called it. "Nah. I'm sure you'll always be gorgeous." He put his arm around her shoulder and pulled her in close as he chuckled. "You know I'm joking, right?"

She knew. She just wasn't in a joking mood. There really wasn't anything to lighten this moment. "Ronnie, I think I want to talk to her." Gloria studied the woman by the window. "Or at least get close enough so she can see me. I don't know why, but I need her to know I was here. That I exist."

Ronnie inhaled and nodded. "I'm right by your side."

She squeezed his hand and they made a slow approach to the fat woman in the wheelchair.

Gloria pulled up a chair beside Naomi's wheelchair and watched her, waiting to see if she'd acknowledge a visitor.

For several minutes, Naomi didn't look at Gloria sitting right beside her. The old woman kept tapping the windowpane with one fat finger, staring angrily with squinted eyes at the tree with the weeping branches and yellowish leaves.

Then Naomi's eyes darted in Gloria's direction. She turned her head and stared hard at her. Her lips moved as she mumbled to herself… or cursed Gloria. Then the old hag looked back out the window, still scowling, still glaring at the sallow tree.

For a moment, Gloria considered getting up and leaving. Maybe it was enough to see the woman. As she assessed her, Gloria noticed some similarities. Their hands seemed to have a similar shape. Maybe their noses were similar, too. It was hard to tell as Naomi was so old and rotund.

Gloria sighed and was about to stand up when Naomi spoke in a creaking voice.

"Ugly thing, a sallow tree. Long, dirty branches hanging down. Notice how nothing can grow near it. It takes up all the space around it, choking everything else out. Filthy tree. Horrible weed. Symbol of death."

Gloria shuddered at the sound of Naomi's voice, but followed her gaze out the window to look at the tree. It was true. It sat in the middle of the courtyard all by itself. Shed leaves and stray branches lay around the tree, dirtying the grounds. No grass could grow beneath it for lack of sunlight. Gloria had read a sallow tree in drought stretches its roots until it can find a water source, greedily undermining a home's foundation if necessary. Quite a force to be reckoned with. Interesting Naomi would feel so agitated by it. It sounded a lot like her.

Gloria felt Ronnie's hand on her shoulder. It gave her courage to speak to the old woman.

"Naomi, my name is Gloria. You are my birth mother." The words tasted odd in her mouth.

Ronnie gave her shoulder a gentle squeeze. She was glad she'd said it. It was done.

Naomi nodded as though she already knew it. She glanced over at Gloria and looked her up and down, then looked back out the window as though Gloria hadn't measured up.

Gloria shrugged. This woman's opinion did not matter to her. She started to stand, but Naomi's voice stopped her.

"You look kinda like me when I was young. Got any kids?" Naomi stared back at Ronnie.

"No." Gloria gripped Ronnie's hand in her own.

"Good," Naomi said. "Because you or your brats can't inherit any of my money, anyway." She turned back to her visual argument with the tree outside the window.

Gloria stared at Naomi for a moment, then felt Ronnie tugging at her.

"Let's go, hon," he said.

For a moment, she wanted to scream at the old woman: *I don't want your damn money or anything to do with you!* Instead, she nodded at Ronnie. It was time to go. Time to let go. To move on. And to be very, very grateful she hadn't been raised by Naomi Talbot.

Yet as they walked out the doors of the mental hospital, Gloria knew deep in her gut she would visit Naomi again someday.

About the Author

Small rural towns and Midwestern perspectives are something G. M. Barlean knows well. She was a farmer's daughter for the first twenty-one years of her life, and a farmer's wife for the next twenty-nine and counting.

It sometimes takes a curious mind and a wild imagination to stay entertained in a one-stoplight town. However, don't be fooled. Interesting things can happen anywhere—especially in Barlean's books. Be assured, all is good in the simple lives of Barlean and her family, but conflict is alive and well in her novels.

Although Barlean's education is in business and many career options she has chosen over the years have enlisted those skills, she's also gravitated to creative endeavors. Barlean is a self-taught photographer who ran a successful photography studio for many years. She managed an opera house where she organized many musically themed events and worked with entrepreneurs as the director of her town's local chamber of commerce.

Now Barlean enjoys mowing her large yard out in the country, a little army sergeant of a Schnauzer, and a couple of shedding cats. She's attended culinary school where she discovered opening a restaurant was not her life dream, after all. She continues to enjoy cooking and entertaining her family and friends. Her husband tolerates all her changing moods and adventures like the good soul he is. Barlean's children are grown and very busy with their own lives. Travel is always on the agenda and mystery and suspense are always on her mind.

GMBarlean.com
Less Traveled Roads Publishing
Amazon
Barnes & Nobel
Kobo
Smashwords

Other Novels by G. M. Barlean

Prelude—Casting Stones
Casting Stones, the Novel
Conclusions—Casting Stones
Casting Stones, Unabridged Version
Recipes For Revenge, A Four Course Novel
Dead Blow

Available in print and digital versions on Amazon, Barnes & Nobel, Kobo, Smashwords, and iBooks.

Other Novels By ... M. Barbara